You
If y
be'
re
v

THE YOUNG ONES

MARY JANE STAPLES
The Young Ones

BANTAM PRESS

LONDON · NEW YORK · TORONTO · SYDNEY · AUCKLAND

TRANSWORLD PUBLISHERS LTD
61–63 Uxbridge Road, London W5 5SA

TRANSWORLD PUBLISHERS (AUSTRALIA) PTY LTD
15–25 Helles Avenue, Moorebank, NSW 2170

TRANSWORLD PUBLISHERS (NZ) LTD
3 William Pickering Drive,
Albany, Auckland

Published 1996 by Bantam Press
a division of Transworld Publishers Ltd
Copyright © Mary Jane Staples 1996

The right of Mary Jane Staples to be identified
as the author of this work has been asserted in accordance
with sections 77 and 78 of the Copyright, Designs and
Patents Act 1988.

All of the characters in this book
are fictitious, and any resemblance
to actual persons, living or dead,
is purely coincidental.

A catalogue record for this book is available from the British Library

ISBN 0593 039688

Printed and bound in Great Britain by
Biddles Ltd, Guildford and King's Lynn.

To Peg

With fond memories of Charles.

THE YOUNG ONES

Chapter One

'Oh, me sad 'eart,' sighed Chrissie Evans of Browning Street, Walworth. She was known all round as Dumpling, simply because she was all round. It was the last Saturday in August, 1934, and her wedding day. It had been fixed originally for Easter, but sensibly her parents had agreed that her bridegroom, Danny Thompson, should be given more time to add to his savings. Danny, wise himself in this respect, felt he should start married life with a useful amount in the Post Office Savings Bank. As for Dumpling, she suggested the ceremony could be put off for ten years so as not to interfere with her involvement with the local football team, Browning Street Rovers. No-one, alas, took any notice of that, so here she was bemoaning her fate.

'But, Chrissie, you look lovely,' said Annabelle Somers, one of her bridesmaids. Dumpling had quite a bevy of bridesmaids: her two sisters as well as Cassie Ford, Alice Harrison, and Annabelle. You're all welcome, she'd said, you can all help to hold me up. Her dad nearly had an unrecoverable fit at having to plonk out money to equip five bridesmaids, but her favourite uncle came up trumps with a donation of twenty-five quid that settled the bill and even left a bit over for the wedding port.

'Annabelle,' said Dumpling, 'it ain't how I look, it's how I feel. It's goin' to ruin me football career.' Dumpling had been utterly gone on football all her life, and still was. 'It's already ruined this afternoon's match.'

'Dumpling, there's no match,' said Alice Harrison, 'the season hasn't started yet.'

'There, that shows what a state I'm in,' said Dumpling, 'it's mucked up me thinkin' amenities. Oh, me sad 'eart.'

'You've already said that,' remarked Cassie, set on having a wedding of her own next year, when she'd be gone nineteen. She had Freddy Brown in mind, of course, and Freddy, having been the recipient of a unilateral declaration, had no idea how to fight it. Well, it couldn't be expected of him, since he was only the male of the species and Cassie was a hundred per cent female. Accordingly, he was putting money into his own Post Office account, and Cassie was periodically checking the interest, intending to let him know when he was affluent enough to officially propose to her.

She and Alice and Annabelle, the three bridesmaids present in Dumpling's bedroom, stood back to observe the bride. Dumpling was in a virgin-white crinoline, a style much favoured by the Duchess of York, prettily plump. The crinoline was kind to Dumpling, although none of her own plumpness was ever an embarrassment to her. Her wayward hair was done up in curls, awaiting her bridal veil.

'Well, look at you, Chrissie, you're a picture,' said Alice.

'I don't feel it,' said Dumpling, 'I can't 'elp thinkin' about what Danny's goin' to get up to.'

The bridesmaids shrieked.

Mrs Evans, Dumpling's mum, who was also present, said, 'Now, Chrissie love, Danny's a nice young man, 'e won't get up to anything a bridegroom shouldn't.'

'It won't be football,' sighed Dumpling, 'I wouldn't mind that. Anything else, well, I'll fight anything else all the way.'

The bridesmaids shrieked again.

Dumpling being a popular figure in the Browning Street locality, it was not surprising St John's Church was packed for the occasion. Danny Thompson, the happy bridegroom, sat waiting for the arrival of his bride with his best man, Nick Harrison, beside him. Nick, a tall and vigorous young man, had found favour with one of the bridesmaids, Annabelle Somers, and he was presently finding favour with Danny in the support he was giving him. Danny, while happy, was also a bag of nerves, and whispering kept taking place.

'Nick, you sure yer sure you've got the ring?'

'No worries, Danny, I've got it.'

'Well, if yer sure. Here, suppose Dumpling don't turn up?'

'She'll turn up, Danny, she's one of the blokes.'

'Not today she ain't. Is me tie straight?'

'Straight as a die, Danny. It's just your face that's any-old-how.'

'Mother O'Riley, 'as me face slipped on account of me nerves?'

'Not so's the people at the back are going to notice.'

'Is Dumpling a bit late, would yer say, Nick?'

'Only five minutes.'

When Dumpling did arrive on the arm of her beaming dad, the congregation rose up in delight, because not only did she sort of float down the aisle in her white crinoline, but five bridesmaids in rose pink followed. Five, would you believe, five. Still, Dumpling being a larger-than-life character, a generous number of bridesmaids couldn't be said to be inappropriate.

Danny, given a nudge by Nick, took his place beside Dumpling in front of the benign vicar.

'Glad you got 'ere, Dumpling,' he breathed in a hoarse whisper.

'Yes, but it ain't 'alf mucked up me career,' said Dumpling in a muffled protest from behind her veil, which comment was so typical of her that it put Danny's nerves to right.

'Tell yer what,' he whispered, 'we'll 'ave a kick-about on Margate beach tomorrer.' Margate was their honeymoon destination, where Dumpling was going to fight anything else other than football to the death.

'Well, that's something,' she said, handing her bouquet to Cassie.

'We are gathered here together,' began the vicar.

The bridesmaids stood in supportive valour of a bride bemoaning the fact that she might have been playing some practice football instead of getting married. But there it was, her good old mum and dad were all in favour, and so was Danny. Mind, she'd have defied them all if Danny hadn't been a footballer himself. Imagine marrying a bloke who wasn't. Some girls actually married blokes who only played ping-pong. 'Orrible.

Dumpling bucked up a bit at thinking how good Danny was as right back for the Rovers, and began to make her responses almost cheerfully. But when she was asked if she would love, honour and obey her bridegroom, she thought some hopes if it interferes with me footballing life. However, out loud she said she would.

When the ring was slipped on to her finger by Danny, the vicar pronounced them man and wife. Danny lifted her veil and kissed her rosy lips.

''Ere, watch it, we ain't at Margate yet, yer know,' she said under her breath.

Annabelle caught Nick's eye. He smiled and winked. Bless him, thought Annabelle, he's nice, and I'm going to keep him just for me.

Great was the acclaim when bride and groom

emerged from the church. It had to be said Dumpling wasn't actually a blushing bride, but she did go pink with pleasure when ten members of the Browning Street Rovers football team formed a triumphal arch for her and Danny with crossed shinpads.

'Good on yer, Dumpling.'

'Bless yer cotton socks, Dumpling.'

'And yer footballin' legs.'

'My life,' said Starving Crow, the Rovers' fast and wily outside left, 'you got as good as two brides there, Danny.'

Well-wishers besieged bride and groom. Up came a brother and sister.

'Good luck, Dumpling, good luck, Danny,' said Horace Cooper.

'Yes, and don't you look lovely, Chrissie,' said Ethel Cooper.

Dumpling beamed.

'Oh, 'ello, Effel, 'ello, Orrice, ain't that kind of yer to wish me luck? Mind, I need it. I never thought about bein' a bride, yer know. Still, it's done now, and I'll 'ave to put up with it. Orrice, you still playin' cricket?'

'That's a fact, Dumpling,' said Horace.

'Well, I suppose it's a lot better than ping-pong,' said Dumpling. 'Oh, me and Danny's goin' to be your near neighbours now we're 'usband and wife, we're rentin' the first floor of a house in your street, Wansey Street.'

'Pleased to have you,' smiled Horace.

'Here, who's pushin'?' asked Danny of crowding guests.

'Everyone wants to wish you luck,' said Ethel.

'Listen, why don't you and Orrice come to the Institute, to me reception?' said Dumpling, who'd known Horace and Ethel for years through the church, but didn't see a lot of them otherwise. But she wished now she'd invited them to be official guests. They were a nice brother and sister. 'You'd be ever so welcome.'

'Oh, ta,' said Ethel, 'but we can't. Orrice has got to get back to the Oval, and I've got to go out. We just thought we 'ad to come and see you married.'

'That's nice of yer, Effel, and you, Orrice,' said Danny, and then bride and groom were pulled aside for some photographs to be taken.

The reception at St John's Institute was a riot of cockney revelry. Roars of applause periodically punctured Nick's delivery of his best man's speech, during which he pointed out that Dumpling and Danny ought to make a fine team together. After all, Dumpling had married a stalwart right back, and Danny had married a girl who was not only one of the blokes, she'd played goalie and centre forward for the Rovers. So between them, a few goals ought to be scored. If not, it would mean one or the other, or both, had lost form. Or that Danny had been injured.

'I'll injure 'im all right, if 'e scores the kind of goals that ain't in the rules,' interjected Dumpling.

Danny was a bit wordy in his own speech when it came to thanking his newly acquired in-laws for the gift of their eldest daughter.

'If I might say so, which I'd like to, if I can remember what it was, well, the fact is, Mister and Missus, what I want to say is that you've done Walworth proud with Dumpling, and it's me pleasure and privilege to thank yer for givin' her away to me. Well, I couldn't be more appreciative, I feel you've done me proud too. Come to that, so 'as Dumpling. I mean, I never thought she'd do me the honour of becomin' me bride. There's a lot about Dumpling that's remarkable, yer know—'

'Well, it's all yours now, Danny,' said someone.

'It's yer legal entitlement now, Danny,' said someone else.

'I ain't listenin' to jokers,' said Danny, 'I'm tryin' to say Dumpling's sort of outstandin' enough to 'ave married a footballer as good as Jimmy Dimmock of Spurs, but seein' it's me that's the lucky bloke, well, it's – well, I ain't sure what it is except I'm lookin' forward to it.'

''Ere, d'you mind?' said Dumpling amid yells of laughter.

'Dumpling, I mean me years of 'appiness as yer better 'alf,' said Danny.

'You'll be lucky,' said Dumpling, 'you ain't gettin' the better of me.'

Oh, me gawd, she thought, but supposing he does when we get to Margate?

Well, of course, the critical moment came much

later that day, at half-past-ten or thereabouts, in one of the bedrooms of a handsome boarding-house in Margate, which Danny had reserved for a week at the crippling cost of three quid. Mind, that was for both of them and included all meals. Having freshened up, cleaned his teeth and donned his pyjamas in the bathroom down the corridor, Danny came back into the bedroom. Dumpling was in the bed, and fully covered up, except for her eyes and head.

''Ere, what you after?' she said. 'Get off.'

'Dumpling, I ain't even in the bed yet.'

'Well, you ain't gettin' in, either, not while I'm in it.'

'Dumpling, we're married.'

'What's that got to do with it? 'Oppit.'

Out went the light then, and into the bed slipped Danny. Dumpling fetched him a wallop.

''Ere, didn't I tell yer to stay out?'

'Dumpling, I'm yer newly-wed 'usband.'

'That's no excuse – oh, me sacred person, leave off, will yer?'

'Dumpling, what're yer wearin'?'

'Me raincoat, and me weddin' corset and me strong elastic knickers, and you needn't think any of 'em's comin' off, Danny Thompson.'

'Dumpling, that ain't fair, yer know.'

'I don't care if it's fair or foul, I ain't goin' to wear just me nightie while you're in bed with me. Crikey, anything might 'appen.'

'Well, I've got to tell yer, Dumpling, that you're

17

nineteen and me lawful wife, and what might 'appen ain't against the rules. Dumpling?' His protectively wrapped-up bride was making funny sounds. 'Dumpling?'

He heard her more clearly then.

Dumpling was giggling.

After that, off came the raincoat, some dewy kisses took place, and a bit later on Danny had no trouble at all with her strong elastic.

'Good old Dumpling, yer lovely,' said Danny sometime afterwards. 'You all right, are yer, me precious?'

'I ain't talkin' to you,' said the amazed and blushing Dumpling. 'You goin' to do this ev'ry night?'

'Only as a sort of celebration,' said Danny.

'Well, all right,' said Dumpling, 'give us a cuddle for now, I've got me knickers back on.'

Chapter Two

Some days later, Sammy Adams, one of Walworth's more dynamic self-made men, woke up in his many-roomed mansion-like house, Victorian vintage, on Denmark Hill, and thought at once of his business. That led him to thinking of George Carter, a competitor, who had a factory not far from his own and was in sore straits. Carter and his business, in fact, were going downhill fast.

An acquisitive thought – based on sound and lawful business practice, of course – made him sit up in the marital bed.

'Susie?'

'Ur?' said his happiest reason for living.

'Susie, you awake?'

'No,' said Susie muffledly.

'Well, try a bit harder,' said Sammy, and Susie opened one sleepy blue eye and looked at the bedside clock. Six-forty. Six-forty? She closed her eye and snuggled down, face buried in the pillow.

'Susie, turn over, I want—'

'You've got a hope, it's the middle of the night.'

'Now, Susie, I'm not after that—'

'Not much. Let go of my nightie.'

'Well, I'll say this much, Susie, your nighties get prettier, which I appreciate, give you me word I do—'

'Sammy, you horror.' Susie, awake now, turned on her back, and Sammy looked down at her. Her fair hair, long and curling, spilled gold over the pillow, which made the pillow look highly valuable. Her blue eyes were sort of morning dreamy. That Susie – what a female woman, what a picture to behold first thing in the morning. Just thirty, she was the mother of their three children. There was Daniel, seven, named after Sammy's late dad. There was Bess, five, named after Susie's mother, and little Jimmy, three. It all made a successful businessman think admiringly of the advantages of profit, and what it could do for him when he had a wife and children to keep in style. On top of which, their healthy bank balance meant they almost had money to burn. Burn? Don't think like that, you lunatic, Sammy told himself.

'Bless you, Susie, I only wanted to talk to you.'

'What?' said his fetching female woman.

'Yes, I've just had a brainwave about George Carter, Susie.'

'What, the man who owns Carter and Company Ltd? Of all the nerve,' said Susie, 'you woke me up at this hour to talk to me about him? Just for that, Sammy Adams, you can leave this bed for ever and live in the garden shed.'

'I don't think I'm very keen on that, Susie.'

'Well, hard luck,' said Susie.

20

'Susie, you awake now? Only I've had this flash of lightning, and it pointed me at—' No, wait a tick, said Sammy to himself, married wives being a bit funny, it might not be too clever talking about business alone. 'The fact is, Susie, what made me flash of lightning liven me up was realizin' it's been fourteen years since I met you, and eight years since I married you.'

'Sammy, couldn't you have told me that at breakfast instead of wakin' me up?' said Susie.

'Well, Susie, I couldn't help remembering that me first sight of you was when you were a bit poverty-stricken in an old frock and ragged drawers.'

'Sammy Adams, I never did, I never wore ragged drawers, not even when Mum and Dad didn't have as much as a penny for the gas. Anyway, you didn't know what I wore, you never saw and I never showed. I wasn't like some girls, givin' boys free looks for a penny.'

'Three looks, Susie? For a penny?'

'Free,' said Susie.

'You can't call it free, Susie, if you charge a penny. Anyway, it's occurred to me that the year we met was the same year the firm took on its first shop. Of course, that wasn't anywhere near to me future advantage as meetin' you, Susie, but what me flash of lightning pointed me at was that I ought to celebrate me good fortune by buyin' out George Carter and his fact'ry.'

'Do what?' said Susie.

'Yes, the acquisition'll be in your honour,' said Sammy.

'I'm daft,' said Susie. 'I'm lyin' here losin' my beauty sleep listening to you havin' a fit about my honour. You've already mucked up my honour by accusin' me of wearin' ragged drawers when I was a growin' girl.'

'You were growin' all right, Susie, you looked a treat in your Sunday blouse,' said Sammy. 'Anyway, I'm pleasured you think it's a good idea to buy out George Carter to celebrate we've been eight years married.'

Susie went a bit soft and sentimental.

'Wasn't it a lovely weddin', Sammy? My mum said they couldn't have done better at Buckingham Palace. Would you believe it's been eight years since you promised to love, honour and obey me?'

'I did what?' said Sammy.

'Yes, good as,' said Susie, 'but you fall down a bit on your promise sometimes. I know why – it's when you think you should be wearin' the trousers. Me and my mum don't believe in husbands wearin' marriage trousers, and I know my late grandma didn't. She set about my grandpa several times on account of him tryin' it on.'

'Tryin' what on, Susie?'

'Answering her back. Mum said Dad tried that on when they were first married, but she soon cured him in her nice way, which is why they've been livin' happy ever after ever since.'

'Well, I'm pleasured for them, Susie, but like I

was saying, we could do with George Carter's fact'ry to expand – Susie, what're you doin'?'

'Reachin' for the clock,' said Susie, 'I'm goin' to hit you with it.'

'That'll set the alarm off,' said Sammy.

'What's that matter? I've been woken up out of me beauty sleep to talk about something we could've discussed at supper tonight, so I've got to hit someone, and you're nearest, and you've asked for it, anyway – oh, hello, love, you're up early.'

Young Bess, in her long winceyette nightie, had entered the large well-furnished bedroom. The little girl, with her chestnut hair, brown eyes and oval features, was more of an Adams than a Brown. And her movements were quick, like Sammy's. But her long nightie let her down on this occasion. She tripped over it.

'Oh, blessed fing,' she said, getting up at once.

'Plum puddin', you hurt?' asked Sammy.

'I'll be better in a minute,' said Bess. 'Can I come in wiv you?'

'Come on, lovey,' said Susie. It was a favourite pastime with little Bess whenever she woke early, to join her mum and dad. She scrambled up into the bed between them and they played guessing games with her until it was time to get up.

Sammy, while shaving, thought, well, Susie didn't get to hit me with the clock, but I've still got a feeling I've been clobbered. That Susie and her marriage trousers, I'll have to have a talk with Boots about how to get them off her. No, I won't, I know what he'll say. He'll say be like me, Sammy, join the club and grin and bear it. Now Tommy, he's well off with Vi, he is. Vi wouldn't wear marriage trousers, not for all the tea in China. Still, Susie is me own personal Queen of Sheba, which makes me overlook what a saucebox she is.

But how had it happened, though? Me, Sammy Adams, getting frequently clobbered by me young Dutch.

The afternoon was sunny, giving a touch of youthful brightness to the old age of Walworth. Mrs Rebecca Cooper, walking briskly home with her shopping, stopped suddenly. Bother it, she'd forgotten to buy a packet of tea. She stepped from the pavement into the road. The quality grocers, Walton, Hazell & Port, had their shop immediately opposite, close to the corner of Manor Place. Unfortunately, and probably because of setting off too quickly, her leading foot gave way and she fell, her laden shopping bag with her. Luckily, the road had been clear enough for her to make the crossing, and her fall put her in no immediate danger. The driver of an oncoming open car saw her well in time, and slowed to a controlled halt. The driver and his passenger both leapt out, reaching Rebecca well in advance of some bystanders.

Rebecca, righting herself, was helped to her feet and found herself looking at two men, both tall and both well-dressed. The older man was of distinguished appearance, the younger good-looking and with energetic blue eyes.

'Are you hurt?' asked Boots. He and Sammy were on the way back to their Camberwell offices from a visit to their select shop in Oxford Street.

'Thank you, no,' said Rebecca, a woman of forty with finely handsome features and blue eyes of her own – strikingly blue. Her light grey costume, worn with a plain white blouse, was entirely in her favour, her close-fitting hat reminiscent of the cloche. 'I think my ankle gave way, but no, I'm not hurt.'

Traffic was by-passing them and the stationary car.

'This way,' said Boots, and put a light hand on her arm and brought her back on the pavement. 'Sammy, pick up the groceries, there's a good fellow.'

'My pleasure,' said Sammy.

'How'd you feel now?' asked Boots of the woman, and Rebecca smiled.

'An ankle twinge,' she said.

'Just a twinge?' said Boots.

'That's all,' said Rebecca.

'Are you on your way home?' asked Boots, liking her lack of fuss and her quite serene air, despite her little accident.

'Yes, except that I was going to buy some tea at the grocer's across the road,' said Rebecca, taken with his naturalness.

'Here we are, one basket of groceries,' Sammy interposed cheerfully with the shopping bag.

'Sammy, pop across to Walton, Hazell & Port, and buy a packet of tea, will you?' said Boots. 'Then we'll drive the lady home.'

'No, no, really,' said Rebecca. 'I can walk quite easily, I live in Wansey Street and it's only just past the town hall.'

'Well, I'll put you down on your doorstep,' said Boots. 'About the tea, Brooke Bonds or Lyons?'

'Brooke Bonds, and it really is very kind of you,' said Rebecca, less concerned about her ankle than what the fall might have done to her stockings. She always liked to feel that everything she was wearing was immaculate.

'There we are, Sammy, hop across,' said Boots.

Sammy was grinning as he crossed the road during a break in the traffic. What with Susie giving him an old-fashioned lecture on who should be wearing the marriage trousers, and now Boots coming it with his Lord Muck stuff, he was being turned into some kind of Aunt Sally. Funny thing about Boots. He always had this easy-going air, and he nearly always looked as if life was a lot more amusing to him than it had ever been to old Queen Victoria, but he was a natural Lord Muck.

Rebecca was sitting in the car with Boots when Sammy returned with the tea. Rebecca immediately foraged in her handbag for her purse.

'No, don't worry, have the packet on Sammy, my brother,' said Boots.

'Thank you, but I really couldn't do that,' said Rebecca, and handed Sammy fourpence-ha'penny.

'Pleasure,' said Sammy. 'Boots, you deliver the lady, and I'll catch a tram back to the offices. I'm up to me eyes, as usual. Good luck,' he said to Rebecca, 'hope you'll beat your twinges.'

'Thank you, goodbye,' smiled Rebecca, who thought both men extremely likeable.

'See you, Sammy,' said Boots. Facing the wrong way for Wansey Street, he drove to Browning Street, turned left and found himself in old haunts. He went down as far as Brandon Street, turned left and then left again into Larcom Street. He passed the Church Institute, where Sammy and Susie had had their wedding reception, and where his precious Rosie had come close to losing her life at the vindictive hands of a psychopathic pervert.

'You seem to know your way around these streets,' said Rebecca.

'I should,' said Boots, 'I was born and grew up around here. My name is Adams.'

'Oh, do you belong to the Adams family one hears so much about?' asked Rebecca.

'Is it favourable, what you hear?' asked Boots. Reaching the Walworth Road, he waited for a chance to slip into the traffic.

'I've never heard anyone say anything unfavourable,' said Rebecca.

'Is that a fact?' smiled Boots, and went, turning right, towards Wansey Street.

'Oh, I assure you,' said Rebecca, and Boots took the right turn into Wansey Street. Rebecca gave him directions and he pulled up outside her house,

27

where the curtains hung crisp and clean, and the front door was painted a very light yellow. 'Thank you so much,' she said, 'won't you come in for a cup of tea, Mr Adams?' In her mould of Christian fellowship, Rebecca put the invitation naturally.

'Are you over your little accident?' asked Boots.

'I think I'm going to live,' said Rebecca.

'Then thanks, I will have a cup of tea,' said Boots. He alighted, went round to the passenger door and opened it. He took Rebecca's shopping bag from her, and she stepped from the car. Her ankle felt just a little tender, but that was all. She put the key into her bright front door, opened it and went into the little hall. Boots, following with the shopping bag, closed the door. Rebecca led the way into her spotless kitchen, which actually overlooked a tiny garden.

'Please sit down, Mr Adams,' she said. 'Oh, I'm Mrs Rebecca Cooper, and I'm lucky enough to have a very kind husband and an adopted son and daughter, who are brother and sister.'

'I've a wife often referred to as a godsend,' said Boots, 'plus a lively young son and an adopted daughter.'

From that point, of course, Rebecca and Boots got on famously, and if Rebecca wondered why a man born and bred in the cockney heart of South London had the easy air of a sophisticate, Boots wondered why an obviously well-educated and fine-mannered lady had chosen to live with her family among the earthy cockneys of Walworth. In reality, all kinds of characters did live there, as Boots well knew, and it didn't surprise him when Rebecca mentioned she was a missionary's daughter. That fitted the polyglot pattern of Walworth's population.

He stayed twenty minutes instead of an estimated ten, and parted with Rebecca on very friendly terms. A mutual liking had been born. Rebecca invited him to call whenever he happened to be close by. She would like him to meet her family, she said. They'd all heard of the Adams dynasty.

'Dynasty?' said Boots.

'Something like that, Mr Adams, and thank you again for being so kind and helpful.'

'How are the twinges?' asked Boots.

'I've forgotten them,' said Rebecca, which she had.

'Goodbye, Mrs Cooper,' he said, and she stood at the door and watched him drive away.

Almost as soon as Boots was back in his office, his wife Emily slipped in. Nearly thirty-six now, two years younger than Boots, she still had a thin ribcage, but much to her embarrassment and her husband's amusement, her bosom had suddenly begun to think for itself and to make itself more positive. Her mother-in-law, known to her family as Chinese Lady, was quite pleased for her. An incurable Victorian with laid-down ideas about what was proper and what wasn't, Chinese Lady had never considered flappers at all proper in cultivating flat bosoms. Well, if there was one thing she thought very proper and natural, it was a positive bosom, such as she had herself. So she really was pleased to note Emily was filling out a bit, even if Emily didn't see it like that herself. Emily, in fact, had a horrible feeling she was going to get buxom. Blow that, she said. Blow all you like, Em, said Boots, but you can't huff and puff those bonny bouncers away. Oh, you common beast, said Emily, and went for him with a hairbrush.

He eyed her now with a little smile. The bodice of her dress stared challengingly back at him.

'Don't say it,' she said, pinned hat sitting nicely on her dark auburn hair.

'Perish the thought, old girl. Say what, by the way?'

'I know you,' said Emily, 'and I can see where you're looking. Listen, my lad, what's all this I hear about you gettin' off with some woman in the Walworth Road?'

'Sammy's been talking?' said Boots.

'Yes, and 'e said that as he didn't feel like playin' gooseberry, he took a tram back to the offices.'

'Thoughtful of him,' said Boots.

'He told me what happened,' said Emily, 'but all this sort of thing 'as got to stop.'

'All what sort of thing, Em?'

'You helpin' women in distress and makin' them go weak at the knees,' said Emily. 'You ought to be locked up.'

'That'll interfere with the family cricket,' said Boots. 'Are you off home?'

'Yes, that's why I've got me hat on,' said Emily.

'Well, so long, old girl,' said Boots, and gave her a light kiss on her lips and something else as well. Emily stifled a little yell. 'Em, is that you blushing?' asked Boots.

'Oh, yer cheeky ha'porth, isn't anything sacred?' said Emily, and escaped to safety, taking her bosom with her. In the passage she ran into one of the general office girls.

'Oh, what's makin' you giggle, Mrs Adams?'

'I suppose something's tickling me, Gwen,' said Emily.

'I've had some of that,' said Gwen, 'me mum used to put me in woolly vests when I was a growin' girl.'

'Woolly vests ought to be locked up, with other things I could mention,' said Emily, and down the stairs she went to collect her bike from the shop below and to cycle home. On her arrival, she gave her son Tim a kiss and a cuddle. She was very demonstrative with her family.

Tim, almost thirteen and just home from school, said, 'Here, excuse me, Mum, d'you mind?'

'Mind what?' said Emily.

'Supposing me friends had seen?' said Tim, a tall slim lad with his father's dark brown hair and grey eyes.

'Seen what?'

'You kissing me,' said Tim. 'It ain't the thing at my age, y'know.'

'If you say ain't in front of your grandma, Tim,

31

she'll tell you not to talk common. You're supposed to be gettin' properly educated at your dad's old school.'

'Mum, we're all common in our families,' said Tim.

'Oh, we are, are we? Who told you that?'

'Dad. We're all from common stock, he said. But sturdy as old oak, and now we're growin' new branches, he said. We might find we've got some decent chestnuts, he said.'

'Decent chestnuts?' said Emily.

'That's me and Rosie and our cousins,' said Tim.

'That dad of yours never talks black and white,' said Emily, 'I never heard of growin' girls and boys bein' called chestnuts before.'

'Oh, Dad's always finding something new to say that other people never think of,' said Tim. 'Anyway, if you wouldn't mind not kissing me, Mum, I expect you and me could get on quite well.'

'Crikey, listen to you, you funny old chestnut,' said Emily, and ruffled his hair and laughed, then went to tell Chinese Lady about Boots coming to the rescue of some woman who'd fallen over in the Walworth Road. A highly picturesque woman, according to Sammy.

'That husband of mine, Mum, there he was, driving along the Walworth Road, and as soon as this woman sees him comin' she falls over.'

'Well, I don't know how it come about, Em'ly,' said Chinese Lady, as trim as ever at fifty-nine and still showing not a single grey hair, 'but that son of mine has got a way with women that could be fatal if he lost his head over any of them.' Mounting one of her favourite hobby-horses, she went on. 'It's to his credit that he never does, nor ever won't, not if I know him. Boots has always got his feet on the ground, even if he still has his airy-fairy ways. That's another thing I'll never understand, his airy-fairy ways. His dad was never like it, and no-one could say I am. Then there's that Sammy, I don't know how I ever come to have a disreputable son like him. I don't know how many times I've told him his dad would never have stood for him tradin' in ladies' undergarments. It's just not decent, I wonder Susie don't spend her days blushin' for him. Still, some mothers could have worse sons, I suppose. As for Boots, well, we both know Polly Simms has got a weakness for him, but she's been a friend of the fam'ly for years, which is the best way of keepin' an eye on her, and I must say I'm very admirin' of how brave she was in the war, drivin' an ambulance for the wounded. And when she was a teacher at Rosie and Annabelle's school, she did a lot for their education. And then there's what she did in goin' to France and findin' out Boots has got a French daughter.'

'Which near caused a fam'ly earthquake,' said Emily.

'Well, we're over the shock now, and hopin' to see the girl at Christmas,' said Chinese Lady. 'As for Polly, we've all got to admit she's near like one of the fam'ly.'

Chapter Three

One of the Adams Enterprises dress shops was in Harleyford Street, Kennington, close to the Oval cricket ground, where the great Jack Hobbs had scored many centuries for the Surrey County Cricket Club.

The shop was stocked with garments designed and manufactured by Adams Fashions Ltd, an associate company that had made a first-class name for itself in the rag trade. The firm was noted for its excellent stitching, its very competitive prices and for being up-to-date in its styles. Sammy had other shops, in Peckham, Brixton, Camberwell, Clapham, New Cross and Stockwell, all catering for the requirements of the girls and women of South London, and the first of those requirements was value for hard-earned money. Sammy knew his customers, he had been born among their kind, grown up with them, and he knew how they had to make a tanner do the work of a bob. His East End factory, where the seamstresses were under the supervision of good old Gertie Roper, turned out garments not only for the quality requirements of Coates of Kensington and their branches, but also for what his South London customers liked and needed, stylish well-made clothes at prices they could afford. His Oxford Street shop, of course, catered for middle-class customers.

The name of each shop was simply ADAMS. That idea had come from Boots, who suggested it sounded right and had promotional value. Sammy latched on to it at once, discarding the stilted look of ADAMS FASHIONS LTD as a shop nameplate, and delivering himself of a compliment to the effect that Boots wasn't just a lordly geezer, that he had a bit up top as well.

'Glad you noticed,' said Boots.

'Well, it's useful, yer know, Boots, a bit up top with an Adams copyright to it.'

'You're welcome, Junior,' said Boots.

'I didn't hear that,' said Sammy, who reckoned he had a certain amount of dignity to uphold.

The Kennington shop was run by the manageress, Miss Hilda Lomax, and her assistant, the latter none other than Sally Brown, Susie's sister. Sally was twenty-two, and Sammy had given her a job as an apprentice assistant after she'd left St John's Church School at fourteen. He started her off at seven-and-six a week in May, 1926, when she was a teenaged flapper. When Chinese Lady found out what Sally was getting, she called Sammy to account. I'm not having that, she said, it's our Susie's own sister, and I won't have you paying her sweatshop wages. Believe me, Ma, I'm not, said Sammy. Don't call me Ma, said Chinese Lady, and don't answer me back. The point is, said Sammy, it's a girl apprentice's recognized wage while she's learning how to turn herself into a valuable assistant. If I paid her more, Ma, on account of her being Susie's sister, I'd gum up the apprenticeship system of the trade, and that could lead to someone dropping a sack of frozen concrete on me loaf of bread. Would you like that, Ma, would you like to see me with me bonce buried down out of sight in me manly bosom? You Sammy, said Chinese Lady, how many times have I told you not to talk disrespectful, and common as well?

Sammy said at once, bless you, Ma, I can't afford to be common, I'm dealing with high-class buyers like Miss Harriet de Vere of Coates, who uses a knife and fork to peel a banana. If I slipped a bit just then, it was unconscious. Well, all right, said Chinese Lady, but make sure you look after Sally. She's your sister-in-law and as good as related to us. Susie grew up very ladylike, and Sally will too as long as she's not paid starvation wages. I take note of that comment, Ma, said Sammy, and will accordingly keep a benevolent mince pie on her. He put himself out of sight and hearing then, leaving Chinese Lady wondering if mince pie wasn't as common as bonce.

Sally received a rise of two-and-six after a year, and a further five bob when the manageress of the Brixton shop, where she was serving as an apprentice, informed Sammy he could consider her qualified. That was when she was sixteen. She took home wages of fifteen bob a week for two years, when she was then given another five bob rise. Later, she was transferred to the Kennington shop to take the place of a girl leaving to get married. It was a lot nearer home for Sally, and she could walk to her work and back, thus saving tram fares. On top of that, Sammy wanted to get her polished up so that he could think about promoting her to be assistant manageress at the Oxford Street shop, which would please her sister Susie and make Chinese Lady say some kind words to him. So Sally polished herself up very diligently, and at the age of twenty-one she was able, when required, to address a customer with what sounded like a born plum in her mouth.

Sammy, highly pleased with his young sister-in-law, thought about rewarding her with yet another rise, this time of two-and-six. Boots interceded. Make it five bob, he said, we've good reports of Sally. Wait a bit, said Sammy, twenty-two-and-six a week is a better than sound going rate. Twenty-five bob is even better, said Boots. Granted, said Sammy, but not till Christmas, say. It's got to be now, I'm afraid, Sammy, said Boots. Orders from above. God? said Sammy. No, Chinese Lady, said Boots, but same as God, I suppose.

So Sally's weekly wage became one pound five shillings, which delighted her, especially as her mum and dad didn't want her to put more than five bob into the housekeeping kitty. The balance enabled her to dress really well, and to wear silk stockings on Sundays and at parties. It was no wonder she liked Boots and Sammy. Perhaps the reason why she was still fancy-free at twenty-two was because she hadn't met anyone who had something of Boots or Sammy about him. Not that she was short of admirers. She had the same kind of fair hair as Susie and had always been pretty. Further, although a tich of a girl at fourteen, she had shot up from then on, and had legs as good as Susie's, and a very attractive figure. But she'd become a bit discriminating. She thought Susie, in marrying into the Adams family, had done wonderfully well for herself, because although they were cockneys they all had real style, in the way they dressed, the way they mixed with all kinds, and the way they didn't bawl or shout. All the same, like all cockneys, they loved a party, they loved a good old rollicking knees-up, and they still liked knocking down coconuts at the Hampstead Heath funfair on some Bank Holidays. She knew, because she'd been with them.

Boots and Tommy, Sammy and Lizzy, and their spouses, and their children, crikey, you'd only got to see them performing at the coconut shy to know their roots went back to Walworth all right. That kind of thing nearly always made Sally think there ought to have been an Adams man for her. And it instinctively made her cautious about what her own Mr Right should be like. He'd got to be out there somewhere, and if she didn't meet him quick she'd get left on the shelf. Blow that. But she didn't want a gorblimey type, or someone with a big head. Someone like Nick Harrison would be nice. Nick was her brother Freddy's best friend, he lived in Browning Street, had a good job and was walking out officially with Annabelle Somers, the elder daughter of Sammy's sister Lizzy. As for Freddy, he was bound to become engaged to Cassie Ford sometime this year, and Cassie was driving him dotty about making his fortune so that she could do her shopping in a carriage with four white horses.

Everyone seems to be going places, thought Sally, and I'm just standing still.

It was nearing five o'clock this Friday afternoon, and she was in the shop window, tightening the back of a dress on one of the dummies. Miss Lomax, presently serving a customer, had thought the bodice looked just a little loose. Business had been good during the day, but was slackening off now, and Sally was looking forward to going to the Tivoli Cinema in the Strand this evening, in company with her friend Mavis Richards. Mavis's young man and her brother Wally were taking them. Sally quite liked Wally, but wasn't serious about him, nor likely to be.

Someone stopped outside the shop, and she glanced. She saw a young man in grey flannels and a cricket shirt. He was bareheaded, had his folded jacket over his arm, and was carrying a long cricket holdall. His face was brown, as if he spent a lot of time in the open air, like weatherbeaten navvies did, and his appearance was cheerful and personable.

Their eyes met through the window. Hello, thought Horace Cooper, what do I see if not a treat of a girl? Blessed cheek, thought Sally Brown, he's staring at me. Worse happened then. He had the sauce to smile at her and to actually give her a wink. Sally delivered a haughty look, as befitted a qualified dress shop assistant with ambitions to be as much of a lady as her sister. She had sent one young man packing on account of him being a bit too forward and a bit too full of himself, a young man called Ronnie, who had once worked for Sammy. But when his parents emigrated to Canada, he went with them, by which time Sally had lost all interest in him.

Having cut the impudent male person dead with her haughty look, she returned to the little task of fixing the tightened dress with pins. Out of the corner of her eye, she glimpsed movement, and as she stepped from the window back into the shop, there the cheeky devil was, entering. Miss Lomax, still attending to the customer at the far end, turned her head to look, then left it to Sally to see what someone in trousers wanted. Sally advanced. Horace advanced. They met.

'Hello,' said Horace, 'how d'you do, pleased to meet you.'

Crikey, this one could be worse than that Ronnie, thought Sally.

'Excuse me,' she said, in her trained shop assistant's voice, 'but this is a ladies' dress shop.'

'Yes, I thought it was,' said Horace breezily. 'I

mean, it looks as if it is. All dressy, you might say.'
Horace was just twenty-four and nearly six feet. Old
friends knew him as Orrice and still called him that,
despite his age, his size, and his adoptive mother's
reminders that his name was Horace. But who in
Walworth would call anyone Horace? He'd always
be Orrice to most people there, just as his sister
Ethel would always be Effel. He was on the ground
staff of the Surrey County Cricket Club, and as a
promising cricketer he often bowled to the team in
the nets. He had hopes of becoming a professional,
starting in the second eleven and going up to the
first. In fact, he'd played for the second eleven
several times during the last two seasons. He had no
regular girl friend, but that didn't mean his social
and recreational preference was for a cricket bat.
Horace was a very normal bloke, and normality had
broken out all over him the moment he'd met this
young lady's eyes through the shop window. He
hadn't been able to help giving her a friendly wink.
Alas that he didn't realize he had got off on the
wrong foot. 'Yes, it looks a very nice ladies' shop,'
he said, taking note of the fact that she wasn't
wearing a wedding or engagement ring.

'Then would you mind leaving?' asked Sally.

'My sister's a lady, y' know,' said Horace. 'She
wasn't at first. More like a holy terror. But our
parents cured her, and now she's a lady. She'd
recognize a shop like this.' Horace spoke fairly well
for a born cockney. Jim and Rebecca Cooper, his
adoptive parents, had worked on his speech,

Rebecca especially. She believed cockneys put limitations on their careers by their slipshod speech, which she thought a great pity, for so many of them were as sharp as needles. But the way they talked closed doors to all kinds of superior jobs. She'd cured Horace of dropping his aitches and other faults, but he still had cockney rhythms to his speech. 'Her name's Ethel,' he continued blithely. 'What's yours?'

'Never you mind,' said Sally, not a bit impressed by the cheeky windbag. Horace was very impressed himself, and certainly Sally looked engagingly pretty in her working dress of navy blue with white cuffs. Her hazel eyes, that could look blue in the summer and green in winter, were clear in their haughtiness. 'If you don't leave this shop at once, I'll call a policeman.'

'What for?' asked Horace. 'I'm a customer.'

'Oh, really?'

'Yes, and honestly as well,' said Horace.

Sally tried being a bit sarky.

'Have you come to buy a frock, then?'

'How much is a blue one?' asked Horace.

'The same price as a pink one,' said Sally.

'I don't think I fancy pink,' said Horace, 'I don't think it's my colour. No, I'll stick to blue. Yes, I'll have a yard.'

'Now look,' said Sally, 'that's my manageress down there, serving a lady, and she's got her eye on you and me as well. So stop larkin' about and go away.'

'Wait a bit,' said Horace, 'that's not very fair, refusin' to serve me because I'm wearin' trousers. What've I got to do to get served, then, go away and come back in a frock?'

'If you come back in a frock, my manageress will 'ave you arrested,' said Sally, dropping an aitch on the shop floor, which she wasn't supposed to. Sammy knew that although most of his South London customers dropped them by the dozen, they expected the compliment of being served by ladylike assistants. Odd, but true.

'But what about my yard of blue, say navy blue?' asked Horace.

'D'you mean a yard of dress material?' demanded Sally.

'Dress material? What would I want dress material for?' Horace was prolonging his time in the shop simply because he liked looking at her.

'How do I know what for unless you do dress-makin'?' asked Sally. 'Anyway, we don't stock materials, only accessories.'

'I'm talkin' about hair ribbon,' said Horace. 'For my lady sister.'

'That's a laugh,' said Sally, correctly suspecting he was trying to make her his best friend.

'I did mention her,' said Horace.

'Yes, I heard you,' said Sally. 'Look, are you askin' serious about hair ribbon? Only we do stock ribbon among our accessories.'

'That's good,' said Horace, 'I'd like a yard of dark blue.'

44

With the customer now in the fitting-room, Miss Lomax called to Sally.

'Do you need any help, Miss Brown?'

'No, the gentleman's made up his mind about what he's come for, Miss Lomax,' said Sally. 'I can serve him now.' She went behind the counter. 'How wide, sir?'

'Wide?' said Horace.

'Yes, what width of ribbon, sir?'

'I didn't know this was goin' to be complicated,' said Horace. 'I thought a yard of blue ribbon would be simple.'

'Well, it would be, wouldn't it, if you'd tell me the width,' breathed Sally, exasperated. Then, in her best shop assistant's voice – that is, with a trained plum in her mouth – she said, 'Does sir wish an inch width, or one-and-a-half, or wider?'

'You've got me there,' said Horace. 'Tell you what, you choose. Well, you and my sister are both ladies, so you're bound to know more about widths than I do.'

'Yes, sir, nice wide ribbon is what you want.' Sally pulled open a tray containing reels, and extracted one of navy blue. 'There, one-and-a-half inches. That width will tie into a really nice bow.'

'Well, it looks champion,' said Horace. So do you, he thought. 'Thanks for being a help.'

'A yard, then,' said Sally. She measured the required length and snipped it off with her scissors. She wound it and placed it in a dainty paper bag. 'That'll be fivepence-three-farthings, sir.'

45

'How much?' said Horace.

'It's silk,' said Sally.

'A bargain,' said Horace and paid up with a silver tanner. He received a farthing change. 'Thanks. What did you say your name was?'

'I didn't say. Good afternoon, sir.'

'It's been nice meetin' you,' said Horace.

'Good afternoon, sir.'

'By the way, I'm often around here, bein' on Surrey's ground staff,' said Horace, 'so shall I look out for you whenever you're not doing much?'

'The door's over there, sir,' said Sally haughtily.

Horace departed with a grin. Sally, not a girl to allow herself to be picked up, forgot him as soon as he left the shop. He might not be a gorblimey type, but he had much the same kind of bigheadedness as that Ronnie of some years ago.

When the shop closed, Sally walked home, as she always did, going along Kennington Park Road and turning right down Braganza Street. That took her into Manor Place, opposite Browning Street, which took her to her home in Caulfield Place. It was a nice exercise, walking home and escaping the crush of crowded trams. If she'd taken a tram she would have had to ride down to the Elephant and Castle, and from there catch another tram to take her along the Walworth Road. As it was, the walk wasn't much more than fifteen minutes, and she was sure it was good for her, even if she had been on her feet most of the day. Sally was a springheeled, long-legged young lady.

46

The evening was balmy, and the warm light bathed her. From the parlour window of a house in Braganza Street eyes watched her, the eyes of a disturbed man. He was always there throughout the year, seated behind the window curtains to observe the street and the passers-by. He was hidden himself, but the graceful gap of the lace curtains allowed the street scene to be visible to him. Ex-Corporal Joseph Burns was a casualty of the Great War, a shellshock case, a 1915 volunteer who had managed the miracle of surviving until the last great German offensive in 1918 opened with an ear-splitting, head-pounding shattering roar of guns. Joseph Burns was dug out of a collapsed trench just in time to escape suffocation, but in a condition that rendered him of no further use to the Army. Once a typical rawboned cockney, loudly extrovert, he had since that day been a silent introvert, making con-versation of a brief staccato kind only with his wife, a woman who had given him care and understand-ing from the moment he was invalided out of the Army. He was a good man, Joseph Burns, a good husband and father, as far as Mrs Burns was concerned, and she nursed him in his condition without any complaint of what it cost her mentally and physically. Their daughter and two sons were married now, and she was able to devote herself to caring for him. He had a small disablement pension, and their sons contributed to her house-hold budget. So did their middle-aged lodger with his rent of seven-and-sixpence a week.

Real trouble only occurred once in a blue moon, when Joseph would suddenly start smashing everything within reach. So Mrs Burns made sure that very little was within reach whenever she became aware that storm signals were brewing. Such signals were perceptible. He would begin to mutter and to twitch, and to periodically let go just a few words. 'That bleedin' sniper, I'll kill the bugger.' Eventually, he would do his raging about, but only for five minutes or so, and then become as quiet as ever. Her lodger, a kind man, said he worried sometimes that her husband might turn on her. No, not my Joe, she said, he would never do that.

He was safe in the parlour. She had removed all the ornaments from the mantelpiece and all the china from the corner cabinet. And there was only the one chair he could smash, his own, which he never did. He sat there all through each day, watching the street, except when he joined her for meals in the kitchen. And in the evenings he listened to the wireless with her. Sometimes he would say that anyone would think the war was over. And she'd say, 'Well, it is, Joe lovey, so don't you worry, nothing's goin' to fall on us and bury us.'

Now he watched the approach of a figure familiar to his brooding eyes. A young woman? So she might be, so she might be, but you could never tell what those Jerry snipers might get up to. He wouldn't put it past any of them to put a skirt on. Sergeant Wilmot had downed a troublesome one once, and when they found him wounded amid brick rubble on the top floor of a ruined house, the crafty sod was wearing a net camouflage over his uniform and some kind of titfer made of leaves, would you believe.

He watched Sally go by. What was she up to? She was always in the street sometime each weekday, always coming up to the house and then going on. She never looked at his window, but he felt she knew he was there all right. She always passed by on this side of the street, as if she was doing a bit of a recce job on him. He'd have to watch her with both eyes skinned, and he'd have to keep his head down. Fatal, that was, showing your head when a sniper was doing a spotting job on you before taking up a hidden position.

Ex-Corporal Joseph Burns frowned. It wouldn't do to get careless.

Horace ran into Dumpling, now Mrs Chrissie Thompson, on his way home. He pulled up, however, before he actually hit her buffers.

'Oh, 'ello, Orrice,' beamed Dumpling, who wasn't finding holy wedlock as much of a trial as she'd thought. It was true Danny did go in for a lot of soppy stuff, but he was very loving and he'd come home from his new job with the London and South Eastern Railway with a bunch of flowers for her on Friday. And although the new football season hadn't started yet, they'd been keeping in form by having kickabouts on the common at

49

Peckham Rye on Saturday afternoons. 'I must say yer do look manly, Orrice.' she said. That meant he looked like a footballer.

'Well, you're a sight for sore eyes, Dumpling,' said Horace, who knew her only through the church. She attended regularly, and so did he and Ethel. Rebecca liked them to go with herself and Jim to most Sunday morning services.

'Oh, d'yer think marriage suits me, then?' said Dumpling.

'You look in the pink,' said Horace, 'and I bet Danny does too.'

'Oh, stop it,' said Dumpling, roundly buxom in a jumper and skirt, 'you'll make me giggle.'

'Is it a giggle, then?' asked Horace, as they turned into Wansey Street together, Dumpling bouncing along.

'What, 'oly wedlock?' said Dumpling. 'Well, I don't know about a giggle, or about it bein' 'oly, neither. That Danny don't hold nothing very sacred. Still, it's done now, I spoke me vows, and I've got to abide by them, or me mum'll come round and give me a talkin'-to. Orrice, I saw Freddy just recent, and mentioned me and Danny 'ad seen you and Effel at me weddin', and he said if you 'adn't taken up cricket, you wouldn't 'alf have made a fine footballer.'

'Freddy?' said Horace. 'Oh, Freddy Brown.' He knew Freddy slightly. 'Well, it was a question of makin' cricket my career, y'know.' He stopped. His home was just across the street. 'Anyway, lots of luck with holy wedlock, Dumpling, and regards to your better half.'

'Well, that's nice of you,' said Dumpling, 'except, like me mum recommended, it's me that's the better 'alf. Mind, Danny's a good right back in our football team, which is playing its first match tomorrer week.' It was September now. ''Ere, would you and Effel like to come and 'ave Sunday tea with me and Danny sometime now we're near neighbours?'

'Anytime, Dumpling,' said Horace, and they parted.

Chapter Four

Jim and Rebecca Cooper's house in Wansey Street put them in one of Walworth's pleasanter-looking residential thoroughfares. Their curtains always looked immaculate, and so did their doorstep. As for the door, Jim himself had applied the paint. Rebecca had been horrified when he chose it, a light yellow. No, no, never, she said, our front door will look cheap and nasty. Well, if it does, said Jim, I'll clean it off and we'll go back to dull old brown. Indeed we will, said Rebecca, or some of those urchins from Brandon Street will throw things at it. But when it was finished, she said my goodness, Jim Cooper, you've painted our door with sunshine. Let's hope the Brandon Street ragamuffins like it, said Jim. Whether they did or didn't, none threw things at it, and some neighbours were highly complimentary. Which made Rebecca feel very pleased with her husband, the most good-natured of men.

Jim had come out of the war minus his left arm, but was inventive and adept at using his one hand to wash, shave, dress, chop wood, carry out odd jobs and generally do as well as fully able people.

Further, with the help of a plumber and his mate, he had converted the small bedroom, the one next to the upstairs toilet, into a bathroom, much to Rebecca's delight. Forty-three years old, Jim was still fit and healthy. Rebecca, forty, was a serene-looking woman who believed the Lord occasionally guided the footsteps of people. She was convinced He had guided Jim to her door thirteen years ago. He arrived on her step with his unofficial wards, the orphaned Ethel and Horace, looking for lodgings. Reluctantly, she took them in, and her ordered life fell to pieces in a way that turned her from a frosty and religious spinster into a warm and caring woman. When she married Jim early in 1922, they formally adopted Horace and Ethel, and she went successfully to work on improving their behaviour, their manners and their cockney dialect.

It was harder work with Ethel than with Horace, for Ethel was an awkward character while Horace was a boy of determination and promise. Rebecca was delighted when he won himself a place at West Square, for there he received a grammar school education.

Ethel, however, while bright, was not much of a scholar, and she left St John's Church School when she was fourteen. Now twenty, she was working as a clerk in the offices of a factory in the Old Kent Road. All her awkward elements had finally taken wing when she at last came to realize how much her adoptive parents cared for her. She had hated girls, she saw them all as a menace to her possessive relationship with her brother. In time she got over that as well, and all she was concerned with now was making sure that when Horace took up seriously with a girl, it would be one who deserved him. Ethel was very attached to Horace, and always had been.

At supper this evening she quite flushed with pleasure when he presented her with a yard of lovely silk ribbon. Dark-haired and dark-eyed, Ethel was a dainty young lady with a very pretty little nose that gave her a piquant appearance. She looked less than her twenty years, and was, in fact, still a little naive.

'But, Orrice, it's not me birthday yet,' she said. No-one could persuade her to call her brother anything but Orrice.

'It's just something I thought you'd like,' said Horace.

'It's lovely,' said Rebecca, who had told of her little accident and her meeting with a member of the well-known Adams family. Jim, Horace and Ethel had all been impressed, since most Walworth residents had heard of this family. In addition, Horace offered Rebecca use of his cricketing embrocation to get her ankle back in order. Rebecca said her ankle had quite recovered, thank you, and that in any case it would never get to be on speaking terms with his smelly embrocation. 'Yes, it really is lovely, Ethel.'

'It's nearly as wide as a Lord Mayor's ribbon,' said Ethel.

'Would anyone fancy me as a Lord Mayor?' asked Jim, day manager of a Servicemen's club in Blackfriars.

'Mum would,' said Horace.

'Mum fancies Dad just as he is, don't you, Mum?' said Ethel.

Rebecca, the most mellow of wives, smiled.

'Let's say it doesn't upset me that your father isn't a Lord Mayor,' she said.

'Oh, I'm not grumblin' much, either,' said Ethel, 'except would Dad like half me ribbon to tie his hair with till he gets his next 'aircut?' Ethel could still drop aitches.

'Jim, you're disgraceful the way you put off going to your barber,' said Rebecca, 'and Horace isn't much better.'

'Oh, I like Orrice and Dad with their hair a bit bushy,' said Ethel. 'Orrice, where'd you get the ribbon?'

'In a ladies' dress shop,' said Horace, enjoying Rebecca's home-made shepherd's pie, hot and spicy.

'In a what?' said Jim.

'Did Orrice say ladies' dress shop?' asked Ethel.

'I believe he did,' said Rebecca.

'Well, I had time,' said Horace, 'there was no match on, and the season's nearly over. It's goin' to be mostly ground work from now on.'

'I like the sound of your cricket more than your ground work,' said Jim.

'We all do,' said Rebecca, a champion of her son's career. She had long since ceased to think of Horace and Ethel as adopted. She regarded them as her very own. They had taken Jim's surname on adoption, and husband and wife, together with the adopted orphans, had become a family in which affection was reciprocated all round. Ethel had originally been in awe of her new mother with her handsome looks, her searching blue eyes, and her smooth abundant black hair worn with a parting down the middle and a large bun at the back. Now, the hair was attractively styled, and the blue eyes given to showing warmth and understanding. 'Horace,' she said, 'you actually went into a ladies' dress shop to buy Ethel some hair ribbon when you left the Oval?'

'Yes, it was about five,' said Horace, 'and I didn't think I could get any in a hardware shop. Are there any seconds, Mum old love?'

'Should I be called "Mum old love"?' asked Rebecca.

'That Orrice, I don't know where he gets 'is language from,' said Ethel. 'Cricket hooligans, I shouldn't wonder.'

'Are there any seconds, Mum?' asked Horace.

Rebecca regarded her son, every inch a young man in his muscular build, his tanned healthy look and the firm line of his jaw. Adolescence had long since gone, but not his cheerful way with people, nor his kindness. He joked a lot, and could tease, but all in all, she was proud of him, and so was Jim.

Rebecca wondered when he was going to bring a young lady home, a young lady who would appreciate just how likeable and good-natured he was. Quite like Jim.

'Yes, there's enough left for seconds, Horace. D'you want all that's left?'

'I'm against that,' said Jim.

'So am I,' said Ethel.

'Seconds all round, eh, Ethel?' said Jim.

'Crikey, not 'alf, Dad,' said Ethel, and Rebecca glanced at her. 'Oh, blow, did I do it in, Mum? I meant yes, please, and ta as well.'

Rebecca brought the large dish from the range hob, and served out seconds to all but herself. Her kitchen was bright, the evening sun slanting in through the window, and the little garden outside showed a border of bright flowers, a magical picture of colour in old grey Walworth.

'Now,' she said, 'can anyone think why Horace had this idea of going into a ladies' dress shop to buy a hair ribbon for Ethel?'

'There was a girl in the window,' said Horace.

'Is that a fact?' said Jim. 'How much was she?'

'Horace, there's no need to answer that,' said Rebecca.

'We ought to know if she was a bargain or not,' said Jim, and Rebecca laughed. In her life with him and Horace and Ethel, she'd had to develop a sense of humour.

'Was she a bargain, Horace?' she asked.

'Now, Mum, don't make funnies,' said Horace, 'this is serious.'

'Pardon?' said Rebecca.

'Did Orrice say serious?' asked Ethel, sitting up. She was all for her brother having a girl friend, as long as she herself approved of his choice.

'Did you say serious, Horace?' asked Jim.

'Yes, I came all over serious as soon as I saw her in the shop window,' said Horace, never one to keep anything interesting to himself. Rebecca always encouraged suppertime conversation, when her family were home after their work and the house came alive for her. 'Did you come all over serious, Dad, when you first saw Mum?' asked Horace.

'Very serious,' said Jim, 'or she'd have thrown us all out.'

'Jim Cooper, that's not true,' said Rebecca.

'Course it's not, Dad,' said Ethel. A little giggle arrived. 'Mum took us all to 'er warm Christian bosom.'

'Ethel, a little respect, please,' said Rebecca, but she smiled. 'Horace, tell us more.'

'Well, I can honestly say the girl was a peach,' said Horace.

'Well, we wouldn't want you to get all serious about a banana,' said Ethel. 'But I don't know I like the idea of a girl showin' herself off in a shop window.'

'She wasn't showin' herself off, sis,' said Horace, 'she was fixin' a dress on a dummy. So I said to myself, Horace, I said, do something about getting to know her. She's a corker, I said to myself.'

'Horace?' said Rebecca, and Jim hid a grin.

'Yes, you know,' said Horace.

'Horace, I thought a corker was a person who put corks into bottles,' said Rebecca. 'I think a dictionary will tell you so.'

'Well, this one didn't come out of a dictionary, Mum,' said Horace, 'this one's a dress shop assistant.'

'And a corker, yes, I see,' said Rebecca gravely. 'Carry on, Horace.'

'So I went in,' said Horace, 'and this girl came up and said as it was a ladies' shop, would I mind leavin'. Leavin' was the last thing I had in mind. Well, you don't—' His little grin showed. 'You don't get to meet a bit of all right every day of your life.'

Jim coughed. Ethel giggled. Rebecca addressed her son in the style of a learned judge.

'Horace,' she said, 'what is "a bit of all right"?'

Horace, who had known his refined mother would ask such a question in just such a way, said, 'Oh, a girl who makes a feller feel serious about her at first sight, Mum. Anyway, as I needed a reason for bein' in the shop, I said I was a customer, and she asked if I'd come to buy a frock.'

Jim roared with laughter. Ethel shrieked. Rebecca smiled.

'And what did you say to that, Horace?' she asked.

'I asked how much a blue one was, and she said the same as a pink one. I don't think she was takin' me seriously, which upset my style a bit.'

'Not good, that, an upset style,' said Jim.

'Not when it was on top of havin' been bowled over to start with,' said Horace. 'Think of something, I said to myself, so I thought of hair ribbon for Ethel, and she sold me a yard of navy blue.'

Ethel, utterly intrigued by the little story, but not sure she approved of some girl too stuck-up to take her brother seriously, said, 'Pink would've been best, it sets off me hair better than navy blue.'

'Ethel, that's a little ungracious,' said Rebecca.

'Oh, I'm not blaming Orrice,' said Ethel, 'it's that girl for sellin' him navy blue when she should have made it pink.'

'But if Horace asked for navy blue,' said Jim, 'she couldn't have insisted on pink.'

'Well, she should 'ave,' said Ethel. 'But of course, I don't really mind blue, it's the thought that counts.'

Rebecca served the afters then, sliced fresh pears stewed in an oven dish and coming hot and melting to the palate, together with everyone's favourite, hot custard that topped the pears like a creamy ocean of pale gold.

'Horace,' said Rebecca, 'did you find out who the girl was?'

'Well, I did ask,' said Horace, 'but she just said good afternnoon, the door's over there.' He grinned at the memory. Actually, he'd liked her spirit, and the fact that she wasn't going to be common enough to allow herself to be picked up, as the saying was.

'Blessed cheek, givin' you the push like that,' said Ethel. 'Well, you don't want to bother about a girl as toffee-nosed as she is. I've a good mind to go to that shop and give 'er an earful.'

'Ethel dear,' said Rebecca, 'young ladies shouldn't talk about giving anyone an earful.'

'Well, a faceful, then,' said Ethel.

'Seems an acceptable alternative,' said Jim. 'Anyway, having been given the push, Horace, is that the end of it?'

'I'm wondering if she's got a steady feller already,' said Horace. 'It wouldn't surprise me, a girl like her. I think I might have a go at findin' out. As for the ribbon, I suppose I was thinking navy blue's a colour I like myself.'

'Orrice, I like it too,' said Ethel, sorry she'd mentioned pink. It was, however, giving Horace food for thought.

Supper over, they were clearing the table when someone knocked on the front door.

'I'll go,' said Jim.

'Oh, it'll be Davy,' said Ethel, 'he's takin' me for a walk this evening.'

Davy Williams, a young man of twenty-three, had met Ethel at a dance in Browning Hall three months ago, and to everyone's surprise, Ethel had actually brought him home a week later. Bringing a feller home in Walworth was a sign that the girl required parental approval of the bloke in question. Ethel had never shown much interest in the opposite sex until then. Her general verdict had been that they were all as interesting as wet flannels or as daft as a kite. Davy Williams, however, actually seemed to find favour with her. It had to be said he was a bit skinny and bookish. He looked a bit clerkly too, with his high stiff collar, bow tie and spectacles, but Horace reckoned he suited Ethel, who'd never gone much on the other kind of Walworth boys, rumbustious and outgoing. In less than a fortnight, he proved very acceptable to Ethel, and there she was, visibly experiencing her first crush, which tickled Horace and Jim no end, because for the next few weeks she was all of a dither every time she heard Davy knock on the door.

'Oh, that'll be Davy. You answer the door, Dad. No, I'd better. No, you go, Dad. Mum, are me stockin' seams straight? Is me hair all right? Oh, wait a bit, don't let him in yet, Dad.' And so on.

But she calmed down and made a name for herself in the eyes of her family by reading poetry with Davy. Great was the astonishment. Ethel hated poetry, and she wasn't exactly alone. In the main, poetry hardly ever crossed more than one Walworth doorstep in ten. Serious poetry, that is. Limericks were all right. Anything that began on the lines of, 'There was a young lady of

Sale who lost her skirt in a gale,' was acceptable, but anything in the nature of 'O! Star-crossed lovers Olympus-bound, wilt thee thy gods with love surround?' was figuratively chucked into the dustbin with the potato peelings on the grounds that it was unfit for human consumption. Mind, the *Pied Piper* and *Charge of the Light Brigade* could get by in some homes, but on the whole most families thought poetry was only for people who wore Bohemian hats and were right off their chumps.

Rebecca was among the exceptions. That is, she liked poetry but wasn't off her chump. But Ethel, well, poetry made her eyes glaze over. Yet, six weeks after meeting Davy she could be heard in the parlour reading aloud to him. Yes, even such lines as, 'Oh, beauteous maiden of mine heart, art thou not my sky-borne lark, soaring in thy wing-ed grace, to sing thy song in heaven's space?'

Such lines were Davy's own, for he had a streak of lyrical Welsh in him, inherited, he said, from his paternal grandfather, and he was always dashing off verses and stanzas of bardic fulsomeness.

It made Horace fall about. Rebecca chided him. Frequently.

'I think it shows a touch of cultural grace in Ethel,' she said once.

'Never heard of it,' said Horace, and continued to fall about whenever Ethel, in the privacy of the parlour with Davy, was heard declaiming his latest epic. Nothing pleased Davy more than hearing Ethel read his poems aloud. Ethel, while wondering what they all meant, liked the moonstruck look that came over him while she was reading. It gave her a sort of complimented feeling, even if his moonstruck look changed to one of pain whenever she stumbled a bit over a line.

'Oh, I'm ever so sorry, Davy,' she'd say.

'Oh, that's all right, Ethel, but it spoils the rhythm. Start again.'

'What, all of it?'

'Yes, start again.'

'We could have some cocoa first, if you like.'

'No, start again.'

'Oh, all right, Davy. "The moorland winds swept o'er the heath, and the heather furred with wild-blown leaf . . ."'

And so on.

This evening he'd come to take Ethel for a walk, and to bring her back in time for cocoa, biscuits and perhaps the reading of an ode or two.

Jim, having let him in, brought him through to the kitchen. Before her marriage, Rebecca had been used to showing all visitors into the parlour, but once the knot had been tied, it didn't take long for her newly acquired family to make informality the order of the day. Rebecca gave in gracefully.

'Oh, good evening, everyone,' said Davy, eyes blinking shyly behind his spectacles, and a lock of brown hair falling poetically over his forehead. 'Oh, hello, Ethel.'

'Hello, Davy,' smiled Ethel, 'I'll just put me hat on, then we can go for our walk.'

'Oh, put your boater on,' said Davy, 'I like it.'

'What, that old Sunday thing?' said Ethel.

Davy shook his head at her and said, 'You mustn't think it doesn't make you look nice, Ethel.'

So when they left for their walk, Ethel was wearing her Sunday boater.

'I've forgotten, what's Davy's job?' asked Horace.

'He's a clerk in a coal merchant's office,' said Jim.

'Well, we ought to order our coal from him, and get a bit of discount,' said Horace, but Rebecca was quite against that sort of thing.

Later, when Ethel returned with Davy, Rebecca made them a pot of tea, served slices of cake with it, and allowed them to take the tray into the parlour. Ten minutes later, as Horace came down the stairs from his room, he heard Ethel's clear fresh voice declaiming.

'Hark, the maiden sings her song
From a hilltop green,
Never was a sound so sweet
Or so fair a maiden seen.'

'Slower, Ethel.' That was Davy.

'Oh, all right, Davy.'

'Start again.'

Horace, entering the kitchen, was grinning all over.

'What's amusing you, Horace?' asked Rebecca.

'Ethel's doing, "Hark the herald angels sing",' said Horace.

'Come again?' said Jim.

'Something like that,' said Horace.

'Is Ethel – um – in love?' asked Jim.

'Could be,' said Horace, 'or she's just enjoyin' her first experience of bein' off her chump.'

Chapter Five

'Sammy's thinkin' of buyin' up one of our competitors,' said Tommy Adams to his wife Vi. They had just put their three children, Alice, David and Paul, to bed.

'Our Sammy's doin' what?' asked equable Vi.

'Thinkin' of how to make Adams Fashions more profitable,' said Tommy, handsome, fit and honest.

'But they're profitable already, aren't they?' said Vi.

'Yes, but when there's a bit more of it waitin' to be picked up,' said Tommy, 'Sammy's against someone else gettin' it.'

'That Sammy's still a caution,' said Vi. 'What competitor is it?'

'Bloke called George Carter,' said Tommy. 'You wouldn't know 'im, Vi, but he's got 'is fact'ry not far from ours. He's losin' orders all right, but I ain't sure he'd sell out to Sammy.'

'Why not?' asked Vi.

'Well, the orders 'e's losin' are mostly comin' our way, so Sammy and Adams Fashions ain't too popular with 'im,' said Tommy.

'What'll Sammy do, then, if Mr Carter won't sell to him?' asked Vi.

''Ave a nervous breakdown,' said Tommy.

'Oh, poor Sammy,' said Vi. 'Never mind, tell 'im I'll come and see him in hospital, and ask him what he'd like me to bring, flowers or grapes.'

'Vi, I think you just made a joke,' said Tommy.

'Oh, did I?' said placid Vi. 'I didn't mean to. Does Boots know about Sammy wantin' to buy Mr Carter's business?'

'Probably,' said Tommy. 'He needs Boots to agree.'

'He'll talk to him, then,' said Vi.

Tommy grinned.

'Anyone can talk to Boots,' he said, 'and 'e'll always listen, but you can't get any change out of him. He's been Lord-I-Am since he was twelve.'

'Yes, wasn't he lordly all the time he was at West Square?' said Vi.

'If I remember right, you were a bit gone on 'im in your teens,' said Tommy.

'A bit gone?' said Vi. 'Crikey, I should say I was, I used to imagine him carryin' me passionately off over his horse to his desert tent, and tellin' me he was mad about my beauty and that he'd order the execution of me mum and dad if I didn't marry 'im.'

'Excuse me,' said Tommy, 'but would yer mind tellin' me how long this lasted?'

'Oh, till you grew up all 'andsome and nice and kind,' said Vi.

'That's my Vi,' said Tommy.

'Mind,' said Vi, 'you didn't ever throw me over any horse yourself.'

'All right,' said Tommy, 'now we're well-britched I'll buy six nags and do some practice runs with yer, Vi. Then I'll buy a bit of desert and a tent, and we'll have a bit of a naughty weekend in Araby.'

'What, all that way when you're always 'aving naughty weekends here at home?' said Vi.

'Good idea, Vi. Let's start one tomorrow. It's Saturday tomorrow.'

'Yes, we'll start early in the afternoon,' said Vi.

'Eh?' said Tommy. He was very fond of his Vi, so good-tempered and amenable, and always compliant whenever he felt like some marital lovey-dovey. But early in the afternoon, with the kids at their most rackety? 'Vi, you sure you know what you're saying?'

'Yes, we've got to do the stripping first,' said Vi.

'Pardon?' said Tommy, now very much taken aback. It wasn't like his Vi to be as saucy as that.

'Well, we said we'd re-paper the spare bedroom this weekend,' said Vi, 'and we could start early tomorrow afternoon stripping the old paper off.'

'Vi, yer teasepot,' grinned Tommy.

'Never mind, Tommy love, I like it that you still like me,' said Vi.

'Well, I won't tell a lie, Vi, re-papering the spare bedroom comes a long way behind that,' said Tommy.

★　　　★　　　★

69

'Hello, Rachel, how's yer remarkable self?' said Sammy over his domestic phone on Saturday afternoon.

'That's Sammy?' said lustrous Mrs Rachel Goodman, Sammy's one and only girl friend in his young and precocious days.

'I have that pleasure,' said Sammy.

'Oh, we all have the pleasure of knowing you're you, Sammy,' said Rachel.

'Don't mention it,' said Sammy. 'Listen, it's eight years since I married Susie, did you know that, Mrs Goodman?'

'I should want to talk about it?' said Rachel. 'And why Mrs Goodman? What's happened to our sacred friendship?'

'Take it from me, Rachel, it's not got lost at this end, and I trust it's holdin' up at yours,' said Sammy. 'Anyway, I thought I'd celebrate me eight years with Susie by makin' an offer to George Carter for Adams Fashions to buy him out, fact'ry included, him bein' financially rocky and unsound of pocket as well. And as you're a shareholder and director, it's me pleasure to ask for your agreement.'

Rachel quickened. The affairs of Adams Fashions were one of her prime interests.

'You'd like the factory for expansion of Adams Fashions, Sammy?'

'My idea exactly, and I'd appreciate you coincidin' with me on the prospect,' said Sammy. 'I've always had a likin' for you and me coincidin'.'

'Sammy, ain't you a love and me old sweetheart?' purred Rachel.

'Well, I won't deny it, but don't say it out loud,' murmured Sammy. 'Susie's in the approximate offing.'

'She's in the what?'

'No, not there, Rachel, just nearby, you might say.'

'Where'd you get "approximate offing" from?' laughed Rachel.

'Oh, you can get anything that sounds educated in this family, if you listen to Boots long enough,' said Sammy.

'Boots doesn't say things like "approximate offing".'

'You sure?' said Sammy. 'I mean, it sounds like him.'

'No, it doesn't, it sounds like my one and only Sammy,' said Rachel.

'I hope your married better half ain't listenin' to that,' said Sammy. 'Anyway, I've got your vote in favour of makin' George Carter an offer?'

'Sammy, it's a must, and have I ever said no to you about anything?' asked Rachel.

'And ain't I always been in favour of female women like you, Rachel?'

'Sammy, you can say that with Susie in the approximate offing?'

'The offing's moved off a bit,' said Sammy.

'Well, love to the offing, Sammy, and all your little ones,' said Rachel, and her laugh travelled like musical velvet over the line and lingered in Sammy's ear even after she'd hung up.

Sammy thought he ought to follow that phone call with one to Polly Simms, a long-standing friend of the family, although a mote in Emily's eye. Polly still carried a torch for Boots. Sammy trusted Boots not to take advantage of that. It would knock nasty holes in the family.

'What d'you want to speak to Polly about?' asked Susie.

'Well, we haven't seen her since well before she went to France,' said Sammy, 'and I thought I ought to tell her she did a good job findin' Boots's French daughter.'

'You mean thank her for it?' said Susie.

'Not a good idea, Susie?'

'Sammy, you know how Polly feels about Boots,' said Susie, 'she's fancied him for years. You don't suppose she liked findin' out he had an affair, do you, and at a time when she was in Albert herself?'

'Well, I'll admit me understandin' of females ain't quite the same as yours, Susie. Still, regardin' how Polly feels about Boots, you can rely on Boots to control the situation.'

'Supposin' he loses control one day?' said Susie.

'Boots?' said Sammy. 'He's never lost control of anything all his life.'

'He lost it in France with the young French widow,' said Susie.

Sammy gave that thought.

'Well, Susie, I wouldn't say he lost control, I'd

say that as he was out of the trenches for a few weeks, he helped himself to a little bit of what he fancied, French style.'

'And I'd say he deserved it, Sammy, and I wouldn't be surprised if the lady thought so too.'

'I share your sentiments, Susie, but life's a lot different for him these days, and if he ever did lose control, Tommy and me would talk very serious to him, and Lizzy would saw his head off.'

'I hope not,' said Susie, 'I don't fancy Boots without his head.'

'Susie Adams, as your legal married husband, I'm against you fancying anyone except me.'

'Well, of course you are, Sammy. There, there, don't worry.'

'Susie, is that you pattin' my head?'

'Bless you, Sammy. Now go and play clockwork trains with Daniel, he's callin' you.'

'I think you're wearin' the trousers again,' said Sammy, 'and for the sake of me self-respect, I'm goin' to have them off you one day, Susie.'

'Yes, Sammy.'

'You sure you're listening?'

'Yes, Sammy, and Daniel's yelling for you now. Off you go, there's a good boy.'

I've got to do it one day, thought Sammy as he went to join Daniel, I've got to lay down the legal marriage law to Susie about me rights, which don't include getting patted on me head.

'Come on, Dad,' said Daniel, 'you can be the porter. I'm the stationmaster.'

'Shouldn't I be in charge?' asked Sammy. 'I'm older than you, me young cocksparrow.'

'But it's my train set,' said Daniel.

Ruddy cockles and mussels, thought Sammy, I'm getting ordered about by everybody. If it gets known, it could ruin me reputation as a formidable businessman.

Sunday evening was balmy. Warm weather was dispensing sunshine over the land, giving the unemployed and the poor a feeling that tomorrow might be more promising than yesterday. A summery day could always do more for the spirits of striving people than the speeches of politicians. Not many down-to-earth Londoners had a lot of faith in politicians. Talking gasbags, that was what most people of Walworth said about them. Still, the country had to have a Parliament, and you had to put politicians into it. But in the words of one of Rebecca's cockney neighbours, it was a gorblimey bellyaching fact that when the elected lot took their seats they always turned out to be as bleedin' retarded as the last lot. He didn't say this to Rebecca, of course, she being a lady, he said it to his wife, who hit him with her frying-pan for using language and for forgetting she was a lady herself.

Rebecca had created a miniature oasis in her backyard. A little lawn four yards square was framed on three sides by flower beds, and against the brick wall that divided the yard from that of her immediate neighbour, sweet peas were still flowering. Rebecca and Jim were seated at their small garden table. They had been to Evensong at St John's Church, and Ethel was making sandwiches and a pot of tea for them. Her poetic friend Davy was helping her. Well, trying to, in between poetizing.

Out came Horace in his open-necked cricket shirt and light grey Sunday flannels. He was eating a sandwich.

'Oh, there you are, Horace,' smiled Rebecca.

'Yes, that's our Horace,' said Jim.

Horace had been out with a friend. He was a good friend, a lively mate, but during the outing, Horace had thought he wouldn't mind swopping him once in a while for the girl in the dress shop. That girl had made her mark on him, and he was honest enough to admit he'd been knocked for six at first sight, which was slightly unbalancing for an up-and-coming cricketer, whose county captain had an interested eye on him.

Ethel opened the kitchen window and put her head out.

'You Orrice,' she yelled, 'you've nicked one of Dad's fav'rite cheese and tomato sandwiches!'

'Not me,' said Horace, 'it's cold pork.'

'That's worse! That's one of Mum's!'

'It's only half a one,' said Horace, finishing what was left.

'Never mind that,' fumed Ethel, 'you're a guts.'

'Ethel, it was just lying about,' said Horace.

'What d'you mean? It was on a plate, with its other 'alf!'

'Pardon?' said Horace. 'I didn't catch that.'

'Yes, you did!'

'Ethel dear,' said Rebecca, 'it's really not important enough for you to shout.'

'Oh, sorry, Mum,' said Ethel. 'No-one can say I'm not dearly fond of me brother, but you 'ave to shout at him sometimes, specially since he's got into a habit of goin' deaf when he shouldn't.'

'It's what they call a defensive mechanism,' said Jim.

'I never heard that before,' said Ethel. Davy's head joined hers outside the window.

'Excuse me, might I say something?' he asked.

'Course you can, Davy,' said Ethel, who sometimes clucked a bit like a mother hen in encouraging Davy to speak his piece.

'Thank you, Ethel. Might I say this? "Summer comes on April's wings, and birds begin to call. Oh, listen to the pearly doves singing peace to all."'

'Oh, what a nice poem, Davy,' said Ethel. 'Did you hear it, Mum? "Peace to all", that's what Davy's saying.'

'Oil on troubled waters?' suggested Jim.

'And no more hollering?' said Horace.

'Mind you, Dad,' said Ethel, 'there wouldn't have been any troubled waters if Orrice 'adn't pinched half Mum's sandwich. I'll make you another half, Mum, and Davy's bringing the pot of tea out now.'

Davy appeared with the tray a minute later, steering a cautious path on account of not having such a strong, confident way of walking as Horace. He always looked as if his mind was on Tennyson instead of his legs and feet. Still, he managed to place the tray on the table without any upset. He smiled shyly at Rebecca through his spectacles.

'Thank you, Davy,' said Rebecca, thinking that he and Ethel made an odd pair together, a quaint pair.

Ethel brought the sandwiches out, then informed Jim and Rebecca that she and Davy were going into the parlour to do some poetry together.

'That's good,' said Horace, relieved that the performance wouldn't take place in the garden.

'Orrice, d'you want to come and listen?' asked Ethel.

'I'd be dead keen,' said Horace, 'but I've got my cricket boots to clean.'

'That's a shame,' said Davy, but when he and Ethel were in the parlour, he let her know that poetry was just for them alone.

'Oh, all right,' said Ethel.

'It spoils it if I don't have you to myself,' said Davy.

'Crikey, have you got it bad?' asked Ethel, experiencing girlish pleasure at wanting to be monopolized.

'You're my dream girl,' said Davy.

'Oh, help,' said Ethel. 'Davy, when can I meet your mum?' She hadn't met his widowed mum yet, or his brothers and sisters.

'Next Saturday,' said Davy. 'Here's the poem I want you to read. Speak it sort of dramatic.'

'Dramatic?' said Ethel.

'Yes, with lots of feeling.'

'Oh, all right,' said Ethel, taking the sheet of paper. She looked at the poem and began to read earnestly, which was as good as being dramatic. '"O, shinin' clouds o'er rooftops red, shall thy tears soon be shed? Bo-Peep casts her sighing eye to the lowering of the sky." Crumbs, Davy, what's it mean?'

Davy's spectacles looked lowering themselves as his short-sighted eyes darkened in reproof.

'I hoped you'd never ask a question like that, Ethel.'

'Sorry, Davy, only is Bo-Peep the girl in the nurs'ry rhyme?'

'It's you,' said Davy.

'Oh, help,' said Ethel again. 'Davy, you do write romantic,' she added. Even if she couldn't make out what much of his poetry meant, she was pretty sure it was romantic.

'Start again, Ethel,' said Davy, leaning back in his armchair and putting his fingertips together. It made him look very much like a young sage with a solemn knowledge of the muse.

Ethel began again. Horace, sneaking into the house, heard her reciting, her young voice piping. The name Bo-Peep kept cropping up, and so did words like beauteous and sighing.

Horace fell about.

Chapter Six

On Monday morning, Percy Fender, captain of Surrey's county side, was talking like a wise old owl to some of the young professionals, Horace among them. At the end of it, Mr Fender let Horace know he could probably look forward to being fully occupied with the second eleven next season, and even to one or two games with the county eleven. Horace, delighted, was subsequently able to take himself off to the Adams shop in Harleyford Street. The manageress wasn't around, but the fetching assistant was. She finished serving a customer just as Horace walked in, wearing his cricket flannels. He remembered something.

'Oh, hello, Miss Brown, long time no see. Well, not since Friday.'

Sally, very well-trained, eyed him with a fair amount of obligatory hauteur, something that was called for whenever a customer was of a dubious kind.

'Excuse me?' There was a plum and a half in her mouth. 'Have you come to read the meter or something?'

'Something,' said Horace.

Sally gave him a toffee-nosed look.

'Oh, it's you,' she said. 'How did you know my name?'

'I remembered your manageress mentioning it,' said Horace.

'I see,' said Sally. 'Well, you can leave now.'

'Yes, I'll have to pop off soon,' said Horace. 'I've got to get back for a bite of lunch.'

'Well, isn't that a shame?' said Sally.

'Yes, I wouldn't mind havin' a chat,' said Horace, 'especially as you're on your own.'

'I'm not,' said Sally, 'my manageress is in the back room havin' a sandwich. Might I be told what you're here for again?'

'It's about that blue ribbon,' said Horace, eyeing her today with a feeling he might have seen her somewhere around Walworth, even if only at a distance. 'Do I know you?'

'I'm sure I don't know you,' said Sally. 'Anyway, what about that blue ribbon, might I ask?'

'Wrong colour,' said Horace, not actually in any hurry to get back for a bite of lunch. He was much more in favour of a day trip to Brighton with this engaging girl. He had no idea that when he entered St John's Church School at the age of ten, she had been one of the eight-year-old pupils. And nor did Sally realize that this forward saucebox had once been the boy known as Orrice, who'd made a name for himself at school by fighting older boys. In any case, he hadn't been long at St John's, he'd left to go to West Square when he was eleven.

'Wrong colour?' she said, and went all hoity-toity. 'Excuse me, but I sold you what you asked for, a yard of navy blue.'

'Yes, wrong colour,' said Horace regretfully.

'Well, I'm sorry, but we can't change it, not when it was what you asked for,' said Sally.

'I wouldn't ask you to change it,' said Horace, 'you're a friend.'

'Not of yours I'm not,' said Sally. Crikey, the sauce of him.

'Well, I suppose we were strangers when we first met,' said Horace, 'but wouldn't you say we were friends now?'

'No, I wouldn't,' said Sally. 'What a nerve. I suppose you think you're God's gift. Some 'opes.' She frowned. 'Some hopes. Kindly leave this shop.'

'But what about some pink ribbon for my lady sister?' asked Horace.

'You're gettin' my goat, you are,' said Sally, her trained plum giving way to cockney forthrightness. 'I'm not changin' what you asked for, d'you 'ear?'

'No, of course not,' said Horace, trying a smile. Sally went all aloof. 'Here's another tanner.' He placed the silver coin on the counter. 'Yard of pink, if you'd be so obliging, Miss Brown. By the way, what's your other name?'

Sally refused to answer. She didn't need saucy blokes like him, even if he was all tanned and healthy-looking. He was too fond of himself, and didn't half fancy his chances. Silently, she

81

produced three reels of wide ribbon, each a different shade of pink.

'D'you want a yard of any of these?' she asked.

'Yes, that one,' said Horace, pointing to a deep pink.

'You sure?' said Sally.

'Sure,' said Horace, liking the shape of her nose. What's it mean, I wonder, liking the look of a girl's nose? I'll have to ask a funfair gypsy one Bank Holiday to tell my fortune. If she says a black cat or a girl's nose is going to cross my path and bring me luck, I'll ask her if she means this girl's nose.

Sally, snipping off a yard of the chosen ribbon, folded it, put it into one of the little white bags printed with ADAMS in tasteful script, and placed the purchase on the counter. She rang up fivepence three-farthings on the till, and gave Horace a farthing change.

'Thank you for your custom, sir,' she said, as Miss Lomax appeared.

'Pleasure,' said Horace. 'I hope you won't mind, but I'm not sure if I'll be able to drop in again, not unless my sister needs some elastic later in the week.'

'We don't sell elastic, sir,' said Sally, plum back in her mouth. 'You'll have to go to a shop that sells ladies' haberdashery, Hi'm afraid.' She added the unnecessary aspirate for good haughty measure.

'What's ladies' haberdashery?' asked Horace.

'Ribbons, tape, elastic, hairpins and so on,' said Miss Lomax.

'I think I'd feel daft in haberdashery,' said Horace. 'Thanks, anyway. Well, I'd better get back. So long.' Off he went. He heard the manageress say something as he left the shop.

'Was that the same young man, Sally?'

Sally. And her surname was Brown. Sally Brown. It rang a bell, not loudly, but with a bit of a little tinkle. Hadn't Ethel mentioned a girl of that name when she'd been at St John's? And somewhere in Walworth, wasn't there a Susie Brown who'd been mentioned in the *South London Press* as having married a self-made businessman called Sammy Adams? And wasn't there another Brown who'd been famous in Walworth for about a week? Yes, that was Freddy Brown, wasn't it? He'd been headlined in the national newspapers as a witness in a murder trial. He was friendly with those young newly-weds, Chrissie and Danny Thompson. And Horace knew him at least well enough to say hello to him if they met. There was a whole family of Browns somewhere in the area around Browning Street. Was Sally Brown one of them?

'Lorst yer way, Orrice?' said the man on duty at the Oval gates.

'Who, me, Albert?' said Horace.

'Yus, you, Orrice. Are yer comin' or goin'? 'Old up, now yer look as if yer walkin' backwards.'

''Ope it ain't goin' to be fatal to me cricket,' grinned Horace, who could revert to cockney at the drop of a hat, but never in the hearing of Rebecca.

'Ain't in love, are yer, Orrice?' said the gateman.

'If it feels the same as being knocked for six, I could be,' said Horace.

'Gawd 'elp yer, Orrice, that's fatal all right. So watch yer cricket, mate. Percy Fender 'isself 'as got 'is eye on yer.'

'Is that gospel?' asked Horace.

'It ain't a fairy story,' said the gateman.

'Well, he did say something encouraging to me this morning, so good on yer, Albert,' said Horace, and went on his way into the ground.

In the shop, Sally was thinking what a daft family he must come from if he had to buy hair ribbon and elastic for his sister. His lady sister, he'd said, as if his family considered themselves posh. Mind, she had to be fair, though. His sister might be an invalid who couldn't do her own shopping. But then, why couldn't the mother do it? Yes, it sounded daft all right. Anyway, with luck, I'll have seen the last of him. All that cheek of his and the way he fancies his chances could easy make me lose me professional poise and throw coat-hangers at him. I could actually throw saucepans and rolling-pins at blokes with big heads like he's got.

On her way home later, and walking through Braganza Street, the front window curtain of a house moved a little. She glimpsed the movement out of the corner of her eye. She smiled as she went on. She guessed some old lady was indulging the favourite pastime of lots of old ladies in Walworth and Kennington, the pastime of watching the world go by from behind curtains.

*   *   *

Horace's hours at the Oval were erratic in the summer, but that went with the job, part-groundsman, part-cricketer. However, as the cricket season proper was as good as over, he was home in time that day to sit down to supper with his family. They always ate in the kitchen, in common with most Walworth families, but Rebecca allowed the parlour to be used for relaxation or recreation at any time. She looked on it as a living-room. Horace liked his home. It always looked as if a bright spirit had been at work in every corner. He especially liked the square kitchen, with its homely range and the dresser full of shining crockery. The window let in a lot of light, despite the fact that Walworth light had much to contend with, having to fight its way through sooty smoke in the winter when chimneys were active, and through the dust-specked air of summer. Still, it put up a good fight as far as Rebecca and her family were concerned. It showed up the gleam of brass on the fender and the fact that the curtains were never allowed to look limp. Attractive potted plants stood on a shelf in the scullery, and on the wall above the mantelpiece hung a large framed photograph of Rebecca's late parents, her bearded father looking like Charles Dickens, her mother a little like Queen Alexandra.

Jim was buying the house now, having been able to afford a mortgage when he was promoted to manager of the club. However, he had promised that when Horace and Ethel were both married, he and

Rebecca would go and live in Hampshire, close to the village where his late mother had been born and bred. That is, if he could find a job in the nearest town. If not, then they'd wait until he retired. Ethel said she and her future husband would go and live in Hampshire too, not far from them. Horace asked if her future husband would agree. Ethel said he better had or he wouldn't be her future husband. At that stage Mr X didn't loom large, anyway.

Over supper, Horace made a presentation of the pink ribbon to his sister. Ethel blinked with new pleasure.

'Orrice, why're you givin' me little presents?' she asked.

'Well, you're not a bad old thing, sis,' said Horace.

'I think you've been in that ladies' dress shop again, Horace,' smiled Rebecca.

'Well, Ethel was right,' said Horace, 'pink suits her hair a lot better than navy blue, so I went in and bought a yard.'

'But I didn't mean to be ungrateful about the blue, honest,' said Ethel.

'Pink or blue, I don't think either was the point of the exercise,' said Jim.

'Yes, tell us, Horace, did the girl in the shop give you a smile today?' asked Rebecca. She was intrigued, of course, thinking a dress shop assistant sounded rather nice.

'More like a suspicious look,' said Horace.

'What a cheek,' said Ethel. 'Fancy anyone bein'

suspicious of Orrice. Orrice, you could've gone to Woolworth's instead.'

'He could,' said Jim, 'but the girl doesn't work there.'

'I don't think I did a lot better for myself today,' said Horace, 'I think she's a bit choosy.'

'Young ladies should be,' said Rebecca.

'But I did get hold of her name,' said Horace, 'it's Sally Brown.'

'Who?' said Ethel.

'Sally Brown,' said Horace. 'Could she be the one you knew at school, Ethel, the one who's got a sister called Susie and a brother called Freddy? Or could she be a Kennington Brown?'

'I didn't know her very well,' said Ethel, 'she was more than a year older than me. I knew Alice French best.'

Jim smiled, remembering young Alice French and how she brought out the worst in Ethel by attaching herself to Horace. Those were the days when Ethel regarded her brother as her private property, more or less. However, Alice's family moved to Lewisham eventually, and she and Horace lost touch.

'I liked Alice French,' said Horace.

'Such a sweet girl,' said Rebecca.

'She used to call Orrice "dear"' said Ethel with a little giggle. '"Hello, Orrice dear" she used to say. "Oh, don't you look nice in your Sunday suit, Orrice dear?" Orrice used to collapse.'

'We've all got happy memories,' said Jim.

Horace grinned and said, 'Never mind Alice. Listen, Ethel, if Sally Brown does belong to the Brown family, d'you know exactly where they live?'

'Orrice, I never went to their house,' said Ethel.

'I believe they live somewhere off Browning Street,' said Rebecca. 'I know Mrs Brown through the church. She attends sometimes and we've met. And I believe I've noticed some of her family with her in the past. She's a very nice person.'

'Glad to hear it, Mum,' said Horace, 'but it's not Mrs Brown I'm after. It's Sally Brown.'

'What exactly do you mean, Horace, you're after her?' asked Rebecca.

'He means he's serious,' said Jim.

'Crikey, Orrice,' said Ethel, 'is it love at first sight?'

'Well, I think I'm in the mood to write her a poem,' said Horace.

'Oh, d'you want me to ask Davy to write one for you?' said Ethel.

'No, I think I'll write my own, sis,' said Horace. 'D'you know, I'm getting vague memories of a Sally Brown now. Wasn't she a bit of a tich?'

'I think you mean petite, Horace,' said Rebecca.

'Well, if petite means a bit of a tich, I'm on your side, Mum,' said Horace. 'But I can tell you the girl in the shop isn't like that, she's up to my shoulders.'

'Five-feet-six?' said Jim.

'About that,' said Horace, 'and with fair hair. She bowled me over again today.'

'What with?' asked Jim.

'Her looks,' said Horace.

'Did you find out if she's already going steady?' asked Rebecca.

'It didn't get sociable enough for that,' said Horace.

'But you're thinking about going into the shop again?' said Rebecca.

'I'm working on it,' said Horace, and Rebecca smiled. Horace had a fair share of determination.

'Good luck,' said Jim.

'Lor', what a palaver,' said Ethel. 'By the way, Mum, me Sunday's boater's gettin' a bit old.' She was fond of boaters. They suited her, and they hadn't yet gone completely out of fashion either for girls or young men. 'I think I need a new one. Davy said it didn't matter, but a new one would be sort of nice.'

'I'll have a look at your old one,' said Rebecca, 'and if you really do need a new one, I'm sure your father and I can put something towards its cost.'

'I like you and Dad,' said Ethel, who didn't earn a fortune as a factory office clerk.

Horace entered the dress shop almost as soon as it opened on Wednesday morning. The head groundsman had given him fifteen minutes to sort out his love problems. Horace said he hadn't got love problems. Well, said the head groundsman, what made you put odd socks on this morning, might I ask? I always wear odd socks, said Horace. Don't give me any rhubarb, said the head groundsman, I had enough for me afters last night, so all you've got is fifteen minutes, and don't come back looking like a bunch of last year's spring onions.

Sally was in the shop, and the manageress was doing something to the till.

'Good morning,' said Horace breezily, a carrier-bag in his hand.

Sally gave him one of her polite shop assistant's looks.

'Good morning, sir,' she said. Miss Lomax glanced and a little smile lightly flitted over her face. It was pretty obvious that this personable young man was taken with Sally. Sally, however, as far as Miss Lomax could judge, wasn't playing. 'We only sell ladies' wear, you know,' said the young lady who wasn't playing.

'Yes, I know,' said Horace, 'I'm a regular customer here. Unfortunately, miss, I can't stay long, I've got to get back in a few minutes. There's a lot of ground work about today.'

'Oh, dear, what hard luck,' said Sally, 'but we won't keep you, sir.'

'Thought you might say that,' said Horace. 'Never mind, I only want to know if you sell straw boaters.'

'We do sell some hats specially designed to go with some outfits,' said Sally, 'and we do have dressy boaters to go with striped blouses. But I don't know we've got one to fit you.' Lowering her voice, she added, 'And I don't know why you keep on comin' in here to make me look silly. I know you're doin' it on purpose.'

'Can I help it if I like you?' said Horace.

'What is it you want, young man?' called Miss Lomax, but with a smile. Horace returned the smile.

'Only a ladies' boater,' he said. 'It's for my lady sister.' He addressed Sally again. 'I've brought her old one, it's in this carrier-bag. I'll leave it with you so's you can match it for size. Then I'll pop back sometime this afternoon.'

'It's early closin' day, at one,' said Sally.

'Yes, so it is,' said Horace. 'Right, I'll pop in about twelve, then, and see what you're offering in the way of a new one. I just don't have time now.' He placed the carrier-bag on the counter. Sally gave him a cool look.

'You'd better not be larkin' about,' she said.

'I'm not,' said Horace, and made for the door. He stopped halfway, then returned, Miss Lomax watching him, the little smile still on her face. 'Excuse me, Miss Brown,' said Horace, 'but did you used to go to St John's School in Larcom Street?'

'That's nothing to do with you,' said Sally, still quite sure he considered himself God's gift and that accordingly he probably picked up girls by the dozen.

'Oh, well, see you later,' said Horace, and left.

'I think you've got an admirer, Sally,' said Miss Lomax.

'I've got several,' said Sally, 'and I'm not mad

about havin' any more, specially one like him. Honest, Miss Lomax, I'm just not gone on young men that think every girl fancies them. That kind take liberties.' Ronnie had eventually taken a liberty with her, and she'd smacked his face. Then he'd done it again, and that was the end of him as far as Sally was concerned. Sally belonged to a respectable family, and was never going to let her mum and dad down by allowing any feller to take liberties with her.

'I thought this one rather nice,' said Miss Lomax.

'He's tryin' to pick me up,' said Sally, 'and I'm not 'aving it.'

The shop's first lady customer of the day walked in then, and God's gift to girls was forgotten. Horace, actually, had never seen himself as God's gift. He'd simply taken a shine to Sally, and was doing his best to earn himself a place in her social life.

Sammy Adams was spending the morning at the Adams Fashions garment factory in Shoreditch, a new factory built in place of an old one destroyed by fire and accordingly an industrial palace compared to the ancient workplaces existing in many parts of the East End. The stone floor of the large machine shop was covered with hard-wearing linoleum of a bright and cheerful pattern. Big windows let in great cubic yards of light. On one side worked the seamstresses, applying themselves to the hand-stitching for which the firm was already famous. On the other side worked the machinists. The factory now employed over a hundred girls and women, all of them under the supervision of Gertie Roper, considered by the older machinists to be the rag trade soulmate of the boss, Mister Sammy Adams. True, there was little Gertie wouldn't do for Sammy in the matter of ensuring first-class quality and maximum production. She offered the same sort of loyalty to his brother Tommy, the factory manager. She had kind feelings for Tommy, a handsome and sympathetic man. She had quite affectionate feelings for Sammy, who had always treated the seamstresses and machinists with a fairness missing from most East End bosses. The girls actually took bonuses home with their Friday wages, something they all kept quiet about in case competitors got to know and arranged for the factory to be accidentally blown up.

Gertie had been a gaunt and scrawny machinist in a sweatshop when Sammy first got to know her. When he acquired the factory, better conditions and better wages came about, and these, together with steady money for her husband Bert, the maintenance and security man, had wrought their happy change. Gertie had filled out and now, in her early forties, looked quite a handsome woman. She dressed well for her job as supervisor, usually in a costume and blouse, and no longer had to operate a machine herself.

At this moment she and her husband were in Tommy's office, and Sammy was holding forth.

'Bein' uninclined, as I am, to stand still while our competitors try to stick their noses in front, I'm presently tellin' meself it's time to buy out George Carter's company. And his freehold fact'ry. In which case—'

'Pardon me, guv,' said Bert, a sinewy ex-docker, 'but as I 'ear it, by way of standin' on a street corner, this here George Carter ain't exactly a friend of yours. In other words, guv, he 'ates yer guts. If he 'as to sell, he'll work 'imself to bleedin' death to—'

'Now, Bert, you ain't talkin' to Monday mornin' leavings,' said Gertie, 'it's our boss and our manager.'

'No worries, Gertie, a spade's a spade,' said Tommy.

'I don't like 'is language in front of Mister Sammy,' said Gertie.

'All right, me old Dutch,' said Bert.

'Carry on, Bert,' said Sammy.

'What I'm sayin', guv, is that the aforesaid geezer ain't likely to sell out to you while 'e's still got two arms and two legs, if yer foller me. I'm beggin' yer pardon if that's bad news.'

'Well, it ain't exactly good news,' said Sammy, who usually made a point of using standard cockney when conversing with his two most loyal East End workers.

'It's a spanner in your intentions,' said Tommy.

'To avoid me intentions bein' gummed up something 'orrible,' said Sammy, 'I'll 'ave to make an offer that's mouthwaterin', although it beats me why the bloke's feelin' unfriendly.'

'It's our prices, Sammy, they're well and truly undercuttin' his,' said Tommy.

'That's hon'rable competition, which is custom'ry in a trade,' said Sammy, 'and worked out for the benefit of the customer. In any case, it ain't good business for any business cove to be guided by who he likes and who he don't like.'

'George Carter's guided by the fact that 'alf his customers have come over to us,' said Tommy.

'The way I 'ear it, guv, the geezer reckons yer nobbling 'im,' said Bert.

'Well, me own reckonin', Bert, is that he's takin' too much out of the business,' said Sammy, 'and at a time when 'is wheels 'ave fallen off and 'is production's up the spout. The silly old sod's got a ruddy Rolls Royce.'

'Which I 'ear ain't properly paid for yet,' said Bert.

'I'll be frank,' said Sammy, 'I'd like 'is fact'ry. But it won't happen yet, not till he recognizes the fact that he's sinkin' fast and needs a lifeboat. If he won't recognize it, then 'is ship'll sink and so will 'is lifeboat. He won't like swallowin' all that water, poor old George. I've heard too much of it can drown a bloke.'

'Mister Sammy, 'is girls 'ud like it if you bought 'is business and 'is fact'ry,' said Gertie.

'I got you, Gertie,' said Sammy. 'Well, if I do we'll 'ave to turn the fact'ry inside-out, in a manner

95

of speakin'. That means I'd like you to reorganize the management side, Tommy, until I find the right kind of bloke to appoint to the job; you to get the girls workin' our way, Gertie; and you to strip the place down and tart it up, Bert, with the 'elp of some local talent. I ain't in favour of girls and women havin' to work in fact'ries that look like sooty railway sheds on a foggy day. I jotted down some ideas on Sunday when I took me fam'ly out for a picnic in the country, which ideas nearly got lost when Susie chucked me notebook in the brambles. Some female wives are a bit funny, 'ave you noticed that, Bert?'

'Well, guv—'

'You goin' to say something, Bert Roper?' asked Gertie.

'Tell you what, guv, I'll give that one a miss,' said Bert.

'Sensible,' said Tommy. 'Listen, Sammy, if you buy Carter out, what's goin' to happen here while Gertie, Bert and me are workin' over there, at 'is place?'

'I'll make arrangements,' said Sammy.

'You'll 'ave to,' said Tommy, 'I'm not havin' Gertie and Bert tryin' to do two jobs at once.'

'Well, some people, I'm happy to say, can do just that, two jobs at once,' said Sammy, 'and if they did it for me, they'd get paid double wages. The first time I get to be unappreciative of human kindness—'

'Eh?' said Tommy.

96

'That's right,' said Sammy, 'the first time I do you can fire me from a cannon.'

'We wouldn't do that, Mister Sammy,' protested Gertie, 'it could injure you something 'orrible.'

'Might blow 'is head off,' said Tommy. He looked at the office clock. It was just coming up to twelve-thirty. On the stroke, he pressed a buzzer, and in the workshop a bell rang. Time for the seamstresses and machinists to knock off for an hour.

'I think I'll have a fried bacon sandwich at Joe's Cafe,' said Sammy. 'It's on me way back to Camberwell.'

Gertie looked at Bert, and Bert rubbed his chin.

'Mister Sammy,' said Gertie, 'if yer goin' that way, I s'pose me and Bert couldn't ask yer to look at an 'ouse in a nice little road by Shoreditch Park, could we? Only we're thinkin' of buyin' it, like you always recommended, and we'd be more'n grateful if you and Mister Tommy could tell us if it's the cat's whiskers or a pig in a poke. Well, it's two 'undred and fifty quid, and you and Mister Tommy know more about buyin' a house than we do.'

Sammy had advised them some time ago that their earnings could be put to good use, that they ought to buy a house instead of renting one all their lives. It almost frightened Gertie, the thought of actually buying a place, but she was ready to take the plunge now, and so was Bert. Sammy, pleased for them, was quite willing to drive them to the house and let them know what he thought of it.

97

Tommy said he'd come too, then go to Joe's Cafe with Sammy afterwards.

So off the four of them went. They passed George Carter's factory on the way, and the bloke himself was standing at the gate talking to a man in a bowler hat. He saw Sammy at the wheel of the open car, and shouted at him.

'Lordin' it, are yer, Sammy Adams, you bleeder!'

'My regards to yer, George,' Sammy called back, and drove on.

'His temper don't sound a bit nice,' said Gertie.

'Well, 'e's got a creditor tryin' to get a hand in 'is pocket,' grinned Bert.

When they reached the empty house, Sammy and Tommy made an inspection, Gertie hanging on to every word they said about it. Tommy thought it as sound as a bell structurally. He knocked on walls, Sammy tested doors and woodwork, and they both examined window frames. The place needed some paint, and the garden – there was actually a garden – needed to be cleared of an accumulation of rubbish. Tommy searched for traces of mice or rats and found none. Sammy said the kitchen was made for Gertie, and that Bert could knock the scullery into shape. He and Tommy recommended the purchase. Gertie and Bert looked at each other.

'Shall us, Gertie?' said Bert.

'Oh, 'elp, why don't we?' said Gertie. 'We got all the savings we've made since Mister Sammy give you yer job, Bert, and 'e said ages ago we could easy borrer what else we needed. It's called a morgidge.'

'Our grown-up kids'll like it, and the park,' said Bert.

'Me and Bert thanks yer both for comin' and givin' us yer kind advice,' said Gertie to the brothers. 'You both been good luck to us ever since we've been workin' for yer, for which we also thanks yer. Now you say, Bert.'

'Say what?' asked Bert.

'You got to speak a piece,' said Gertie, 'you're 'ead of the fam'ly.'

'Me?' said Bert and grinned. 'What, just for now, like?'

'Get on with it,' said Gertie.

'Well, gents,' said Bert, 'Gertie's right. We owe yer, and we ain't afraid to say so. It ain't just workin' for yer, it's knowin' yer, and would yer give our regards to yer older brother, who's also a gent, when you next see 'im.'

'It's all mutual,' said Sammy. 'Come on, let's all have a fried bacon sandwich before I make me way back to Camberwell.'

'Mister Sammy,' said Gertie, 'I like yer something chronic.'

Chapter Seven

Early closing meant the dress shop shut at one.

'Let me see,' said Miss Lomax at five minutes to, 'has that young man been back?'

'No, Miss Lomax,' said Sally, who'd taken the trouble to find a very nice boater, the same size as the old one, and to put it aside.

'Well, I'm closing up now,' said Miss Lomax, a single woman of thirty who had a gentleman friend of thirty-five. 'I suppose he was serious about buying a boater for his sister, was he?'

'I'm sure I don't know,' said Sally, fuming a little because she was certain he was having a game with her. He was probably laughing his head off. His big head. 'He's not worth bothering about, Miss Lomax.'

'He seemed quite likeable, I thought,' said Miss Lomax, emptying the till.

'Oh, I think he likes 'imself all right,' said Sally, not too keen on the manageress making the kind of remarks that implied his comings and goings were worthy of notice, which they weren't. Nor was he. In fact, he was the kind of bloke who shouldn't be noticed by anybody at all. That would shrink his big head. Him and his lady sister. If he did manage to arrive before Miss Lomax locked the shop, she'd tell him to buzz off.

But he didn't show up, and she and Miss Lomax left to go their separate ways. However, by the time she was halfway home, Sally had put him out of her mind.

She herself, however, was still in the fermenting mind of a shellshocked man of the Great War, and he drew back in his chair as he saw her approaching. He took his head out of the way, as it were, but not before he'd glimpsed she was carrying something long.

There'd been a threat of rain all day. It hadn't come to anything, but Sally had her umbrella with her.

To ex-Corporal Joseph Burns, who still lived in the dark, thunderous days of war, it could have been a disguised rifle, a sniper's rifle. He drew back in his chair, breath escaping in a hiss as she passed by. It didn't fool him, the fact that she neither glanced nor stopped. She was doing a recce on him all right, he was sure of that. He waited for her to retrace her steps. Well, she wasn't carrying a rifle for nothing, she was ready today to get him in her sights, curse her. But she didn't reappear, and he sighed with relief.

Sally walked on, refusing to think about the young man who was playing her up. Horace, actually, was innocent. He simply hadn't been able to get to the shop before it closed. Nor did he get home until eight, after Rebecca, Jim and Ethel had had supper. As he let himself in, he realized Davy was there again, in the parlour with Ethel, because Ethel was reciting. Davy had wanted her to read his poem 'The Lady of the Shining Waters'.

'But, Davy, I'm always readin' that one to you,' Ethel had said.

'I hope you're not saying you don't like it, Ethel,' said Davy.

'Yes, course I do,' Ethel assured him, 'I was only saying about it, that's all.'

'Begin,' said Davy, and Ethel began.

'All in white the lady stood on the shimmering sheet,
The sky above her dark-haired head, the water,
         'neath her feet.
Lilies floated on the lake and crowned her tresses
         bright
Their petals draping beauteously her gown of purest
         white.'

It was at this point that Horace entered the little hall and heard his sister.

'Oh, far beyond the misty vale the waters of the
         lake
Spread their shining surface, oh, come, ye sprites,
         awake.
There stands the lilied lady, sighing in her dreams,
Pointing to the waters, where dwell the mermaid
         queens.'

Horace rolled in the aisles, good as. Ethel said, 'Davy, you sure she should be standin' on the lake? I mean, she's not Jesus, is she?'

'Ethel, it's poetry, I should think you'd understand that.'

'Yes, all right, Davy.'

'Continue,' said Davy.

'Alas, the sun of evening flushed the radiant sky,
And once again the lady gave forth a soulful sigh.
Behold the trees in mourning upon the bright green
*   bank,*
Their leaves were softly trembling as the lady slowly
*   sank.'*

'Yes, quite good, Ethel,' said Davy, 'but you should try to make your voice quiver a bit.'

'I don't know how I could do that,' said Ethel.

'It's just a question of feeling, Ethel,' said Davy.

'Well, I had a lot of feeling for the lady sinkin',' said Ethel.

'There you are, then,' said Davy, 'put that feeling into your voice.'

'I'll try,' said Ethel, although she thought it might make her sound daft.

Horace, grinning, went through to the kitchen to catch up on his belated supper.

'Horace, why are you looking so pleased with yourself?' asked Rebecca.

'It's Ethel,' said Horace, 'I think she and Davy are tyin' each other up in poetical knots.'

'Well, it's one way of passing the time,' said Jim.

'It's killing me,' said Horace, and laughed.

Rebecca, setting his supper before him, said, 'What progress have you made today?'

'With my cricket?' said Horace, getting to work

with his knife and fork. 'Well, I may be a regular member of the second eleven next season. With a chance of one or two games for the county side.'

'Congratulations,' said Jim.

'That's splendid, Horace,' smiled Rebecca. 'And what about your interest in Miss Sally Brown?'

'Oh, I'm still interested,' said Horace, 'but progress is at a bit of a standstill. I took Ethel's old boater in first thing this morning.'

'You did what?' said Jim, looking up from his evening paper.

'Fact, Dad,' said Horace, 'I took Ethel's old boater in this morning.'

'No wonder I couldn't find it when I wanted to look at it,' said Rebecca.

'Well, it gave me the chance to go into the shop again and ask about a new one, seeing Ethel said the old one's had its day,' said Horace. 'I left it with Sally and said I'd call back midday, but I couldn't get away.'

'Does Ethel know you took it?' asked Jim.

'No, I thought she might read me some poetry if she'd known I'd snaffled it,' said Horace. 'I'll have to go back to the shop tomorrow, if I can.'

'Horace, you're using extraordinary methods to see this young lady,' said Rebecca.

'Yes, in and out of a ladies' dress shop like a yo-yo,' said Jim.

'Well, I'll keep goin',' said Horace, 'something hopeful might happen.'

Rebecca said, 'I'm quite fascinated by all this.'

'Mind you, it's taxin' my credentials,' said Horace.

I really should like to take a look at this young lady myself, thought Rebecca.

In the parlour Davy was frowning as he advised Ethel her voice didn't have any quiver at all.

'But I'm tryin' all I can,' said Ethel.

'What you ought to do is get emotional,' said Davy.

'Er what?' said Ethel.

'A lump in your throat would help,' said Davy.

'Oh, I do get a lump in me throat at the cinema sometimes,' said Ethel earnestly.

Davy looked disgusted.

'Oh, films,' he said, 'that's all artificial, not poetry. Think of the lady being drawn under the lake by the limpid hands of fate.'

'The what hands?' said Ethel.

'And the lady's you yourself, Ethel,' said Davy, 'pure and beauteous and sighing.'

'Oh, crikey,' said Ethel, 'are all your poems about me, Davy?'

'Well, of course,' said Davy, gravely owlish.

'And I'm all pure and beauteous and sighing?' said Ethel, who had a sudden terrible feeling she was going to giggle. Davy wouldn't like that, it wouldn't half pain his poetic soul. Still, she liked his poetic soul a lot more than the vulgar minds of costermongers or Billingsgate fish porters or blokes from Brandon Street who called out, 'Oi, Effel, 'ow's yer Sunday bloomers?'

'Ethel, you inspire my poetry,' said Davy.

'Well, that's really nice of you, Davy, but I don't go around doin' a lot of sighing, do I?'

'You ought to when you're reading my verse,' said Davy. 'Anyway, read this poem again.'

'All right,' said Ethel, 'and I'll really try to quiver this time.'

But she didn't get top marks from Davy for her efforts. Still, he did say he was sure she'd improve, which was a comfort to her.

'Good morning, modom,' said Miss Lomax at a little after eleven the following morning. She had a weakness for the West End pronunciation of 'madam', something which Sammy discouraged in his South London shops on the grounds that what was acceptable to West End customers didn't do anything for the ladies of Lambeth, Southwark, Peckham and so on. They liked his shop assistants to be ladylike, but 'modom' was coming it a bit, and had toffee-nosed implications. However, it did slip from Miss Lomax sometimes, usually when the customer was well-dressed.

'Good morning,' said the customer in return, and with a smile that was all of serene. Rebecca looked stylishly handsome in a grey costume and velour hat. 'You have a rather nice silk scarf with the outfit worn by one of your window dummies. Do you sell them as accessories?'

'We have an excellent range of them, madam, and at very economical prices,' said Miss Lomax. 'May I show you?'

'Thank you,' said Rebecca, and glanced at the young woman who was attending to a customer of her own. The light of another smile showed in the eyes of Horace's adoptive mother, for the young woman's appearance and looks were indisputably attractive. Her features stirred little chords of recognition. Rebecca felt sure she had seen her in the neighbourhood somewhere in the past, and also, perhaps, in the East Street market.

Yes, she's Sally Brown, I'm certain she is. My word, she really is attractive, and Horace, alas, may be right in feeling she already has a steady young man.

'Here we are, madam,' said Miss Lomax.

Rebecca's inquisitive call at the shop cost her the price of a light-blue silk scarf. Sally glanced at her only when she was on her way out.

I know her, thought Sally, she's local. What's her name now? Cooper, yes, Cooper. Isn't she the woman who brought up that funny pair of kids, Orrice and Effel? I think I've heard they're still around, but I don't know if I'd recognize them.

Her working day eventually approached its close. It had been quite a busy one. There might not be much money about, according to the newspapers and the wireless, but there was always some of it making its way into the tills of the Adams dress shops. That was because of the right kind of prices, helped by the absence of any middlemen for most of the wares, and the excellent finish of garments.

Brother-in-law Sammy really did employ first-class machinists, and an intelligent designer too, a woman who knew what was attractive and saleable to South London customers. Next year sometime, Sally's transfer to the Oxford Street shop was on the cards, unless she was married by then. Some hopes. Well, she was always looking for someone like Sammy or Boots, and that kind of someone hadn't crossed her path yet.

The other kind of someone, that joker, hadn't appeared in the shop. That joker was all washed up, as far as Sally was concerned. He'd had his laugh at her expense and left her with an old boater. Well, that old boater was now in the dustbin at the rear of the shop. The dressy boater she'd selected was now on general display.

Oh, blow him. Ten past five, and there he was, entering the shop, looking as fond of himself as ever with that smile of his. A cat's grin, more like. There was just one customer present, and Miss Lomax was attending to her. Horace, looking very healthy from a long day in the open air, advanced breezily on Sally. Sally drew herself up and pre-sented a haughty front to him. Of course, all it did to Horace was to make him think what a nice proud figure she had.

'Hello,' he said.

'Beg your pardon?' said Sally.

'It's me,' said Horace.

'Really? How interesting, I'm sure.' It sounded as if Sally had a very well-trained plum in her mouth. 'Are you the new window-cleaner?'

'You asked if I'd come to read your gas meter before,' said Horace, liking her looks more each time.

'Well, we don't wish it read again,' said Sally. 'You can leave now.'

'I think you're cross with me,' said Horace, 'but I honestly couldn't get back here yesterday, my services were in demand all day. Sorry about that, Sally.'

'Miss Brown, if you don't mind,' said Sally, 'and how did you know my name, might I ask?'

'I heard your manageress use it,' said Horace.

'Have you come to mess me about again?' whispered Sally fiercely.

'No, I've come about my sister's boater,' said Horace. 'Where is it?'

'In the dustbin.'

'Pardon?'

'In the dustbin.'

'I didn't hear that,' said Horace.

'I didn't think you were comin' back,' said Sally crossly, 'I thought you were larkin' about.'

'Me?' said Horace.

'Yes, you, you've been doin' it to me all the time.'

'Hold on, wait a minute, half a tick,' said Horace, 'd'you mean you've chucked my sister's Sunday boater into your shop dustbin?'

'Yes, didn't you hear me tell you it was because I didn't think you were comin' back?'

'Well, I just don't know what to say, Miss Brown, I'm amazed.'

'No, you're not,' said Sally, casting an eye at Miss Lomax. Miss Lomax was still busy with her customer. 'You're larkin' about.'

'Well, blow my head off,' said Horace cheerfully, 'I don't think much of that, comin' from someone who's given my sister's boater to the dustmen.'

'Oh, you're gettin' my goat, you are,' breathed Sally, who'd mislaid her trained plum.

'Never mind, no hard feelings, I expect it can be rescued,' said Horace. 'Unless, of course, you've found the new one I asked for.'

'Look, are you bein' serious?' demanded Sally.

'Cross my heart,' said Horace.

'D'you need any help, Miss Brown?' called Miss Lomax.

'No, it's the customer for the boater,' said Sally.

The other customer, a housewife in her thirties, blinked at Horace.

'Well,' she said in the direct way of her kind, 'I never 'eard of a young man buyin' a lady's boater in a ladies' shop before.'

'It's my first time,' said Horace, 'and it's for my sister. Mind you, I've shopped here for other things.'

'He's barmy, poor bloke,' whispered the housewife to Miss Lomax, who smiled.

Sally, pulling herself together, brought the plum back into her mouth.

'I'm pleased to inform you, sir, that the selected boater's on display,' she said. 'Over there.'

Horace took a look. It was a crisp golden yellow, with a green and gold band and two little trailing extensions.

'I like it,' he said. The customer, leaving, steered cautiously wide of Horace on her way out. 'Yes, I'll have it,' he said. 'Thanks for all your trouble, Miss Brown.'

Miss Lomax, emptying her till, reminded Sally they were closing in a few minutes. Sally, after giving Horace a challenging look, which he returned with a smile, silently took the boater off the display stand and offered it to him for closer inspection.

'No, I'm happy with it,' he said. 'How much?'

'Three shillings and sixpence,' said Sally.

'Well, that sounds fair,' said Horace, and dug into his pocket. He brought out some silver and placed half a crown and a bob on the counter. 'Wait, though, I think I'd better take the old one back. As you're closing now, I'll drop in sometime tomorrow and pick both boaters up. Is that all right?'

Seeing he'd paid for the new one, and seeing she'd got to rescue the old one from the dustbin and probably give it a clean, Sally didn't feel she could argue. All the same, he was coming back again? Again?

'Very well, sir.'

'You've been really helpful,' said Horace, who now had an excuse for seeing her again. 'Can't thank you enough. See you sometime tomorrow, then.'

Off he went. Well, it could be worse, thought Sally, there could be two of him.

'A sale, then?' said Miss Lomax.

'Yes, but he's not pickin' it up till tomorrow,' said Sally.

Miss Lomax smiled.

'What a very nice young man,' she said.

'Beg your pardon, Miss Lomax?'

'Is he a soldier?'

'What makes you ask that?'

'He's conducting a campaign, isn't he, Sally?'

'Blow that,' said Sally. And now I've got to go and dig in the blessed dustbin, she told herself.

Horrors, the bin was empty. The dustcart had been round today. Oh, crikey.

The tormented war casualty saw her again. It was always again, she never stopped doing her recce job on him. Well, he'd got to keep watching her, or she'd get him. The Jerries had recruited her all right. Some women were good with a rifle, and the really good ones could be trained to become crackshots.

There she was, going by now, but not carrying anything except her handbag. She disappeared from his sight and he drew his usual breath of relief.

'Mum,' said Ethel that evening, 'I can't find me boater.'

Rebecca, glancing at Horace, said, 'Oh, I'm arranging to buy you a new one, Ethel dear.'

'But where's the old one?' asked Ethel. 'It's still got a bit of life in it.'

'I can't think what I did with it,' said Rebecca. 'Can you think, Horace?'

'It's probably in the dustbin,' said Horace.

'Well, that's not very nice,' said Ethel. 'Davy might want me to wear it if we go out for a walk this evening.'

'Not if it's full of potato peelings,' said Horace, tickled at the thought of giving her a nice surprise tomorrow, and looking forward to seeing Sally Brown again. He'd got to persevere with her, he wasn't going to give up, not unless she was committed to some other bloke. If she was, some other bloke ought to fall off Beachy Head.

'Ugh, I'm not lookin' in any dustbin that's got potato peelings in it,' said Ethel.

'Or tea leaves,' said Horace.

'Ugh, that's worse,' said Ethel.

However, when Davy came round he didn't invite Ethel out for a walk, he invited her to read his lastest poem, all about a fair maiden who dwelt by a limpid pool.

'*O, sun above in heavens blue,*
Cast thy radiant light
On lustrous maiden sweet and fair
With tresses dark and bright.'

'Slowly, Ethel, slowly.'

'Yes, all right, Davy. Is the maiden me again?'

'Of course.' Davy's spectacles showed a sorrowful light at her need to ask.

'Crikey, I—'

'Crikey's not very poetical, Ethel.'

'No, but I mean, you're writin' about me again. Davy, how can I be fair when I've got dark tresses?'

'Fair means pure of heart, Ethel.'

'Oh, 'elp,' said Ethel, then read on.

'By limpid pool she dwells each day,

Rose petals form her gown – Davy I can't just be wearin' rose petals. They'd fall off.'

'Not in poetry, Ethel.'

'But what about poetical breezes, Davy? They'd blow me petals right off.'

'Well, if you must be contradictory, Ethel,' said Davy gently, 'I suppose you're only being like most girls.'

'Davy, I wasn't bein' contradict'ry, I was just askin', that's all.'

'Are you sure you want to read this poem?' asked Davy, spectacles showing the grey light of doubt.

'Yes, of course, Davy.'

'Well, that's nice, Ethel. Continue, then.'

Ethel continued by reciting from the beginning of the second verse.

'By limpid pool she dwells each day,

Rose petals form her gown,

The limpid pool reflects fair face

And eyes of dream-filled brown – oh, my word, Davy, I've never thought about my eyes bein' dream-filled.'

'Ethel, you simply must use your imagination,' said Davy.

'It's not my imagination,' said Ethel, 'it's havin' you write poetry that's so flattering.'

'I'm glad you like it, Ethel. Carry on.'

Ethel carried on.

'Water lilies dip their heads
In a manner beckoning,
O! If she should accept their nods,
What shall be the reckoning? Oh, help, Davy, she's not goin' to sink under water again, is she?'

'To become a water sprite?' said Davy.

'What's a water sprite?' asked Ethel.

'Well, didn't you ever read *Water Babies* by Charles Kingsley?' asked Davy.

'What, when I was young?' said Ethel. 'No, I just read comics.'

'Never mind,' said Davy, 'you've got lots of promise now you're much older.'

'I'm only twenty,' said Ethel, whose conversational simplicity made her sound much younger.

'Yes, that makes you very promising, Ethel. But I was going to say water babies could be called water sprites. Carry on.'

'I just hope the maiden fair doesn't go under again,' said Ethel. Alas, the maiden fair did. The poem described how the water lilies kept beckoning until the mesmerized petal-clad, dream-filled young thing slid slowly into the depths of the limpid pool to become a water sprite. 'Well, Davy, I don't think much of that.'

'I beg your pardon?' said Davy, spectacles blinking with shock.

'Oh, I didn't mean I didn't like the poem,' said Ethel, 'only that it was rotten hard luck on the maiden fair, specially as she was supposed to be me.'

'No, you mustn't think of it like that,' said Davy. 'But next time I bring a poem, it'll be full of happiness. Read this one again, Ethel, and try to get that quiver in your voice when you reach the last two verses.'

'Oh, lor',' said Ethel.

'Pardon?' said Davy.

'Yes, all right, Davy.'

Chapter Eight

At ten minutes past noon on Friday, when a certain person in trousers walked into the shop, Sally said oh, bother it to herself. She was serving a customer and Miss Lomax was attending to another, so Horace could only stand and wait. He managed to do this without looking awkward or out of place. In fact, he inspected some dresses on display. Sally, knowing she'd got to tell him his sister's old boater had been tipped into a dustcart, went all edgy the moment her customer left the shop. Horace then presented himself in his cheerful way.

'Here I am, Miss Brown, and how's yourself, might I ask?' he said.

Sally opted for being what she was, a well-trained assistant.

'Good morning, sir, you've come to collect the new boater?'

'Yes, and the old one, just in case the new one doesn't fit,' said Horace, highly appreciative of her professional poise.

'Oh, the new one's exactly the same size as the old, sir,' she said, 'I was very careful about that.'

'Well, good on yer,' said Horace in fine old

cockney fashion, 'but I'd better take both.'

Miss Lomax glanced, and a little smile showed. She was aware of Sally's predicament and was on Horace's side. She couldn't think why Sally hadn't given him some encouragement. In an acceptable and respectable way, of course. Sally Brown was against being forward.

'Well, I—' Sally's plum took an embarrassed dive. 'Look, could we talk low so's Miss Lomax's customer doesn't hear?'

'Low?' said Horace. 'D'you mean common and gorblimey?'

'No, course I don't,' breathed Sally.

'I used to talk very common and gorblimey, and still can, if you want,' said Horace.

'Well, I don't want, I meant not to talk loud.'

'Sort of confidential and about going out together?' whispered Horace.

'You've got a hope.'

'Can I help it if I like you?'

'I don't want you to like me, thanks very much.'

'All right,' said Horace, 'let's get back to the boaters, then. Can you let me have 'em?'

'Look, what's happened isn't my fault,' said Sally.

'What isn't?'

'What I did with your sister's boater.'

'D'you mean it's still in the dustbin?' asked Horace.

'The way you kept actin', I was sure you were larkin' about,' said Sally.

118

'Don't worry,' said Horace, 'we've been through all that, and there's no hard feelings, y'know. Look, just show me where the dustbin is, and I'll dig into it for the boater meself.'

'It's not there,' said Sally.

'Where, then?' asked Horace.

'It's – it's – oh, blow it, the dustmen took it yesterday.'

'Hello, hello,' said Horace, 'what have we here, might I enquire? A shock for me sister?'

'I just didn't think you were comin' back,' breathed Sally, wrathful at being at a disadvantage.

'Oh, well, never mind,' said Horace cheerfully, 'up and down, in and out, which way, that way, all in a day's work. Can't be helped.'

'Look, I'm sorry, really,' said Sally.

'Well, I suppose the boater could've gone into a Salvation Army jumble sale,' said Horace, 'but now that it can't, let's—' He checked. 'Mind you,' he said after a second's flashing thought, 'my sister might still want it as a spare for weekdays. She's fond of boaters. They might be going out of fashion a bit, but they suit her. I think the best bet is the Corporation rubbish dump near the gasworks. We'll go there Sunday morning and have a look for it.'

'What, you and your sister'll turn all the rubbish over on Sunday morning just to find an old boater?' said Sally.

'No, you and me,' said Horace, at which point Sally had forty fits and Miss Lomax's customer departed. The shop door swung open again, and a dour-looking woman entered, making straight for Miss Lomax after a disapproving frown at the presence of a person in trousers. 'Where were we?' murmured Horace.

'I know where I am,' whispered Sally in utterly ferocious fashion, 'but I don't know where you are, except off yer daft rocker. If you think I'm goin' to the dustcart rubbish dump with you to look for some old boater, you can think again. Me turnin' rubbish over and on a Sunday morning? You're potty.'

'Well, it seems a fair suggestion,' said Horace, 'seeing you put the boater there. Not directly, of course, no, I'm not sayin' that, but sort of indirectly through the help of the dustmen. Where d'you live? I could call for you at ten, say, and we could go there together.'

'Oh, I'd like to bash your 'ead in,' fumed Sally, 'I never knew anyone that got my goat more than you. I hate you, I never hated anyone more, and I'm not goin' to any rubbish dump to look for an old boater, not with you, nor anyone else, not even if Old Nick comes to haunt me, d'you 'ear? Look, I'll pay for the boater. Not that it's worth more than tuppence.'

'What's wrong?' said Horace. 'You sound upset.' Actually, he thought her ferocious mood encouraging. Well, he'd read a very interesting novel once, in which one of the characters, a wise old female bird, had said that if a woman gets good and shirty with a man it's because she's really very fond of him. 'You're not cross with me, are you?'

'Oh, you're comin' it, you are,' said Sally, 'and if you don't go away, I'll go outside and look for a policeman.'

'What about the new boater?' asked Horace.

'Here.' Sally reached under the counter and brought out a green and white striped box containing the purchase. 'That's it, and kindly don't come back again. Oh, and 'ere's tuppence for—'

'No, don't worry,' said Horace. 'Look, tell you what, I'll write a note to your dustman and ask him if he can find the boater for me. I'll bring the note in on Monday, say, and you could pass it to him. How about that?'

'I'll scream in a minute,' breathed Sally.

'Well, you're obviously upset,' said Horace, 'so I'd better shove off, I suppose. Of course, if my sister starts mourning the loss of her old boater, I'll try to think of something to solve the problem and pop in about—'

'Listen,' hissed Sally, 'if you ever come in this shop again, I will bash your 'ead in, d'you 'ear me?'

'I'll have to go now, I've got to get a bite of lunch,' said Horace, and off he went, having had a very enjoyable time getting to know more about Miss Sally Brown, mostly concerning what a lot of dash and fire she had, which he liked.

Later, Sally was able to tell Miss Lomax of her nerve-racking conversation with that Charley-Harry character. When she came to the bit about going to the rubbish dump on Sunday morning, the manageress shrieked with laughter.

'Well, I don't think it's funny,' said Sally, whose lively sense of humour had been completely ruined for the time being.

'Of course it is, it's a scream,' said Miss Lomax.

'What, trying to drag me off to a smelly old dump to look for that old boater?'

'You didn't take that seriously, did you?' said Miss Lomax.

'It got my goat,' said Sally. 'Anyway, I don't think he'll come back this time, not after the earful I gave him.'

'I wouldn't bet on it,' said Miss Lomax. 'Mind you, Miss Sally Brown, I can't allow him in the shop except as a customer.'

'Well, if he does come in,' said Sally, 'couldn't we borrow someone's mad dog and set it on 'im?'

Ethel was delighted with the new boater, but said she didn't want Horace to keep spending his money like this when he ought to be saving up. Horace said he was saving up, so Ethel asked him what he was saving up for.

'The girl in the dress shop, probably,' said Jim.

'Orrice, have you got it bad?' asked Ethel. 'You must have the way you keep goin' to the shop. By the way, she must be the Sally Brown that used to be at St John's. I remembered this afternoon that someone told me ages ago she works in one of the Adams shops. Well, she's the sister-in-law of

Sammy Adams that started the business. Still, that's no reason why she should turn her nose up at you. Orrice, how much was this boater?'

'Oh, only a few bob, and you're welcome,' said Horace.

'Well, it's really nice of you,' said Ethel, 'but it's a bit barmy, isn't it, spendin' money on presents for me just to give yourself an excuse to go into the shop and talk to 'er.'

'I suppose we're both a bit barmy at the moment, Ethel,' said Horace.

'You and Sally Brown, Horace?' smiled Rebecca.

'No, me and Ethel,' said Horace.

'Me, why me?' asked Ethel.

'That's a tricky one, Horace,' said Jim.

'Slip of the tongue, Ethel,' said Horace, who wasn't going to tell his sister she'd gone potty over poetry.

'I should 'ope so,' said Ethel. 'What 'appened to my old boater, by the way?'

'It fell under a bus,' said Horace.

'D'you mean you dropped it in the road?' asked Ethel.

'Sorry, sis.'

'Oh, well, never mind,' said Ethel, 'the new one's lovely. You could go round to Sally Brown's house and tell her thanks for helpin' you choose it.'

I could, thought Horace, but she might bash my head in.

'I think she lives in Caulfield Place, off Browning Street,' said Rebecca, who felt Sally Brown was just the kind of young lady she'd have picked herself for Horace.

'The point is,' said Horace, 'does she already have a bloke?'

'You mean a young man,' said Rebecca.

'Orrice, haven't you found that out yet?' asked Ethel.

'I'm still a bit behind making progress,' said Horace.

'Crikey, Mum, would you believe it?' said Ethel. 'I think our Orrice is shy.'

'I've never noticed it,' said Jim.

'No, well, you're not a lady shop assistant, Dad,' said Ethel. 'I think I'd better find out for you, Orrice, I know lots of people that live around Browning Street.'

'I don't need any help,' said Horace.

'Yes, you do,' said Ethel.

Well, it's a hard life, thought Horace, when a bloke's soft on a young lady who only wants to bash his head in. I've gone wrong somewhere. On the other hand, all that flashing fire might mean she's getting fond of me but doesn't know it. Well, I wouldn't be what Mr and Mrs Cooper have made of me if I didn't keep trying.

★ ★ ★

Dumpling and Danny entertained their close friends, Cassie Ford and Freddy Brown, in their newly-wedded abode in Wansey Street. They had three very nice rooms and a lav and handbasin on the first floor of the house. Danny, good at fitting things up, had turned the back room into a cosy kitchen, having had a gas oven installed in the recess to one side of the fireplace. He'd re-papered the walls, painted the ceiling, given an old standing dresser a smart look and well above the gas oven he'd fitted a two-door cupboard for use as a larder. When he finished it all, Dumpling gave him a kiss.

'Well, that's nice of yer, Dumpling,' he said.

'Yes, but don't get soppy,' said Dumpling, who considered kissing, cuddles and all that came a daft second to football. Still, whenever she started giggling in the marital bed, Danny knew she'd forget football for five minutes or so.

They entertained Cassie and Freddy in their living-room, which was the front room and over-looked the street. The four armchairs were plump-looking, like Dumpling herself. She'd chosen them from a houseful of furniture Mr Eli Greenberg had acquired. Mr Greenberg was the well-known rag and bone merchant, a friend to the families of Walworth, who could supply any kind of second-hand furniture at a knock-down price to hard-up cockneys. It kept him poor, he said, and so did his wife and three stepsons, but if a man could make his gentile friends happy, should he worry about starvation?

Dumpling held forth.

'I been tellin' Danny that now Herbie Briggs and

Alf Bargett 'ave moved away, the team could do with some new blokes for this season.'

'Oh, how is Danny?' asked Cassie.

'Well, he's 'ere, you're lookin' at 'im,' said Dumpling.

'Yes, but how is he now 'e's married?' asked Cassie.

'Daft,' said Dumpling. 'You can ask 'im yourself.'

'How are you, Danny, as a married man?' asked Cassie.

'Daft,' grinned Danny.

'If it does that to all married blokes, count me out,' said Freddy.

'It didn't do it to Danny,' said Dumpling, 'he's always been daft.'

'I'm thinkin' I might emigrate,' said Freddy.

'Dumpling, you're nearest, give 'im a kick,' said Cassie, as eccentric as ever.

'Can't we talk about something sensible?' said Dumpling. 'Like our football team? Only I've been thinkin' Orrice Cooper used to be good at football when 'e was at school, and we don't want 'im to waste 'is talents.'

'I don't know I've ever met 'im to talk to,' said Cassie.

'Oh, I know him a bit by sight,' said Freddy, 'and I've heard he's goin' in for serious cricket these days.'

'But you can't play cricket in the winter,' said Dumpling.

'I concur, Dumpling,' said Danny. 'On top of which, Orrice 'as got the right build for a footballer.'

'Well, so 'ave you, Danny,' said Dumpling generously.

'Oh, I think Danny's also got the right build for a married man,' said Cassie. 'Of course, you'd know that better than me, Dumpling. D'you think Freddy has too?'

'Freddy what?' said Dumpling.

'Yes, d'you think 'e's got the right build for a married man?' asked Cassie.

'Cassie, I dunno what you mean,' said Dumpling. 'Mind, me mum once said married men come in all sizes, and wives 'ave to take pot luck, and me Aunt Hilda said 'er pot luck needed some Iron Jelloids.'

'Did you ask your mum what that meant?' enquired Cassie.

'No, course not,' said Dumpling, 'she was talkin' to me Aunt Hilda in the parlour at the time, and she didn't know I was listening. Besides, it all sounded daft to me.'

'Well,' said Cassie, imagination at work, 'I 'ope Freddy doesn't turn out to be pot luck.'

'Well, we all 'ave to take 'em for better or worse,' said Dumpling. 'Still, as long as you can get them doin' something to improve themselves, like readin' a book in bed instead of muckin' about, you can put up with their funny ways. Look, shall we ask our captain, Nick 'Arrison, to talk to Orrice about joinin' Browning Street Rovers?'

'What about askin' me if I regard meself as pot luck?' said Freddy.

'Freddy, we've gone past that bit,' said Dumpling, 'we're on about something sensible.'

'Oh, sorry I spoke,' said Freddy.

'That's all right,' said Dumpling, her blue sweater full of goodies. 'Mind, if I see Orrice, I'll ask 'im official meself as I'm a committee member. 'Ere, did yer know 'is sister Effel's got a young man? Me and Danny's seen 'er out with 'im, poor girl.'

'Why poor girl?' asked Freddy.

'Well, anyone could see 'e couldn't play football for toffee,' said Dumpling. 'Crikey, what an 'orrible fate for Effel if she marries 'im. Still, lots of us get unlucky. I mean, I 'ad to meet me own dire fate on me weddin' day, and I asked me dad what I could do about it, and me dad said just grin and bear it, which I did. I'll make a pot of tea now.'

'Good on yer, Dumpling,' said Freddy.

'Oh, yer a bloke after me own 'eart, Freddy,' said Dumpling.

'Excuse me, Dumpling, but Freddy's exclusive to me,' said Cassie.

'Yes, I'm her exclusive bit of pot luck,' said Freddy.

'I'm expecting my mother in an hour,' said Davy Williams to his landlady early on Saturday afternoon.

'Oh, yer widdered mother?' said Mrs Albright, and Davy's spectacles regarded her gravely.

'Yes, that's the one, Mrs Albright,' he said. 'She's my only one, you know.'

'Well, we all only ever 'ave one,' said Mrs Albright. Sixty, she was widowed herself, but had children and grandchildren. Her little house in Surrey Grove, near the Old Kent Road, was just right for her. Young Mr Williams, as her lodger in the upstairs back, was just right too, paying her a welcome five bob a week and being a nice quiet bloke. No trouble at all. What he liked about the house was that it actually had a bathroom. How it got there, Mrs Albright didn't know. She'd only been living there forty years, since she and her late husband, as newly-weds, had moved in. He'd installed a gas geyser, and they'd enjoyed lovely hot baths once a month regular. Mr Williams paid her thruppence every time he used it, which was a lot more regular than once a month. He liked a good wallow, with a large cake of yellow Sunlight soap to keep him company. He wrote poetry as a hobby. He'd read a poem to her once, but as it wasn't a bit like 'The Wreck of the Schooner Hesperus' that she'd learned at school, it went right over her head, and he didn't read any more to her. 'I'll be that pleasured to meet yer mum,' she said now, 'I expect she misses not 'aving you at 'ome.'

'Oh, she's still got my brothers and sisters,' said Davy. 'It was because I secured this job in Walworth that I left. I couldn't get work in Woolwich. By the way, I'm bringing my young lady to meet my mother.'

'That's nice,' said Mrs Albright, 'and it's nice too that you've got yerself a young lady, seein' you're always livin' so quiet, like. I'm pleased you took me advice and went to that dance, where you met 'er. A young man ought to get out and about a bit, that's what I always say, and 'aving a young lady 'elps. Me son Johnny was sort of married to 'is stamp album for years, and 'ardly ever went out till 'e met a very nice girl at 'is work, and after that he as good as forgot he 'ad a stamp album at all. When yer mum and yer young lady are both 'ere later, I'll bring up a nice pot of tea for them.'

'You're not going to the market?' said Davy.

'Well, I always do, Saturday afternoons,' said his landlady, still an active and independent kind of woman. 'It's me fav'rite time, Saturday afternoons, it's when the market's really lively, and I've always liked a bit of liveliness as much as a nice drop of port at Christmas. I'll make the pot of tea when I get back about four, as I always fancy a nice cup meself then.'

'Well, thanks, Mrs Albright,' said Davy, 'you're very kind.'

'Not at all, I'm sure,' said the good lady. 'We're all 'ere to be as kind as we can to each other.'

'What a nice thought,' said Davy, and his spectacles looked shyly grateful.

Chapter Nine

'Oh, this is where you live, Davy?' said Ethel, as she and he turned into Surrey Grove. It was a bit empty-looking, with no street kids about, but the old houses still stood up valiantly to time, and none of the doorsteps seemed scruffy.

'Yes, here we are,' said Davy, halting at the door of his landlady's house. There was a latchcord dangling from the letter-box, something familiar to many Walworth front doors. Davy pulled on it and the door opened. 'There, go in, Ethel.'

Ethel stepped straight into a living-room.

'Oh, it's like some of the 'ouses in King and Queen Street,' she said. 'They don't have passages, just front rooms. Is your mum expectin' me?'

'Well, no, I'm expecting her,' said Davy, closing the door. 'I did tell you I only lodge here.'

'Oh, yes, so you did,' said Ethel, 'I forgot.'

'My family lives in Woolwich,' said Davy, 'and my mother's coming to visit this afternoon. You'll be able to meet her when she arrives.'

'It's a shame Woolwich is a long way away, but I like what you've told me about your mum and your brothers and sisters, except I'm sorry your mum's been widowed,' said Ethel. 'Oh, are we in your landlady's living-room, then?' she asked, looking at the little ornaments on the mantelpiece.

'Yes, and she's a nice person,' said Davy, 'except that she doesn't have much of a clue about poetry. It's a pity some people can't see the beauty of poetry. My room's upstairs. Come on.' He took her up to his room, furnished with a bed, a little table, some chairs, a cupboard and a gas ring. Ethel thought my goodness, I've never seen anything more tidy. I didn't know young men could be as tidy as this.

'You do keep your room nice, Davy,' she said.

'Oh, thanks, Ethel,' said Davy, and looked at the tin clock on the mantelpiece. It was just after half-past two. 'Mother ought to have been here by now. I thought, in fact, she might have been waiting on the doorstep, my landlady being out. Never mind, she'll get here any moment. Sit down at the table, Ethel, and I'll show you one of my poetry books, the Robert Browning one.'

Ethel, neat in a light coat and little hat, took the coat off and Davy hung it on the doorpeg. Then they sat down with the book of Robert Browning's poems. Ethel did her very best to look and sound fascinated as Davy quoted from various epics. Well, she was always working hard to become a poetical soulmate of Davy's, since he was the only young man she'd met who was a bit of a gent. Ethel didn't have the make-up to identify with the boisterous and rumbustious nature of most of Walworth's young men. She liked quiet blokes. Whereas Cassie often thought about Freddy going romantically mad and carrying her off on a white charger to somewhere thrilling, Ethel would have died before the horse got anywhere near the destination. Cassie at eighteen was a lot more imaginative and outgoing than Ethel was at twenty. However, Davy appreciated Ethel's similarity to the pure young lady of his sonnets, and Freddy appreciated Cassie's similarity to a potty madcap. He knew he was never going to live a quiet life with Cassie. But then, he wouldn't have to live with sonnets, either. He and Cassie were soulmates of a different kind.

'Your mum's still not come, Davy,' said Ethel after twenty minutes.

'She's probably been held up,' said Davy. 'I'll go down and see if she's wandering about in the street.' Down he went, and back he came after a few minutes, a forlorn look to his spectacles. 'No, she's not anywhere about. Still, she does this sort of thing sometimes, she writes to say she's coming and then forgets.'

'Don't you ever go to see her?' asked Ethel.

'Oh, yes, every so often,' said Davy. 'I'll take you with me one Sunday. Well, let's do some more reading. I must say it's very uplifting, reading poetry with you, Ethel.'

'Oh, thank you, Davy,' said Ethel, but wouldn't have minded just sitting and talking.

Time went by without any sign of Davy's mother, and when Mrs Albright returned from the market, she called up to him.

'Is yer mum there, Mr Williams?'

'No, she forgot to come, Mrs Albright. There's just my young lady up here with me.'

'Well, don't do anything yer mum wouldn't like,' called Mrs Albright with a perceptible chuckle. 'Anyway, I'll still make a pot of tea and bring it up.' Which she did, and Davy introduced her to Ethel. 'My, ain't you a nice-lookin' girl?' she said. 'I'd like to 'ave met yer mum, Mr Williams, but meetin' yer young lady makes up for it. Look, I've brought you up some of me home-made cake as well. What's that book? Oh, poetry.'

'Yes, it's poems by Robert Browning,' said Ethel.

'Oh, I've 'eard of 'im,' said Mrs Albright. 'I 'ope he wasn't 'ard goin' on a nice afternoon like this. Never mind, I'm sure you'll like me cake.'

'Yes, I'm sure,' said Ethel, 'thanks.'

'Are yer takin' yer young lady to the pictures this evenin', Mr Williams?' asked Mrs Albright.

Pain seemed to darken Davy's spectacles.

'Films are artificial, Mrs Albright,' he said.

'Are they?' said the good lady. 'I thought they was real. I mean, there's people in them. Well, I'll leave you to the tea and cake, and go down and 'ave mine.'

Down she went, and Ethel poured the tea.

'I wouldn't actually mind goin' to the pictures, Davy,' she said. 'I won't worry about the film bein' artificial.'

'Well, if that's what you'd like,' said Davy.

'Thanks ever so,' said Ethel.

So they went later, and in the cinema they held hands, which made the big film very enjoyable for Ethel and helped Davy to put up with its artificial nature.

On Sunday morning, Dumpling popped round to Browning Street to see Nick Harrison, leaving Danny to peel the potatoes for dinner, and the apples for afters. Well, as Dumpling had to put up with a fair amount of marital goings-on, she made sure she had her own back by keeping Danny under her thumb for the rest of the time.

'Hello, Dumpling, what can I do for you?' asked Nick on opening the door to her.

'It's about the football team,' said Dumpling, brightly overflowing in a colourful Sunday frock.

'What about it?' asked Nick, as Dumpling bounced in and took herself into the parlour.

'We're short of reserves now we've lost Briggs and Bargett,' said Dumpling. 'Of course, we've got Alice's young man Johnny Richards to make up for Briggs, but we ain't got no-one to take Bargett's place, and there's always got to be a reserve. Mind, I could be yer standin' reserve, if yer like, and take me turn playin' in some matches.'

'I don't think our rules allow us to include a married woman in the team,' said Nick.

'Course they do,' said Dumpling. 'Well, they

don't say we can't. And what's bein' married got to do with it?'

'Well,' said Nick, 'there's – um –'

'What's um?' asked Dumpling.

'I don't know, I'm not a married woman myself,' said Nick. 'It's just something I've heard about.'

'Um?' said Dumpling.

'Well, er and um,' said Nick.

'Nick, you feelin' all right?' said Dumpling. 'You 'ad quite a few nasty turns with the team about the end of last season, and we all thought it was on account of you bein' in love. Was it Annabelle? Well, you're goin' out official with 'er these days.'

'I suppose I did lose a bit of form in some games,' said Nick.

'Yes, and me 'eart bled for yer,' said Dumpling. 'I admit I like Annabelle, but she's got a lot to answer for if she made you lose yer form. You don't want to take love too serious, yer know, Nick.'

'All right, I'll try not to,' said Nick.

'Yes, it's best you don't, it sort of interferes with things that matter,' said Dumpling. 'I mean, if I took Danny serious, it could muck me whole life up. Anyway, d'you know Orrice Cooper that lives near Danny and me in Wansey Street?'

'Not much, no,' said Nick.

'Well, 'e used to be a good footballer before 'e took up cricket, and he's a nice bloke and looks like he's got smashin' legs. I like fellers' legs, yer know, with all them muscles. Anyway, would yer like to

136

call on Orrice this afternoon and ask if 'e'd like to join the Rovers this season?'

'Sorry, Dumpling, I'm playing tennis this afternoon with Annabelle.'

Dumpling nearly fell over.

'Yer doin' what?' she said, aghast.

'Yes, she's helped me to learn how to use a racquet.'

'Oh, me gawd, when?' asked Dumpling, nearly turning pale.

'Saturday and Sunday afternoons during the summer,' said Nick.

'You been playin' tennis all this time?' said Dumpling. 'I'm 'orrified for yer. No wonder we ain't seen much of yer at weekends. What's the team goin' to think, their captain playin' tennis? It'll soften yer muscles, Nick, and make yer talk like a floorwalker in Selfridges. And what about yer footballin' leg muscles, which all us supporters is proud of? I said to me mum once, I said I wished I 'ad leg muscles like Nick's. Mind you, mine ain't so bad. Would you like to feel 'em? No, p'raps not, now I'm a married woman. Nick, you ain't goin' to play tennis all yer life now, are yer? All the street kids'll start cat-callin' yer.'

'Well, Annabelle's keen,' said Nick.

'But don't she realize what it'll do to yer?' said Dumpling in some sort of anguish.

'She hasn't mentioned it.'

'Well, I'm sorry, but I'm goin' to 'ave to,' said Dumpling, 'I'm goin' to 'ave to talk to 'er. Crikey,

137

we voted 'er on the committee and now she's makin' you play tennis. I'll do me best to make 'er understand we don't want our famous captain turned into a cissy.'

'That's very kind of you, Dumpling,' said Nick.

'Well, I got my affections for yer, Nick, and I don't like to think of a manly bloke like you pattin' tennis balls over a net. If Cassie knew, she'd faint, and she'd 'ave nightmares that Freddy might take it up. Excuse me, Nick, but it ain't nothing to grin about, yer know.'

'Sorry, Dumpling.'

'Oh, that's all right, I forgive yer, but if yer don't mind me sayin' so, you ought to stand up to Annabelle and let 'er know you was born to be a footballer, not a tennis fairy.'

'Um, I'll have a word with her,' said Nick.

'So will I,' said Dumpling. 'Nick, could yer deputate me to ask Orrice Cooper meself if 'e'd like to join the Rovers?'

'Certainly, Dumpling, you ask him.'

'Oh, good on yer, Nick. I'll take Freddy with me while Danny's doin' the dinner washin'-up. How's yer dad gettin' on now 'e's been home out of the Navy for a bit?'

'He's doing fine,' said Nick.

'Oh, that's good, I like yer dad and all 'is stories of 'is time in the Navy,' said Dumpling. 'Me mum's very admirin' of his sailor's walk. Well, goodbye for the time bein', Nick, and I won't forget to 'ave a word with Annabelle.'

* ★ ★ ★

Horace, due to go out in fifteen minutes to meet a friend, answered a knock on the door that afternoon. He found Dumpling on the step, a picture of rotund buoyancy. Despite what her mum called her condition of lingering puppy fat, no-one could have said Dumpling wasn't mobile. She was light on her feet, she bobbed and bounced around, and even when she was standing still – a bit of a job for her – she appeared to be full of jolly quivers.

'Oh, 'ello, Orrice,' she said.

'Afternoon, Dumpling,' smiled Horace.

A young man emerged from Dumpling's large round shadow and stood beside her.

'Oh, this is me friend, Freddy Brown,' said Dumpling. 'You know 'im, don't you, Orrice?'

'Slightly,' said Horace. 'How d'yer do, Freddy?'

'I'm standin' up,' said Freddy, and they shook hands.

'I 'ope yer don't mind us callin', only—' Dumpling stopped. The parlour door was ajar and a voice was heard.

'With sails aloft the graceful ship
Swam o'er silvery sea,
On shining deck Queen Aisha sat
While mermaids served her tea.'

'Crikey, Orrice, is that yer wireless?' asked Dumpling.

'No, it's Ethel,' said Horace.

'Behold, the sea breeze cometh
To speed the royal ship,

139

O! Listen to the mermaids
As the prow doth dip.'

'Oh, blimey,' breathed Dumpling, 'is that really Effel? All that doth and cometh?'

'She's reading her young man's latest poem,' said Horace.

Ethel was heard to say, 'Oh, the ship's not goin' to sink, is it, Davy?'

And Davy was heard to say, 'Just read on, Ethel.'

'Oh, that's her young man?' whispered Dumpling, while Freddy straightened out a grin.

'That's her young man,' agreed Horace, 'name of Davy Williams.'

'Oh, me gawd,' breathed Dumpling, 'she's walkin' out with a poet?'

''Fraid so,' murmured Horace.

'Oh, poor Effel,' whispered Dumpling, 'it never ought to 'appen to a nice quiet girl like 'er. I've seen 'er out with 'im, and I said to meself he don't look much of a bloke, more like a ping-ponging one, if yer know what I mean. But a poet, oh, me 'eart aches for Effel. That's the second 'orrible blow I've 'ad today. Can me and Freddy talk to yer for a minute, Orrice?'

'Come through to the kitchen, Mum and Dad have gone to the park,' said Horace. Dumpling tiptoed like a dancing balloon past the parlour door, leaving Ethel and Davy talking about the poem. 'What's the other horrible blow you've had today, Dumpling?' asked Horace.

'Yes, what?' asked Freddy.

'It's Nick 'Arrison,' said Dumpling.

'Do I know him?' asked Horace.

'You must've seen something of 'im,' said Dumpling, ''e's the Browning Street Rovers football captain. He talks a bit posh on account of 'aving a clerkin' job, but he's still one of the blokes.'

'Oh, yes, I think I've seen him around,' said Horace.

'Well,' said Dumpling, 'what do you blokes feel about a manly bloke like Nick takin' up tennis with Annabelle Somers? Ain't it a shock to yer?'

Horace coughed.

'Tennis?' he said.

'You know, that patball game cissy blokes play,' said Dumpling. Horace coughed again. 'Orrice, you got a chest cold?'

'No, I'm fine,' said Horace. 'Tennis, did you say?'

'It's no secret to me that Nick's been playin' with Annabelle,' said Freddy.

''Ere, you never said,' complained Dumpling. 'Ain't you alarmed?' she asked. 'There's all kinds of other games 'e could play with 'er.'

Freddy and Horace coughed together.

'Who's Annabelle?' asked Horace.

'Nick's steady,' said Freddy. 'Er, what other games, Dumpling?'

'Well, there's running races and throwing the 'ammer,' said Dumpling. 'Still, I'd best not say too much about it, we don't want everyone to know. What me and Freddy's really come about, Orrice, is to ask if you'd like to join our Rovers team this season. We know you've got a cricket career, but you don't play it in winter, and Freddy, who's our right 'alf, remembers 'earing you talked about as a natural footballer.'

'Well, I did play a bit early on, Freddy,' said Horace. 'That reminds me, d'you have a sister?'

'Two,' said Dumpling, who never minded answering up for her friends. Still, she had nothing on Cassie, who could answer up for everybody. 'Susie and Sally. Susie's married, but I don't know why Sally ain't. D'you know why, Freddy?'

'Well, since you ask, Dumpling,' said Freddy, 'she's—'

'Mind, I do know Sally's got sev'ral blokes, but no-one serious,' said Dumpling.

'Kind of yer to let Orrice know, Dumpling,' said Freddy, 'it sort of saves me the trouble.'

'Oh, that's all right,' said Dumpling generously.

'Freddy, does she work in an Adams dress shop?' asked Horace.

'Yes, the Kennington one,' said Freddy.

'Well, I've met her lately,' said Horace. 'If I came round to your house, could you introduce me?'

'What for, if you've met 'er?' said Freddy.

'Well, I'd like a proper introduction, as she seems a bit funny about that sort of thing,' said Horace.

'Sally?' said Freddy. He grinned. 'Never 'eard of it. Still, come round anytime, Orrice, it's Caulfield Place, number two.'

'Here, 'old on,' said Dumpling, suspecting something soppy was floating about, 'you ain't mentioned if you'd like to join the Rovers, Orrice. They're important in Walworth, yer know.'

'Well, I'm highly complimented, Dumpling,' said Horace, 'except I'm not always free Saturday afternoons, even in the winter. I'm on the ground staff. But I'll think about it, the Rovers bein' important.'

'Well, the invitation's official,' said Dumpling. 'We could find out what yer made of, Orrice, by doin' a kickabout with you on Clapham Common when you're free. Me and Danny and Freddy could go with yer one Saturday afternoon.'

'Sounds friendly,' said Horace.

Dumpling, eyeing him a bit uncertainly, said, 'I 'ope you won't relegate yer talents on account of yer feelings for Sally, only there's an 'orrible lot of that kind of thing goin' on round 'ere lately. You don't want to lose a sense of proportion, Orrice.'

'Oh, I'll fight that, Dumpling,' said Horace, 'and I'll think about the Rovers.'

'Well, I 'ope so,' said Dumpling. 'Now I'd best get back to Danny and see if 'e's finished washing-up the dinner things,' said Dumpling. 'I'll keep in touch, Orrice.'

'Right,' said Horace.

'So long,' said Freddy, 'nice to 'ave had a face to face with you, Orrice.'

Dumpling tiptoed again as she and Freddy left. From the parlour came the sound of Ethel's voice.

'And the rainbow flushed the silvery sea
As it closed around Queen Aisha.'

'That's good, Ethel, very good.'

'But, Davy, she's gone down under the sea with the mermaids. She'll be drowned.'

'Oh, me achin' 'eart, poor Effel,' breathed Dumpling, and left in company with Freddy, who was wearing a grin. 'Freddy, I ain't too 'appy, yer know,' she said.

'About Effel and 'er poet?' said Freddy.

'No, about Orrice and Sally. I got a forebodin' feelin' he's more interested in yer sister than the Rovers.'

'Can't 'ardly believe it, can we?' said Freddy gravely.

'It just ain't natural,' said Dumpling.

Ten minutes later, Davy heroically put poetry aside and took Ethel for a tram ride to Ruskin Park, the September weather still balmy.

It made a nice change for Ethel. Earnest though she was in trying to become Davy's poetic soulmate, going up the park on a Sunday afternoon was much more her style.

'Out!' called Annabelle, picturesque in her white tennis dress. She was partnering Boots against Rosie and Nick on one of Ruskin Park's public tennis courts, and Nick had just served to her.

'Out?' he said. He was quite good at the game now. 'You sure?'

'Fault,' said Annabelle, 'so get on with it.' Nick hit his second service. Annabelle, an energetic and useful player, returned it with a forehand wallop. Rosie, at the net, cut it off and the ball plopped back over and died a death. 'Hate you,' said Annabelle.

Rosie, still on vacation from Somerville, laughed. Nick served to Boots, who played a lob. Rosie pedalled backwards on legs still golden from the sun of a Salcombe holiday, and hit a winning smash.

'What a partner,' said Nick.

'Uncle Boots,' said Annabelle, 'letting Rosie go to university hasn't improved her. Did you see what she did to us then? Isn't she horrible?'

'If she keeps it up, we'll drive to Clapham Common afterwards and chuck her in the pond,' said Boots.

'Yes, the deep end,' said Annabelle. Nick served to her, a fizzer. She missed it altogether as she swung her racquet at it.

'Forty-love, Miss Somers,' called Nick.

Annabelle marched to the net.

'Come here,' she said. Nick walked up, and they met with the net between them, Nick in a white cricket shirt and grey flannels, his expression solemn.

'Yes, Miss Somers?'

His young lady, soon to be eighteen and accordingly very much on her mettle, gave him a scornful look.

'Stop showing off,' she said.

'Me?' said Nick, with Boots and Rosie looking on and winking at each other.

'Yes, you and your cannonballs,' said Annabelle. 'And stop looking at me like that.'

'Like what?' asked Nick.

'Like there's something to laugh about,' said Annabelle.

'Oh, like this, you mean,' said Nick. Not the famous captain of the Browning Street Rovers for nothing, he leaned over the net and kissed her. Spectators looking on from the path yelled their approval. Annabelle, delighted, hit him over the head with her racquet strings. More yells.

'Take that,' she said, 'how dare you kiss me in public?'

'Forgot myself,' said Nick, 'I thought it was Christmas.'

'Are we in the way, Daddy?' asked Rosie.

'Slightly,' said Boots, 'but we'll stick it out.'

'Come on, Uncle Boots,' said Annabelle, 'play up, don't stand about.'

The game was resumed. Strollers in the park stopped to watch, all four courts being used. Ethel and Davy had arrived to join the strollers, Davy saying there was a poetic atmosphere about parks.

'Yes, and it's nice as well,' said Ethel.

'Oh, more than just nice,' said Davy.

They halted to watch the tennis, eyes on the game being played by Nick and Rosie against Boots and Annabelle.

'I know that man,' said Davy, looking at the long-legged figure of Boots. 'His name's Adams, he's got a business in Camberwell. I asked him for a job once, but he didn't take me seriously. He turned me down.'

'Oh, I'm sorry about that, Davy,' said Ethel. 'The whole fam'ly's in business, you know. My mum met two of the brothers a little while ago. One of them drove her home after she slipped over in the road. She said it was Mr Robert Adams.'

'Yes, that's him, on the court,' said Davy, 'he's the one who didn't take me seriously. Still, he did give me a smile.'

'Their business is ever so successful,' said Ethel. 'Orrice has got a crush on Sally Brown that works in one of—oops, look out, Davy.'

Rosie had mishit a ball, and it came sailing over the wire to bounce in front of Ethel. She caught it on the bounce, and took it forward to the wire. Up came Boots, a smile on his face.

'Thanks,' he said, as Ethel lobbed it over the surround.

'My mum met you a little while ago, Mr Adams,' she said ingenuously.

'My pleasure, I imagine,' said Boots.

'She's Mrs Rebecca Cooper,' said Ethel with informative friendliness.

'Oh, yes, I remember her,' smiled Boots, 'give her my regards. But I don't think I met you, did I?'

'I'm Ethel Cooper, and me young man just told me who you were. He saw you about a job once, he said.'

'Come along, Ethel, come along,' called Davy, who had drifted away. Boots glanced at him, and his eyes flickered in recognition. Yes, there had been an interview about a possible job. He might have spoken to him now, but this wasn't the place.

'Are you with us, Uncle Boots?' called Annabelle.

'Coming,' said Boots. He smiled again at Ethel and returned to the tennis.

'What a nice man,' said Ethel when she caught Davy up.

'Very nice,' said Davy, and he and Ethel went on a pleasant Sunday afternoon saunter around the park.

After the tennis match was over, Annabelle and Nick said goodbye to Boots and Rosie, then began their walk to Annabelle's home in Sunrise Avenue, not far from the park.

'By the way, about this tennis lark,' said Nick, 'Dumpling's against it.'

'Dumpling's what?' said Annabelle.

'Against me playing tennis. She thinks it'll ruin my footballing muscles and turn me into a fairy on a rockcake.'

Annabelle shrieked. A middle-aged couple, passing sedately by, looked at her, and the male half said, 'You all right, miss?'

'Not half,' said Annabelle, 'I'm having the time of my life.'

'That's nice, I was young once,' said the female half, and went on with her partner.

'Chrissie wasn't serious, was she?' said Annabelle.

'Yes, and shocked as well,' said Nick. 'She's

going to give you a talking-to. Hope you'll be the better for it.'

Annabelle laughed. Life was at its most enjoyable for her.

'Nick, have we ever had a serious conversation?' she asked.

'Serious about what?'

'Oh, you know, about life and the unemployed and the state of the world,' said Annabelle. 'Whenever I'm in Walworth with you and I see how shabby and peaky some of the street kids are, I feel a bit guilty because I've always had nice clothes myself, and never gone hungry. I think it's rotten that MPs always look so well-dressed and well-fed but never do anything about seeing everyone else is.'

'Well, you're a working woman,' said Nick, 'and I'm a working bloke, and we could talk about all these problems until the cows came home, but we'd never solve anything. Everyone gets to vote when they're twenty-one, but you can only vote for politicians, and you're right, they never solve anything, either. Everyone knows it, so everyone makes do with attending to their own problems. I've got this problem of how to stop you beating me at tennis.'

'That's just what my dad or my Uncle Boots would say,' said Annabelle. 'D'you know, I don't think anyone in the Adams families or the Somers family ever has a serious conversation, either.'

'That's why they never come to blows,' said

149

Nick, 'and why they're all so sociable. And remember, they got where they are by their own efforts, by a lot of hard work. That's why I like them.'

'Nick, you are a love,' said Annabelle. 'It's going to be official on my birthday, isn't it?'

'An official serious conversation?' asked Nick.

'Oh, aren't you the funny one?' said Annabelle. 'I mean our engagement.'

'Well, I know I'm going to officially propose to you then,' said Nick.

'Promise?'

'Listen, you gorgeous girl, if I don't get the ring on your finger on your birthday it'll only be because it doesn't fit.'

Annabelle hugged his arm.

'Mum's forgiven your Pa for letting your family down,' she said. 'Well, she can't help herself, she likes him.'

Nick's Ma and Pa had been entertained more than once by Lizzy and Ned, and Ma and Pa had reciprocated.

'Pa's a lady's man,' said Nick, as they turned into Sunrise Avenue.

'So are you,' said Annabelle.

'Me?' said Nick.

'Yes, you're mine,' said Annabelle, 'I'm a lady.'

'Bless you,' said Nick, 'you're a peach of a girl.'

'Oh, bless you too, Nick lovey, you're one of the family already. All my aunts and uncles are always saying bless you to each other. I think Aunt Vi and Uncle Tommy say it to each other six times a day.

Nick, are you still getting on well in your new job since you've had your rise?'

'Imports and exports? Better than the insurance job, and a lot more prosperous for me. I've got my own little office now, my own telephone, and my own shorthand-typist.'

'Not the kind that sits on your lap, I hope,' said Annabelle.

'Not so far,' said Nick. 'But with all that, I'd feel important if your Great-Uncle John hadn't warned me against getting above myself. He said once that the whole world is full of pipsqueaks, and that I was one of them. I'll never understand why he pulled me out of the claims department and sent me into imports and exports.'

'He likes you,' said Annabelle.

'He what?'

'He likes you,' said Annabelle, 'you're his favourite pipsqueak – Nick!' She was running for home then, Nick in pursuit, and the autumn leaves of Sunrise Avenue stirred in the light September breeze.

Chapter Ten

There was a letter for Boots on Monday morning, written in French.

Dear Papa, I wish on you a hundred thanks for writing to me. I was so happy to hear from you and have you tell me that all your family, everyone, will be delighted to see me when I visit you at Christmas. Aunt Marie and Uncle Jacques are being very good and making no loud speeches about my coming to live with you after Christmas. They understand I belong to you and that it is only right for me to be with you. It would be very strange for a father and daughter not to be together, but it is right too that I should spend this time with them before I leave them. It is to get them used to the idea that I have to be with you. Mercy me, Papa, I keep thinking can all this be true, that you are alive and we have found each other. I like you very much and will soon come to love you, as a daughter should, you are much to be admired, I think. Also I think my sister Rosie is beautiful and kind, and I hope we can be very special friends. Also I admire Mademoiselle Polly to whom I owe so much. Please remember me to her,

and please give my respectful wishes to your wife
who is to be my new mother, and my greetings to your
son who is my brother. I am very excited and
sometimes forget what I'm doing, which makes
Uncle Jacques say my head is already in England.
Please send me more letters.

See, I sign myself your loving Eloise.

PS. I forgot to say in English cheeri-o and gawd
blimey. My Uncle Jacques showed me how to spell
it, he speaks the English of the Tommies and also
knows how to write it.

The letter was passed around the breakfast table, first to Emily, then Chinese Lady, then Mr Finch and on to Rosie and Tim. Only Mr Finch and Rosie were able to read it. Emily said it was all double Dutch to her, and Chinese Lady said she didn't really hold with foreign languages, especially Frenchified ones, and that it was time everyone used English. Everyone could understand every- one else better then, she said. There was an awful lot of misunderstood language in the world, she said, which led to a lot of ruinous happenings, which wouldn't come about if everyone spoke English. Perhaps someone might be kind enough to read Eloise's letter out loud. In English, mind.

Rosie did the honours, translating as she read. She was very solemn when she quoted 'cheeri-o and gawd blimey.' Chinese Lady blinked. Mr Finch coughed, as was his wont on certain occasions. Tim grinned. Emily giggled. Boots kept a straight face, because Chinese Lady was looking at him.

'I'm sure I don't have to ask who taught the girl that common bit of language,' she said. 'Still, except for that, well, what a nice letter. I never heard anything more ladylike. I'm sure we're all proud she's an Adams, and we won't say anything concernin' how she come about.'

'The same way as they all do, Maisie,' murmured Mr Finch.

'Put some marmalade on your toast, Edwin,' said Chinese Lady, which meant he wasn't to enlarge on his remark, not with young Tim present.

'I've got a nice feelin' we're goin' to like the girl,' said Emily, who hoped she would herself, because her job as a stepmother would be much easier then. In private, she'd asked Boots her own kind of questions about the girl's late mother. Well, as his wife she naturally wanted to know exactly why he had made love to the woman. Boots simply said that Cecile Lacoste had been an attractive if slightly tempestuous Frenchwoman, that at the time he'd been a slightly corkscrewed soldier, and the one fell in with the other. Corkscrewed? What d'you mean, corkscrewed? Slightly insane, said Boots. Boots, you've never been insane all your life, said Emily. I was then, said Boots, I caught it in 1915. Caught what? Trench insanity, said Boots. Emily asked if he meant French. No, trench, said Boots. It was a complaint, he said, that made a whole battalion of blokes forget their manners when they were out of the line. Forget their manners? said Emily.

Afraid so, Em. Oh, were you all like it? All, said Boots, and it made thousands of Frenchwomen run screaming for help. An exception was Cecile Lacoste. She stood her ground and let it happen. Emily didn't fall for that. Oh, you daft ha'porth, she said, think I'm simple, do you? No, said Boots, I just think you're a godsend, old girl. Oh, bless you, Boots, smiled Emily, I'm glad you said that.

Tim said now, 'Has anyone thought about the problems we're going to have if Eloise doesn't speak English and most of us don't speak French? Myself personally, I can still only string a few words together at school, and Mr Ainsley always says it would offend his ears a lot less if I didn't bother. He says I'm a painful reminder of you, Dad.'

'Well, we managed to part friends when I left in 1913,' said Boots. 'It amazes me he's still teaching. I thought he was about sixty even then.'

'He still is,' said Tim, 'everyone says he's been sixty for about fifty years.'

'Perhaps he's Peter Pan's grandfather,' said Rosie. 'And perhaps Eloise is taking English lessons. Ask her when you next write, Daddy.'

'Yes, if she's not speakin' any English when she comes over at Christmas, I'll just be saying parley-voo to her all the time,' said Emily.

'I've heard about parley-voo,' said Chinese Lady, 'and I'm not sure I like the sound of it, Em'ly.'

'Well, it's the only French I know, Mum,' said Emily. 'Rosie, is that you laughin'?'

'No, I've finished now, Mum,' said Rosie, and

thought just how much her family meant to her. She had her new friends at university, intellectual friends, likeable friends, and amusing ones, but no friends, however special to her, could ever diminish the deep affection she had for her family and all the Adams clan.

'Good on you, Rosie,' said Tim. His sister was due to return to Somerville in a little while, and the family would miss her again. It would be as if one of the brighter house lights had gone out.

Later that morning, Rosie phoned Polly and read Eloise's letter to her over the line. The PS, of course, made Polly laugh.

'I think Eloise is going to fit in with the Adams',' she said. 'Rosie, do you have something on today?'

'Only a few summer rags, Aunt Polly.'

'There speaks your father,' said Polly, 'except he'd have said an old grey suit. I meant are you busy today?'

'No, I'm not doing anything special, except a little studying,' said Rosie.

'Well, would it stop you coming to town with me so that we could have lunch together?'

'I'd love to,' said Rosie.

'Shall we go mad and try the Ritz?' said Polly.

'Aunt Polly, I'd love that even more.'

'Good,' said Polly, 'I'll pick you up at twelve. And would you do me a favour, sweetie?'

'Ask, and I'll say yes.'

'Would you cut out Aunt Polly, old thing? I've

decided that coming from you it makes me feel ancient.'

'Polly, then,' said Rosie.

'That's better,' said Polly.

The Ritz was a splendour of white and gold. Polly had reserved a table for two, and Rosie thought the deference of the maitre d'hotel was touched with pleasure as he led them to it. It was like Polly to be known here. For all that she had chosen to sublimate her wayward self to the sober nature of teaching, she never lost touch with gaiety. Emma, Annabelle's twelve-year-old sister, was at West Square School now, and Polly was keeping an affectionate eye on her progress. Rosie knew why Polly had such an affinity with the Somers and Adams families, she had known for years, but kept it to herself.

The September day was fine and warm, and Polly was in a dress of yellow silk gauze with a round black neck trim and patterned with black polka dots of varied sizes. The sleeves, elbow-length, were loose with floating points, and a wide black sash with trailing ends adorned her waist. Her long gloves were black, and so was her pillbox hat. Rosie thought she looked superbly elegant. Her hair, the same kind of dark brown as Boots's, was worn in a style that never varied, a bob that ended in curling points that lightly touched her cheeks and gave piquancy to her vivaciousness. She seemed years younger than thirty-eight.

Rosie herself was in a turquoise dress of classic simplicity, and a close-fitting hat. Boots had opened a bank account of a generous kind for her, and she had her own cheque book. She was able to buy whatever clothes took her fancy, except that most Somerville undergraduates were such earnest young ladies that frumpish outfits were the thing with them. They wished to be appreciated for their intellect, not their appearance. Rosie was among the few who said blow looking like someone's grandma.

They sat down. Polly, drawing off her gloves, ordered aperitifs. The restaurant was a glitter of silver and glass on white damask. The grey of gentlemen's morning suits politely refused to clash with or to rival the colourful nature of ladies' exquisite raiment. A gentleman's sartorial duty was to help set off a lady's apparel. Only a bounder would do otherwise.

The aperitifs arrived and with them, the menus, and Polly and Rosie were left to study the extensive list of à la carte offerings.

Over the top of her menu, Rosie said, 'Polly, you look frightfully dashing and elegant.'

'Do I, darling? Not too old, you mean?'

'How would you feel if the waiters thought we were sisters?'

'Giddy,' said Polly. 'Cheers.' She raised her glass.

'Yes, cheeri-o and gawd blimey,' said Rosie, and Polly laughed.

'You have an entertaining sister now, Rosie.'

'Eloise? Yes.' Rosie began to enjoy her aperitif

158

while studying the menu. 'I have so much that I sometimes wonder why fortune especially favours me. There are so many people who have so little. Sometimes I feel fortune will turn her face away and take back the best of what she's given me.'

'I doubt if Boots would allow that,' said Polly lightly, 'he'd go to war with the devil himself on your behalf, never mind mere fortune. You'll never lose what you have, sweetie. Ah me, I've never had what I've most wanted.'

'And what is it that you've most wanted?' asked Rosie, who was sure she knew.

'Something, sweetie, that I can't have. Shall we order? Are you ready to?'

They ordered, and Polly chose a wine.

Then Rosie said, 'Speaking of our Lord of creation—'

'Who?'

'Boots,' smiled Rosie.

'Your father?' said Polly. 'Oh, he's the Lord of creation, is he?'

'Yes, according to the family,' said Rosie, and laughed. 'I've something to give you. Daddy meant to let you have it when he next saw you. I knew it was there at home, so I rang him at the office this morning, told him you were taking me to a glamorous lunch at the Ritz—'

'What did he say to that?'

'Oh, that he'd be having a pub sandwich himself, but that neither of us was to sorrow for him. Anyway, I asked if I could give you this packet myself, and he said yes and to tell you it was with the compliments of the family. Here you are, Polly.' Rosie took a flat packet from her handbag and passed it over the table to the family's aristocratic friend.

'Oh, I say, a sealed packet?' murmured Polly. 'Are the contents serious, then?' She broke the seal, opened up the wrapping and disclosed a flat velvet-covered box. She sprang the lid and there, nestling in its white silk bed, was a string of pearls. She stared, losing her breath for a moment. 'Rosie?'

'It's from all the families,' said Rosie. 'Aunt Lizzy's, Uncle Tommy's, Uncle Sammy's and ours. It's to let you know you're special to all of us for everything you did in finding our French relative and arranging for Daddy and me to meet her. Everyone wanted to chip in, and did. D'you like them?'

Polly stared again at the necklace.

'Oh, ye gods,' she breathed. Without affectations or prejudices, it had never been difficult for her to identify with Chinese Lady's extensive family. The friendship she enjoyed with them was a very real one, but there was always something missing. Fortune, she thought, may have given Rosie a great deal, but it's never given me what I most want. These pearls are intended to let me know I'm special to these families? They're Boots's idea of a consolation prize? Consolation has got a hat on with holes in it, but all the same, I'm touched. 'Whose idea was it, Rosie?'

'Oh, you'll have to guess that,' said Rosie lightly, and Polly thought yes, I'm right, they're a consolation prize from Boots, even if every family did chip in.

'Rosie,' said Polly, 'they're beautiful, and I'm overwhelmed. To whom should I address my letter of thanks?'

'To Grandma Finch,' said Rosie, and smiled. 'Of course, you probably think it should be Boots. Well, you and he share something that's very special to the men and women of the Great War. You're old comrades, aren't you?'

'Boots has said that, has he?' said Polly, her brittle smile showing.

'It's simply something I understand,' said Rosie.

'Do you, Rosie, old thing?'

'Well, you know, Polly,' smiled Rosie, 'you're one of my very favourite persons.'

'Thank you, sweetie,' said Polly, 'I can say snap to that. Here come our first courses. Let's let our hair down when we get to the wine. I need to do that to celebrate how special I am to your grandmother's family.'

Rosie thought there was something self-mocking about that, but because she understood, she smiled again and said, 'I'll celebrate with you.'

Had he been present himself, Boots would have thought back to 1920, to the days when five-year-old Rosie, a neglected and lonely waif, sat with him on his doorstep to become his quaintly talkative little pal, he as blind as a bat at the time. He would have marvelled at the way the waif-like child had turned herself effortlessly into the kind of young lady who could absorb the cultured atmosphere of the Ritz to the manner born. He would have wondered again about the man who had fathered her, a man who'd been an Army officer at the time.

Tuesday morning. Boots's office door quietly opened to allow the entry of a woman. She closed it just as quietly. Boots turned his head.

'Polly?' he said. Polly put a finger to her lips, a request for a discreet silence. She crossed to his desk, and as he looked up at her, his expression wary, she bent her head and chucked all discretion, figuratively, into his wastepaper basket by kissing him with demonstrative immodesty. After which, Boots said, not without good reason, 'What happened?'

'Oh, just a sweet kiss, old sport, for everything you've given Rosie and for bringing her up to be what she is. And for giving me that consolation prize.'

'What consolation prize?' asked Boots.

'The pearls, dearly beloved, to make up for my not being awarded first prize,' said Polly.

'What first prize?'

'You,' said Polly. 'Cursed fate has much to answer for, and so have you, come to that, for doing what you did to Cecile Lacoste and not to me. Oh, well, san fairy, I suppose other people suffer too, and the pearls are divine. I've just posted a letter to your mother in which I've thanked everyone. Can't stay longer, must dash. I'm meeting Sir Somebody or other, but you can call anytime I'm in bed. There's always room for you there. Cheeri-o and gawd blimey, old soldier. That's the password now, I believe. So long, keep the home fires burning.'

Exit Polly in a swirl of light garments. Boots shook his head and smiled. Brittle charmer had come and gone without doing any damage. She'd be back at her teaching post in a day or so. And Rosie would soon be back at Somerville.

★ ★ ★

'What, again?' said the head groundsman first thing Wednesday morning.

'What d'you mean, again, guv?' asked Horace.

'I mean this is the second time.'

Horace pointed out the first time had been so long ago he'd forgotten it. The head groundsman said don't come it, sunshine, you haven't been promoted to the second eleven yet. Then he asked Horace if he'd mind not bringing his troublesome love life to the cricket ground with him as well as his odd socks. Horace said he didn't have any love life, not even a troublesome one, and that he was only asking to dodge off for fifteen minutes to see a man about a dog. The head groundsman said he'd heard about dogs like that, and they all wore frocks and fancy stockings. The heavy roller had got to perform this morning, he said, and if Horace wasn't back to give a hand with it in twenty minutes, he'd sack him.

Miss Lomax had only just opened the shop when Horace walked in. The manageress at once effaced herself to allow Sally to deal with him.

Sally, of course, said, 'Oh, no, not you again.'

'Good morning, Miss Brown,' said Horace, 'I thought I'd just pop in to let you know the new boater fits my sister a treat, but that she's got a sentimental attachment to her old one, as she was wearin' it when she met her young man. So I thought—'

'Stop,' said Sally.

'OK,' said Horace, 'what d'you want to say?'

'Hoppit,' said Sally. 'That's all.'

'Is that fair, Sally?'

'Fair? Fair? You can talk. Comin' in here, playin' games with me and larkin' about, what's fair about that?' Playing games and larking about were what got Sally's goat, she being of an age when she required to be treated seriously, especially as she was in line for that assistant manageress's position in Oxford Street of all places. Brother-in-law Sammy wouldn't think anything of an Oxford Street assistant manageress who let amateur comics take the mickey out of her. 'I still 'aven't – haven't forgot about you havin' the sauce to ask me to go to the Corporation rubbish dump on Sunday to look for that boater. That did it, that did. Yes, and who said you could call me Sally, you – you – you faceache.'

'Well, I must say you're in form this morning,'

said Horace. 'But about the boater, I thought I'd do what I said, write a note to your dustman and let you have it tomorrow so that you could pass it on to him. Afterwards – well, later this week, on Saturday evening, say, d'you think you'd like to come to the pictures with me?'

'I'd rather fall to me doom off Blackfriars Bridge,' said Sally.

'Look,' said Horace, 'if I got a proper introduction to you, would that help?'

'Miss Lomax,' called Sally, 'could you please ask this gentleman to leave the shop?'

'Why, what's the trouble?' asked the intrigued manageress.

'No trouble,' said Horace, 'I've got to dash off, anyway, or the head groundsman'll break my leg. I'll drop in tomorrow, if you wouldn't mind me doin' that to give Miss Brown a note for the dustman. Thanks very much.' It was as well he left then, because Sally was so far gone with umbrage she was about to take a shoe off and chuck it at him.

Miss Lomax was laughing.

'Miss Lomax, I still don't think it's funny,' said Sally.

'My dear, where's your sense of humour gone?' asked Miss Lomax, arranging a new display.

'It's not my sense of humour, it's his rotten jokes. Did you hear him say he was goin' to bring me a note tomorrow to give to the dustman?'

'I don't know how I kept my face straight,' said

Miss Lomax. 'On the other hand, I really can't have him using the shop to romance you.'

'Romance me?' said Sally.

'That young man's in love with you. Or near to it.'

'Oh, he is, is he? Well, I hate him something rotten,' said Sally, 'and if he does come in tomorrow, I'm goin' to scream the shop ceiling down.'

'Oh, he'll come,' said Miss Lomax.

I'll be sick, thought Sally. He's in love with me? That comedian? I bet he's only in love with himself. Well, he's always more pleased with himself than any other bloke I know.

She prepared herself mentally for a real up-and-downer with him, if he came in early and no customers were present. I could bring in a fish that's gone rotten, I could bring it in well wrapped up, and then as soon as he opens his mouth I could fill his face with it. No, I couldn't, the shop would smell all day. I'll bring a rotten tomato instead. What's his name? Has he told me? I can't remember, but he did say his sister's name was Ethel. If he thinks he can get me to pass a note to the dustman that'll make me look silly, he can think again. Just wait till he comes in tomorrow, he'll walk straight into that rotten tomato.

'Who's that?' barked an irritable voice from the Shoreditch end of the line.

'Sammy Adams here, George. Business any better for you?'

'Spoil your lunch, would it, if I told you it was?'

growled George Carter, factory owner and a competitor of Sammy's. 'I know what you're after, Sammy bleedin' Adams, and you're not gettin' it, not even over my dead body.'

'Sorry about your headache, George.'

'So you should be, you're responsible for it, you've been undercuttin' me for years.'

'Now be your age, old man,' said Sammy, 'you know as well as I do that long-term undercuttin' is suicidal. We're competitive, I grant you that, but we've still got to cost out every contract to make sure of a fair profit, or we might as well shut up shop.'

'You're full of bleedin' fairy stories,' said George Carter.

'I don't go in for those, either,' said Sammy. 'Look, if you have to sell, I'll top that offer I made yesterday with another monkey. And you can rely, George, on every quid bein' gilt-edged, which means ready money. Hard cash. Bank of England white fivers, if you fancy same.'

'Listen, you're not gettin' my business or my factory,' said George Carter. 'The last thing I'd do would be to help make you top bloody dog in the rag trade. You got that?'

'Your headache's hurtin' me,' said Sammy, 'but I forgive yer. I know how you're feeling. And my offer's stayin' on the table. Don't wait till the liquidators move in, they'll do a bankruptcy job on you. Just phone me before they start treadin' all over your office carpet.'

'Sod off,' said George Carter, and slammed the phone down.

'Now he's hurt my ears,' said Sammy, and replaced his own receiver. He got up from his desk and went into Boots's office, acquainting him with the news that George Carter was still playing hard to get. Like a croquet set.

'I think you mean "coquette",' said Boots.

'Same thing, except you talk better French,' said Sammy, perching half his rump on the corner of his brother's desk. 'We could do with that fact'ry of his, we could do with knockin' it down and buildin' a modern one, puttin' the machinists into rented premises while it's being built.'

'You can feel a new challenge coming on, can you, Sammy?' said Boots.

'I'm against standin' still, Boots.'

'You haven't stood still since you opened the first shop,' said Boots, 'you're the equivalent of perpetual motion.'

'Sometimes, y'know, Boots, I ain't sure I approve of all that educated language of yours. Anyway, I'd like us to buy George Carter out before his creditors move in and pinch all his assets.'

'Would you?' said Boots.

'Yes, take the firm over while it's still a goin' concern. Well, half a goin' concern.'

'Apart from the fact that he won't sell to us, you're losing your touch, Sammy.'

'Steady on,' said Sammy, 'that could cause me a

sleepless night. Me losin' my touch? You're grievin' me.'

'Sammy old lad, is anyone else likely to buy George Carter out except at a giveaway price? Let the liquidators move in, and as soon as they've done so, then make your offer. The liquidators will have to accept your price for the shares and the factory on behalf of the creditors, especially if the amount's large enough to give them a hundred per cent settlement. And it'll give George Carter no say in the matter.'

'Well, drop me down a manhole,' said Sammy, shifting half his rump a couple of inches, 'I see now what we all had in mind when we sent you to a good school, a blind hope that it would make you smart. Might I offer you me irrespective compliments?'

'Might I suggest you should have seen the obvious yourself?' said Boots.

'Sometimes just lately, I've had trouble wondering if I'm comin' or goin',' said Sammy.

'Is there a reason?' asked Boots.

Sammy grinned.

'That Susie,' he said.

'Got you by the nose, has she, Sammy?'

'Got me by the trousers as well,' said Sammy, 'she's wearin' them.'

'Join the club,' said Boots.

'Knew you'd say that,' said Sammy.

'Best thing, Sammy, and you can always count your blessings.'

'How's Rosie?' asked Sammy.

'Still enjoying her vacation,' said Boots.

'Vacation? Leave off,' said Sammy, 'it's school holiday round these parts. Vacation sounds like the doctor's been.'

'I think you mean vaccination,' said Boots.

'That definitely sounds like the doctor's been,' said Sammy. 'Anyway, I'm fond of Rosie, but I suppose you realize that with her looks and style, and now this education, she could get to marry a millionaire and live on a yacht a long way from Denmark Hill and Southend-on-Sea?'

'She's hasn't mentioned the possibility, Sammy.'

'Put a crease in your noble brow if she did,' said Sammy, 'and I wouldn't go much on it myself. Losin' our Rosie to some swell always halfway round the world? I'm against that, even if your French daughter does turn out to be compensatory. Well, back to work, I'm up to me ears, as usual. But regardin' George Carter and his sinkin' ship, we'll wait for it to happen, Boots, then launch the Adams lifeboat.'

'That'll give you what you want, Sammy.'

'And what's that?' asked Sammy from the door.

'Another challenge,' said Boots.

'Well, like I mentioned, Boots, you can't stand still,' said Sammy, and departed for his office.

It was Boots's unspoken contention that Sammy shouldn't have let the scrap metal business go. He missed it, Boots was certain. He missed what the extra workload meant, a stimulus for his active brainbox. Scrap metal was going to come into its own in the not too distant future. Nazi Germany was rearming, no doubt about it, and Britain would have to make up its mind to stay ahead of Hitler and his warlords. Parliament, however, seemed indifferent to necessity, and Winston Churchill, that cavalier of a politician, was almost a lone voice in warning of the menace posed by a revived Germany.

Damn another war, thought Boots.

Chapter Eleven

Ned Somers, answering the phone that evening, called Annabelle. Out she came into the hall.

'It's for you,' said Ned.

'Who is it?' asked Annabelle.

'A public phone box,' said Ned, 'I heard the pennies drop.'

'That's interesting,' said Annabelle, 'I've never had a public phone box ring me up before.' She took the receiver from her smiling dad. 'Hello?'

'Oh, 'ello, is that you, Annabelle,' asked Dumpling. 'It's me 'ere.'

'Is that Chrissie?' said Annabelle, recognizing the voice.

'Yes, it's me. I 'ope you don't mind me phoning, like, but I'm in an 'orrible state about Nick.'

'What? Chrissie, what d'you mean? Has he had an accident?'

'No, did someone say he 'ad?'

'I thought – well, why're you in a horrible state about him?'

'Annabelle, I've got to speak me mind for the good of the Rovers, I've got to say I don't think much of you gettin' Nick to play tennis. I can't 'ardly believe he's been at it all summer. 'Ave you thought of what it might do to 'im? It could ruin 'is footballin' legs, yer know, and if some of the street kids find out he's goin' in for patball they'll be askin' 'im if he'd like a teddy bear for Christmas or a tennis frock.'

'Chrissie, tennis isn't patball.'

'It is round our way,' said Dumpling. 'I told Nick I felt it was me duty to speak to you. Crikey, if it got around that he was goin' in for tennis, it might get in the local paper or even on the wireless. He wouldn't 'ave any reputation left.'

'Chrissie,' said Annabelle, 'I promise you that if Nick can't kick a football as good as ever, I'll see that he gives up tennis.'

'Oh, blimey,' breathed Dumpling, voice quivering over the line in a way Ethel's Davy might have liked, 'you ain't saying Nick's goin' to play tennis ev'ry summer, are you, Annabelle?'

'But, Chrissie, it's jolly good exercise, and Nick can really biff a ball.'

'But ev'ry summer? I'll 'ave a nervous breakdown. Annabelle, couldn't you and Nick do football kickabouts on Clapham Common instead? You've got to 'ave some thought for 'is leg muscles.'

'Honestly, Chrissie,' said Annabelle, struggling not to split her sides, 'I've got a lot of thought for them. I've never admired anyone's leg muscles more.'

'Well, I can understand that,' said Dumpling, 'and I can only 'ope that if it's tennis ev'ry summer with you and Nick, you'll keep a sort of medical eye on 'is legs to make sure they ain't gettin' rundown or anything.'

'Oh, I'll keep a very good eye on them, Chrissie, I promise,' said Annabelle.

'The whole team's got to put its trust in you,' said Dumpling. 'Mind, only Danny and Freddy know. If I told all the blokes, I dunno what they'd do. Oh, I nearly forgot, could yer make sure Nick ain't seen about in Walworth carryin' any racquet or tennis balls?'

'Oh, he brings them in a holdall,' said Annabelle.

'Well, that's some relief,' said Dumpling, 'but like I mentioned to Freddy, there's all sorts of other games you and Nick could play, yer know.'

'Pardon?' gulped Annabelle.

'Not ping-pong, of course, that's even more cissified than tennis,' said Dumpling.

Annabelle, fighting to recover, said, 'I promise there'll be no ping-pong, Chrissie.'

'Well, all right,' said Dumpling, then grumbled in an undertone that love didn't half do 'orrible things to people.

'What was that, Chrissie?'

'I've got to go now, me time's up.'

'Oh, I was going to ask how Danny was,' said Annabelle, but found herself talking to a dead line. Dumpling had had her tuppence-worth. Annabelle put the phone down and hastened into the family sitting-room, which was the Sunrise Avenue equivalent of a parlour. There she collapsed on the sofa and muffled her shrieks of laughter.

Her immediate future with Nick promised to be hilarious if she was to inspect his leg muscles after every game of tennis. Let's see, would that include thigh muscles? Yes, why not? But Nick would have to drop his trousers.

Annabelle stifled more shrieks.

Ethel and Davy, having been out for an evening walk, were hurrying back to Wansey Street by way of the Walworth Road. Clouds were running about, some as white and soft-looking as swansdown, and some dark and heavy with rain. Ethel was wearing her mackintosh, Davy carrying his. A tram, coming from the Elephant and Castle, clanged to a stop at Browning Street. From it alighted two young ladies and two young men. One of the young ladies, the better-dressed of the two in a smart raincoat and hat, detached herself to cross fast to the pavement and to enter Browning Street at a very quick pace. One of the young men called.

'Oi, come on, Sally, I was only jokin'.'

'I'm off jokin',' called the young well-dressed lady over her shoulder.

Well, I'm blessed, thought Ethel, I believe that's Sally Brown. My, hasn't she grown attractive? And she dresses well too. No wonder Orrice has fallen for her. But she isn't half in a paddy, you can tell. Is that what she's like with Orrice? And is that her bloke, the one who called to her? He's not bothering to hurry after her. I should think his number's up, from the way Sally spoke and looked. I think I'll have to tell Orrice.

Her brother, however, was out with old school friends. He ought to be romancing some girl by now, thought Ethel, and if Sally Brown hadn't grown so stuck-up, she'd see Orrice was a lot better than the bloke who got off the tram with her.

Having escaped the deluge of a shower that fell from the sky a minute after they were indoors, Ethel and Davy, with the approval of Rebecca and Jim, retired to the parlour for one more poetry session. This time, the happy poem promised by Davy materialized, and he himself read it.

'*When Ethel Cooper was but ten, she lived in a little house,*
And who do you think she was friends with? Why a funny little mouse.
Up and down the stairs it ran, with Ethel close behind,
Her golden locks a-dancing as up the stairs she climbed.'

'Davy, I don't have golden locks,' said Ethel.

'Ethel, those sort of differences don't count in poetry,' said Davy.

'I see. Oh, all right.'

'*The mouse's name was Pinky, what d'you think of that?*
Its whiskers were that colour, and that's an honest fact.
And every day on Sundays, if you'd like to know,

176

Ethel took him walking, and to the park they'd go.
Happy were the people, to see them in the park,
Pinky looked so perky, and dogs would at him bark.
Alas that on one Sunday, when Pinky had grown
    fat,
He got a bit too perky, and was eaten by a cat.'

'Well, I don't call that a happy ending to a poem,' said Ethel.

'Ethel, where's your imagination?' said Davy. 'It was happy for the cat, wasn't it?'

'In any case,' said Ethel, 'it was more like a nurs'ry rhyme, and I've gone past them a bit.'

Davy's spectacles took on a sorrowful look.

'Ethel, I hope you don't think I write nursery rhymes,' he said.

'But that was just like one,' said Ethel, 'and reminded me of those Orrice used to read to me when I was six. You've noticed I'm a bit older now, 'aven't you?'

'Ethel, I like you being a bit older,' said Davy. 'I like you being old enough to appreciate poetry. I wouldn't write my poems for you if you were still only six.'

'I'd be thankful, Davy, if you wouldn't write any more about me bein' only ten and havin' a pet mouse. Actu'lly, I hate mice.'

'Well, there you are, then,' said Davy, 'it was a happy ending for you, with Pinky getting finished off by a cat.' Ethel laughed. Davy peered darkly at her. 'Ethel, have I said something funny?'

'Well, it sounded funny,' said Ethel.

Davy, frowning, looked as if he thought Ethel was out of order.

Sally went to work the following morning feeling in just the right mood to deal with any funny stuff from the young man she thought of as Bighead. She hadn't had much of a social outing last evening with Mavis, Mavis's young man and her brother Wally. For some reason, she'd found she'd gone right off Wally, who while he wasn't the last word as a Romeo, had always been good company. But last evening he'd irritated her to the point where she'd walked off after alighting from the tram. Her mood was upsetting to herself as well as Wally. She was hardly ever irritable. Help, supposing it meant she was already turning into a sour old maid?

Today she was ready to give that other young man an earful that would send him packing once and for all. If he actually did bring a note for her to give to the dustman, she'd take it and then fill his mouth with it. She'd decided a rotten tomato simply wouldn't do, not in the shop, even if it would make a suitable faceful for him.

Horace, however, did not show up. All day Sally consciously waited for him to appear, but Horace was trapped by his work. The ground staff were busy repairing the ravages of the county cricket season that was now at its end, and only the minimum time was allowed for a break. Horace spent all day sweating at ground work.

Sally went home in a kind of rageful mood that

she hadn't had the opportunity to give him either an earful or a faceful, and when she passed the house of the watching man his eyes, guarded and hooded by his lowered lids, were peering slits of glinting light as he noted her expression. Bloody hell, he thought, it's all guns firing, she can hear 'em and she ain't too pleased, she's out in the open, and they're her own bleedin' Jerry guns. Down he went to the floor, crouching, his hands over his ears. His wife came in.

'Joe? Joe? Now what're you doin' down there, Joe?'

'Ruddy guns,' he breathed hoarsely.

'No, course not, love, the war's over. You're safe now, and your supper'll be ready in a bit. Get up now.'

He got up. He put his arm around her.

'It's funny,' he said.

'What's funny, Joe?'

'When you're 'ere, there's no guns.'

'What's up, love?' asked Sally's dad over supper that evening.

'What's up with me?' said Sally. 'Nothing.'

'You've been very quiet since you got in,' said her plump and placid mum.

'I'm sure I don't know what you mean,' said Sally, who couldn't think why she was wild that that cheerful Charlie hadn't turned up. After all, if he'd decided not to bother her any more, she ought at least to feel relieved. Instead, she felt sort of angrily frustrated. Well, he'd cheated her of the chance of sending him packing once and for all.

'Must be love,' said Freddy.

'What, our Sally's in love?' said Mrs Brown, whose homely kitchen was the family melting pot.

'I'll go barmy if anyone takes Freddy seriously,' said Sally.

'There's a lot of it about, y'know,' said Freddy, who worked in a Southwark brewery with his dad. The brewery was owned by Adams Enterprises, Sammy's first limited company. 'Well, there's Nick and Annabelle, and Danny and Dumpling to start with.'

'That's it, let's all go barmy,' said Sally.

'And now it looks like there's Sally and some bloke we don't know about,' said Freddy. 'Well, I'll bet my bicycle it's not Wally Richards, he's too thick. She's probaby met the sort of bloke she can't bring 'ome, like Lord Archibald.'

'Who's he?' asked Mr Brown.

'Don't ask, just hit him, Dad,' said Sally.

'Freddy, I notice you didn't say anything about you and Cassie,' said Mrs Brown.

'I'm tryin' to lie low,' said Freddy.

'You won't get any change out of that, Freddy,' said Mr Brown, 'Cassie'll dig you out even if yer lyin' low down a manhole.'

'If she had any sense she'd leave 'im there,' said Sally.

'That's not nice, Sally,' said Mrs Brown.

'I told you, it must be love,' said Freddy.

'Hit him twice, Dad,' said Sally.

'There's a lot of it about, y'know,' grinned Freddy.

'You've already said that.'

'I'm only—'

'Leave off,' said Sally.

'Yes, stop your teasin', Freddy,' said Mrs Brown. She would have liked Sally to take up with a nice young man. She agreed with Freddy that Mavis Richard's brother Wally wasn't up to scratch. Sally was deserving of someone more special, and seeing she was now twenty-two it was time she started walking out steady with the right young man. But Mrs Brown wasn't going to worry her about it. Mrs Brown wasn't that kind of a mum.

Friday went by without incident for Sally, leaving her still feeling frustrated.

Horace, home late that evening, was asked by Rebecca if he'd called at the dress shop again. Horace said he hadn't had a chance to, he'd been too busy. In any case, he said, he needed a reasonable excuse to go there, or he'd simply get slung out. Jim asked what an unreasonable excuse would do for him.

'Don't answer that, Horace,' said Rebecca.

'Where's Ethel?' asked Horace.

'In the parlour with Davy,' said Jim.

'I can't hear a sound,' said Horace.

'No, Davy's composing a new poem,' said Rebecca.

'And Ethel's twiddling her thumbs?' said Horace. 'What a life. Listen, Mum love, do ladies' dress shops sell stockings?'

'Some do, yes,' smiled Rebecca.

'Well, it's Ethel's birthday next month,' said Horace,

'Hello,' said Jim, 'are we getting desperate, Horace?'

'I need an excuse or two in reserve,' said Horace.

'Horace,' said Rebecca, 'I really think you should avoid the possibility of becoming an embarrassment to Miss Brown. She may be finding your visits to the shop very embarrassing, particularly if her manageress disapproves, and that may be why you're getting a cold shoulder. I must say that although your admiration for the young lady is perfectly natural, your way of courting her affections is very unusual.'

'You're not happy about it, Mum?' said Horace.

'Oh, I'm not in the least unhappy,' said Rebecca. 'That is, I don't disapprove of the unusual.' Her former self would have disapproved instantly. Her married self actually found a little delight in the cavalier nature of Horace's advances. What she feared was that that very attractive young lady might begin to consider him an irritating nuisance. 'Why not attempt the obvious? Why not present yourself at her family's door and ask her brother Freddy to formally introduce you to her?'

Jim said, 'It's a fact that while most Walworth girls, on the whole, don't mind a wink from across a crowded dance floor, followed by a bit of saucy slap and tickle, there are—'

'I beg your pardon, Mr Cooper?' said Rebecca.

'Have I said something, Mrs Cooper?' asked Jim.

'Yes, I don't think Mum liked the bit about slap and tickle,' said Horace.

'I didn't,' said Rebecca.

'There you are, Dad, she didn't,' said Horace.

'Fair comment,' said Jim. 'Anyway, there are some girls who don't favour getting come-on signs from young men they've never been introduced to, and Sally Brown might be that kind of a girl.'

'Believe me, she is,' said Horace.

'Then do what's right and proper,' said Rebecca.

'I've already had a word with Freddy about that,' said Horace, and accordingly he went out later that evening.

Freddy, answering a knock on the door, found Horace on the step.

'Evening, Freddy.'

'Pleased to see yer, Orrice.'

'Is your sister Sally in?'

''Ello, is this it?' grinned Freddy. 'Have you come to be properly introduced to her?'

'I'd like to be,' said Horace.

'She's a bit ratty this evening,' said Freddy.

'Don't like the sound of that,' said Horace.

'Well, I grant, it's not promisin',' said Freddy.

183

'Still, I'll take a chance,' said Horace.

Freddy turned and called.

'Sally, come out a minute, would yer?'

Sally came out of the kitchen, advanced along the passage and stopped halfway as she saw Horace on the step.

'What's that person doing here?' she demanded.

'He wants to be introduced,' said Freddy, 'so might I do the honours and present 'im? He's—'

'He's got a hope,' said Sally. 'Ask him how he found out where I lived.'

Freddy put the question.

'You told me, Freddy,' said Horace.

'Oh, so I did,' said Freddy.

'Ask him why he's got the nerve to come knockin',' said Sally.

'Might I ask why – 'ere, what'm I doin', I don't have to ask,' said Freddy, 'I know already. He's come to be properly introduced.'

'Well, 'ard luck,' said Sally. She walked to the door and closed it. It rattled. Then she went back to the kitchen. Freddy opened the door again. Horace looked at him.

'Told you she was a bit ratty,' said Freddy.

'Not my evening,' said Horace.

'Yes, 'ard cheese, Orrice, but good luck next time, if you're keen,' said Freddy.

'Got your blessin', have I, Freddy?'

'Well, Dumpling reckons you've got a good build,' said Freddy, 'and Sally's never been in favour of skinny blokes.'

184

'Well, good on yer, Freddy, some other time, then,' said Horace.

'So long, mate,' said Freddy.

'D'you know that character?' asked Sally when her brother returned to the kitchen.

'Yes, he's Orrice Cooper from Wansey Street,' said Freddy.

'He's who?' said Sally.

'Orrice Cooper. Don't you remember him and 'is sister Effel when they were at school together?'

'Well, I'm blessed,' said Sally, 'I liked 'im a bit for the way he set about boys who made fun of Effel, I never thought he'd turn into a bighead.'

'I used to hear about Orrice and Effel,' said Mrs Brown. 'Of course, they're grown up now. What's Orrice grown up like, Freddy?'

'He's on Surrey's ground staff at the Oval, and a bit of a cricketer,' said Freddy. 'Good-lookin' bloke, yer know—'

'Back of a bus, more like,' said Sally.

'Good build too,' said Freddy.

'Skinny ribs, more like,' said Sally.

'I've got a torso like that meself,' said Freddy. 'Slim, yer know. It's part of a good build in a bloke.'

'You got what, Freddy?' asked Mr Brown.

'Skinny ribs,' said Sally.

'I ain't heard Cassie say so,' said Freddy.

'Poor girl, she's moonstruck,' said Sally.

'Sally, have you come to meet Orrice Cooper lately?' asked Mrs Brown.

'He's been in the shop sev'ral times,' said Sally, 'playin' daft games with me over hair ribbon and a boater for his sister. He doesn't 'alf fancy his chances.'

'I heard he used to be a good footballer,' said Freddy.

'I hate football,' said Sally.

'And he's supposed to be a good cricketer, too,' said Freddy.

'I hate cricket worse,' said Sally.

'My, you do sound out of sorts, Sally,' said her mum.

'Told you, it's love,' said Freddy, 'and we know who now.'

'I'll scream in a minute,' said Sally.

Cassie arrived then and took Freddy out for a walk. Freddy asked where she was taking him to. Round to the church, said Cassie. Freddy asked what for. Cassie said she'd met the vicar and he'd informed her a large basket of flowers had been presented to the church. So she and Freddy were going to do flower arranging in time for Sunday morning service.

'Me?' said Freddy.

'No, both of us,' said Cassie, turning into Walcorde Avenue. 'I promised the vicar. I said – here, wait a minute, where've you gone?' Freddy wasn't with her any more. He was beating a retreat down Browning Street. 'Well, what a funny bloke,' said Cassie, and went after him. Supple, athletic and fast, she caught him in Turquand Street. 'Here, where'd you think you're goin'?' she demanded.

'Well, I know where I'm not goin',' said Freddy, 'and that's to the church.'

'Freddy, of course you are, I promised the vicar.'

'Well, tell 'im I couldn't get there on account of breakin' me leg,' said Freddy.

'Sometimes, Freddy, I don't think you understand about obligations,' said Cassie.

'Who said that?' asked Freddy.

'Me, I did,' said Cassie.

'Obligations?'

'Yes, you're obligated to help me arrange flowers in the church,' said Cassie.

'Now, Cassie, blokes don't get obligated to arrange flowers, and I'm like iron in refusin' to.'

'Freddy—'

'No, for once, I'm puttin' me foot down, Cassie.'

'Well, I like you bein' manly, Freddy, of course I do, but we did promise the vicar.'

'Not me, I didn't.'

'Yes, you did, I promised for both of us, and the vicar said to thank you. What a nice helpful young man Freddy's grown into, he said.'

'I can't 'elp that, Cassie, I'm not havin' anything to do with arrangin' flowers in church vases.'

'Now, Freddy.'

'Cassie, can't you spot me look of iron determination?'

'Yes, of course I can, Freddy, and it doesn't 'alf suit you, you're ever so good-lookin' when you're like iron.'

Freddy looked at her. Her raven hair, thick and healthy was worn long as usual, and ribboned at the nape of her neck. A new halo hat sat on the back of her head, and her orange-coloured sweater showed that at eighteen she'd grown up very nicely. Crikey, thought Freddy, I'm done for if I don't stiffen me sinews.

'Cassie, I'm not departin' from me iron resolve,' he said.

Cassie smiled.

So Freddy and his iron resolve spent an hour helping Cassie decorate the church with flowers. He could only hope the street kids wouldn't get to hear about it.

As for Ethel, she made the mistake of giggling over one or two of Davy's poetical phrases, which caused his spectacles to take on the dark hue of upset sensitivity. Ethel, who simply hadn't been able to strangle her giggles at birth, said she was awfully sorry, only a fair maiden seated on a dewy throne of sun-kissed water lilies had made her think of the time when Mrs Blossom of Brandon Street had slipped and sat in an April puddle.

Davy said perhaps she didn't really like his poetry. Ethel said oh, but it's so romantic, and that she hadn't meant to think about Mrs Blossom, poor woman. Well, if you're sure, Ethel, said Davy. Ethel said she was, and that she felt very drawn towards his fair maiden who liked limpid lakes and pools and water lilies. Well, it is you, said Davy, and Ethel asked if the fair maiden oughtn't to wear

188

a bathing costume sometimes. I mean, if it's me, she said, I'd feel more comfortable in a bathing costume than in ivy leaves. Bathing costumes aren't poetical, said Davy, spectacles sort of glooming at her. Oh, all right, Davy, said Ethel.

Chapter Twelve

At his Shoreditch factory on Saturday morning, George Carter spent a difficult hour figuratively wrestling with three angry creditors who'd called in person to collect what he owed them. In the end, to avoid being summonsed he gave them all cheques in full settlement of their accounts. At their insistence, the cheques were drawn on his private bank account.

At the Kennington shop, a hand-delivered letter was among the mail Miss Lomax picked up from the mat when she arrived. It was addressed to Sally, and she handed it to her when she came in.

'I think that can only be from your latest admirer, Sally.'

'If you don't mind, Miss Lomax, he's just a headache,' said Sally, and opened the letter.

Dear Miss Brown, I'm sorry we didn't get properly introduced, as I thought that if we could it would be to our advantage.

Our advantage? Ours? Oh, the saucy devil, he was getting worse.

*I still hope we can be friends, especially as I now
know I was at the same school as you for a while,
and that I like your brother Freddy. I know you
might think it potty, but I couldn't help writing you a
poem. Ethel's going in for poetry with her bloke, and
I've caught the bug. My poem's as follows:
A pretty girl called Sally Brown
Always greets me with a frown,
I think it's going to get me down
Getting no smile from Sally Brown.'*

Sally had never read such daft drivel.

*I suppose it's not much of a poem, and Ethel could
probably write a better one, but if it helps to let you
see I'd like to take you to the pictures or to hear the
band in Hyde Park, or both if you're keen, then I'll
try writing some more. Yours in hope, Horace
Cooper.
PS. I think my mother would like to meet you if
we could get properly introduced.*

Well, breathed Sally to herself, if he thinks
writing to me as if I'm fourteen years old does anything for me, he can think again. And what does he
mean, his mother would like to meet me? He's got
bats in his belfry. He's drivelling. He's about as
grown-up as he was at ten.

'Is it a love letter, Sally?' smiled Miss Lomax.

'It's ugh,' said Sally. I bet he'll pop in sometime
today with that silly grin all over his face, she

thought. I'll make him eat his silly poem if he does.

But he didn't.

For some reason that made her rattier than ever.

That's funny, thought Dumpling. Something private and personal should have happened by now. It was three weeks since her wedding day, and five-and-a-bit weeks since – well, never mind that. It never worried her, anyway, it didn't give her headaches or anything like that. Still, she'd never been late before, she was very regular. Oh, well.

'Danny,' she said to her lesser half after he'd come home from his morning's work and they'd had their Saturday midday meal, 'you needn't clean the winders this afternoon.'

'Well, Dumpling, to be honest, after me 'ard labours this mornin', I wasn't thinkin' of doin' any winder-cleanin',' said Danny.

'No, all right, you can do it later on,' said Dumpling. 'We'll go to Clapham Common this afternoon for a kickabout, and ask Freddy and Cassie to join us. Four of us could get a good kickabout, specially as it's our first match next Saturday.'

'Oh, all right, Dumpling,' said Danny, devoted to her companionable self and her cheerful way of ordering him about.

However, Freddy and Cassie weren't available. They'd gone out, so Dumpling and Danny went by themselves, and people sporting themselves on Clapham Common blinked to see a jolly fat girl kicking a football about with an upstanding male specimen.

As for Cassie and Freddy, well, it was a fact that Cassie had marriage on her mind. She was already eighteen. Her sisters Annie and Nellie were both married, and she was an aunt to Annie's two little boys. Fancy being an aunt and not even engaged. She had pointed out to Freddy what a disgrace this was. Freddy said he couldn't see it was a disgrace, but if it was, whose fault was it? Yours, said Cassie. How could it be mine, asked Freddy, when it's not me but me brother Will that's married to Annie? Yes, but no-one's married to me, said Cassie, and that no-one's you. Aunts ought to be married, she said, or people would look at them.

Freddy said he didn't mind looking at her himself occasionally, as she was just as good to look at as a potted plant. Cassie asked if he meant an aspidistra. No, me mum's potted African violets, said Freddy. They're pretty, he said, like you. Yes, I know I'm pretty, Freddy, said Cassie, but I'm still an unmarried aunt. Freddy pointed out he naturally thought about getting married eventually, that he was saving up for same, and that when he'd saved enough he'd look around to see who he ought to marry. Cassie went for him. Wisely, Freddy fell down. He knew he'd suffer damage if he stayed on his feet. Cassie told him to get up. Freddy asked what for. You're looking at my legs from down there, said Cassie. Well, I'm not complaining, said Freddy. Well, I am, said Cassie, it's not nice. Well, it is from where I am, said Freddy. Get up, said Cassie, so I can talk to you properly. Freddy said that at the moment he was better off where he was, and that he didn't mind postponing any talk. Cassie said he was playing hard to get, which was daft, as only girls had the right to do that. Her dad, known as the Gaffer, appeared then and asked what Freddy was doing on the parlour floor.

'Lyin' doggo,' said Freddy.

'Yes, and it's private, Dad,' said Cassie, 'so you can go back to the kitchen.'

'But what's up?' asked the Gaffer.

'Cassie's complainin' about bein' an unmarried aunt,' said Freddy.

'Ah,' said the Gaffer. 'Ah,' he said again. 'Well,' he said. 'I see,' he said. 'Yes, you sort it out, Freddy,' he said. 'Like Cassie said, it's private.'

But it was nothing that didn't happen regularly, in various ways, between Cassie and Freddy. They were one in their own kind of cross-talk, which Cassie enjoyed immensely, while always keeping the upper hand. In any case, Freddy, like Danny before him, was actually making sense in wanting to put a fair bit of oof aside before asking Cassie to name a date. However, after taking a young man's natural note yesterday evening of the fact that she'd grown up a treat, and having forgiven her for breaking his iron reserve, he'd taken his irrepressible young lady up West this afternoon and was in Oxford Street with her.

Cassie, looking sweetly gift-wrapped in her one

194

and only lightweight autumn coat, an attractive mint green, asked for the umpteenth time why he'd brought her here.

'Well, I couldn't come by meself,' said Freddy, 'I've got to make sure the size is right.'

'What size? Size for what?'

'Not a liberty bodice,' said Freddy.

'Here,' said Cassie, 'what do you know about liberty bodices?'

'I've got two sisters, and I've had 'em all me life,' said Freddy, 'and I'm like Sherlock 'Olmes, I'm observant.'

'Sherlock 'Olmes doesn't observe liberty bodices,' said Cassie, 'he looks in hansom cabs to see if a criminal's left some clues, like a body and a blood-stained chopper. My dad's got a chopper,' she added, 'but it's not blood-stained. Well, not yet it isn't. Freddy, what're we stoppin' for?'

'Well, we're here,' said Freddy.

'Yes, but what for?'

'It's Bravingtons,' said Freddy.

Cassie turned her head and saw the bright window display of the jewellers.

'Freddy?'

'Would you honestly like to get engaged, Cassie?'

With Saturday afternoon shoppers milling around them, Cassie blinked.

'What, here, now, in Oxford Street?' she said.

'D'you want to try the Zoo, then?' asked Freddy.

Cassie looked at him. He was doing his best to hide a grin, she could see that. There he was, a young man now, and she'd known him since she was ten, when he'd made her his best mate and they'd gone about together around the streets, she with her school boater lopsided and her gymslip a bit crooked, and he with his large peaked cap on the back of his head. He'd left those years well behind, he was five feet ten now, slim but with fine square shoulders and whipcord muscles, and he never lost his temper except with affluent MPs who, fortified by a good lunch, enjoined everyone to tighten their belts to help the country out of recession. Apart from that, he had his mum's temperament, and his own way of being protective. She felt they understood each other in a way neither of them would ever understand anyone else. She still had to threaten to kick him sometimes to let him know that his place in life was next to her. Now he'd accepted that, and here outside Bravingtons in Oxford Street, he was telling her they ought to get engaged. Cassie was actually lost for a moment, because of a lump in her throat.

Swallowing it, she said, 'Freddy, why couldn't you 'ave asked me before we left home?'

'Well, that was an hour ago,' said Freddy, 'and we're a bit older now, and you need to be a bit older to get engaged.'

Cassie laughed. Oxford Street was alive with shoppers, and buses, taxis and posh cars were charging about. Fancy being proposed to on a Saturday afternoon in Oxford Street. Trust Freddy to do it in this fashion.

'If I say yes, do I get a kiss?' she asked.

'Might I suggest on the bus goin' 'ome, if no-one's lookin'?' said Freddy.

'Freddy, I haven't checked your account lately, so how much 'ave you got saved up?'

'I can't tell you 'ere, with all these people about,' said Freddy. 'Some crooked geezer might listen in and pinch me Post Office book.'

'Never mind that,' said Cassie, 'just tell me.'

'With the interest, a bit over fifty quid,' said Freddy.

'Fifty?' Dreams floated into Cassie's eyes, dreams, probably, of bridal silks and satins. She was still very imaginative, and wrote fanciful stories with a pencil in exercise books. They were usually on Elinor Glyn lines. 'Did you say fifty?'

'Cassie, not out loud, not here—'

'Well, you should've told me at 'ome,' said Cassie. 'Freddy, it's all of fifty pounds?'

'And a bit more,' said Freddy. 'Well, I get two quid a week at the brewery, and overtime, and a bonus at Christmas—'

'Yes, all right, Freddy, we're engaged to be married, then.'

'You say when, Cassie.'

'Next Easter,' said Cassie. 'You'll 'ave a hundred pounds saved up by then, and we'll be nearly rich. I don't mind bein' an aunt now I'm engaged. Let's go in, then, and I'll let you spend as much as two pounds on the ring. We can get a lovely one for that.'

'I thought thirty bob—'

'Freddy,' said Cassie, with a tide of shoppers breaking around them, 'it's me you're engaged to, not someone you found under a market stall.'

'All right, as I found you in a fact'ry yard, I'll go up to two quid, then,' said Freddy.

In they went, and when a polite bloke who looked like a Buckingham Palace butler asked what their pleasure was, Freddy said he'd like to look at some engagement rings for an aunt he was going to marry, which made the bloke twitch a bit. Cassie, however, helped him to recover by explaining how she came to be an aunt, an unrelated one. Freddy said an aunt couldn't be unrelated.

'Of course she can,' said Cassie, 'I'm unrelated to you, aren't I? That's why we can marry. Could we see some rings, please?'

'Suitable for an unrelated aunt,' said Freddy, and the polite bloke let it be known then that he liked these particular customers. His dignified countenance worked itself into a smile, and he became a kind help to Cassie. Well, she and Freddy were a tonic, even if they hadn't come to buy a diamond solitaire.

When they left the shop Cassie was wearing a very nice sapphire ring, which had cost Freddy two pounds, six shillings-and-elevenpence, and which Cassie loved dearly.

'Now,' said Freddy, 'what about tea and fruit buns at a Lyons?'

'Freddy, an engagement ring, and a fruit bun,

and a pot of tea all at once?' said Cassie.

'Well, I've never been engaged to you before,' said Freddy.

Cassie slipped her arm through his and they walked to find a teashop.

'Freddy?'

'I'm still here,' said Freddy.

'I feel ever so pleased with you and your Post Office savings,' said Cassie.

'I just feel short of two pounds, six shillings-and-elevenpence,' said Freddy. 'Worth it, though.'

'Honest?' Cassie was sort of limpid-eyed for once, like the lady in Davy's sonnets. 'Honest, Freddy?'

'Every penny,' said Freddy.

'Well, I suppose you're quite lucky to have me really,' said Cassie. 'Listen, when we're married you'll get a ten-bob rise. Sammy always gives that sort of rise to any of his men who get married. Susie told me when I was talkin' to her once. She said Sammy says it's his responsibility to see his workers don't 'ave to start married life in a watchman's hut or a pawnbroker's shop. Freddy, you'll be gettin' two pounds ten a week then. That's nearly rich, isn't it? Still, I won't want a winter fur coat to start with, we'd best find a house to rent first, say in Wansey Street. Wansey Street's nice. Well, sort of more select than our streets, with nicer gates and railings.'

She went on like this in a quick and engaging way, and was still at it when they turned into Lyons and found a table in the popular teashop. They sat down. Cassie stopped talking then and looked at her new ring. Freddy looked at her. She glanced at him, and he had a quite sober moment wondering just how she'd managed to change from a dotty madcap into a real treat of a girl. Crikey, he thought, her eyes look all misty. What's that for?

'Cassie?'

'Freddy, I'm ever so glad you found me in that fact'ry yard when I was lookin' for our cat.'

Dumpling laid on a young people's tea party on Sunday to celebrate the engagement, inviting Horace and Ethel – because they were now neighbours and Horace might join the football team – and Nick and Annabelle, and Cassie and Freddy themselves, of course. Ethel asked if she could bring Davy, who might write a poem to Cassie and Freddy. Dumpling felt she could put up with a poet for the duration of the party and for the sake of Ethel, so she said yes, he could come.

A whole bowl of shrimps and a whole bowl of winkles stood on the kitchen table, along with a large dish of bread and butter, jars of jam and a fruit cake baked by Dumpling herelf.

Nick and Annabelle met Horace and Ethel for the first time, as well as Ethel's young man, Davy. Then they all sat down to tea around the table in Dumpling's kitchen, and they all talked at once, except for Davy. Annabelle thought him nice but shy, his spectacles sort of blinking modestly when Ethel said what a good poet he was, and that he was going to compose a sonnet in honour of Freddy and Cassie. Cassie said Freddy had proposed to her in Oxford Street, would you believe, in the middle of people and with a bus going by. Still, it showed initiative, which a girl liked, she said, as long as he kept it to himself on the top deck of a London bus.

'Excuse me,' said Freddy, 'but wasn't it you that—'

'Eat your bread and butter up, Freddy, there's a dear,' said Cassie, treading on his foot.

The hunger of the young began to decimate the mountains of shrimps and winkles, eaten with bread and butter, and festive chat created an atmosphere that was very celebratory. Well, everyone was happy about the engagement, and even Dumpling said marriage wasn't daft all the time. Growing rounder and rosier by the minute when she started to consume bread and jam, she told Davy that Nick was good at making up poems, his education and clerking job had done it for him. Mind, he wasn't actually a poet, he was a footballer, but he could probably make up a poem before they got to the cake. Horace said give it a go, then, Nick.

Nick gave it thought, then came up with his effort.

'Two people called Freddy and Cassie
Went to their wedding by taxi,
The cabbie said, "Oi!
Kindly mind me eye,
You ain't married yet, me lassie."'

The girls shrieked. Horace and Danny roared

with laughter. The slight disapproval of a serious muse glimmered through Davy's spectacles. He didn't think much of doggerel or limericks.

'Did you like that, Davy?' asked Ethel.

'I hope Nick won't mind if I say it's not poetry,' said Davy.

'No, I don't mind,' said Nick.

'Not a bad effort, though,' said Horace, 'and quick as a flash, almost.'

Davy hastened to say, 'Mind, it was all right in its way.'

'Oh, it was such a giggle,' said Ethel, and Davy looked as if it was a half a giggle full stop.

'Myself,' he said, 'I'd do the happy couple the honour of beginning with something like, "With apple blossom awaiting Cassie's beauteous form divine." And so on.'

'Me beauteous what?' said Cassie.

'Oh, me gawd,' gurgled Dumpling and giggled. It was catching enough for Ethel to join in. Nick and Horace kept their faces straight. Danny grinned. So did Freddy.

'Lovely, Davy,' said Annabelle, sympathetic to the serious young man, who was regarding Ethel in sad disappointment.

'I shall do my best to complete the sonnet,' he said.

Oh, that poor Effel, thought Dumpling, fancy her having a poet like that for a young man. It didn't ought to be allowed, not with a nice girl like her. There's one or two blokes in our football team that might be glad to take up with her if I could get her to come and watch some of our matches.

After tea, willing hands helped with the washing-up, and then Dumpling ushered everyone into her bright living-room, the front room that overlooked the street.

'It being an 'appy occasion, we'll honour Freddy and Cassie with a singsong,' she said. 'Get yer mouth organ, Danny. Mind, if you'd all rather talk about football—'

'Blow that for a lark,' said Freddy.

'Football's rather boring, isn't it?' said Davy.

Shock registered itself all over Dumpling's jolly-looking face.

'Oh, yer poor feller,' she said.

'Well, football's not Davy's style,' said Ethel.

'Yes, there are other things,' smiled Annabelle.

'Oh, I suppose so,' conceded Dumpling.

'I think we'd better 'ave a singsong,' said Danny.

'Yes, would you like a singsong, Davy?' asked Ethel.

'It might be an improvement on football and giggles,' said Davy, and then his spectacles blinked with sensitivity as some of his new friends gave him funny looks. 'Well, I—'

'I'll collapse in a minute,' said Dumpling.

'Catch her before she hits the floor, Danny,' said Nick.

''Ere, everyone sit down,' said Dumpling, 'and you get busy with yer mouth organ, Danny.'

Everyone found a seat, and Danny, grinning,

blew a few chords in the direction of Cassie and Freddy, and Dumpling led the way into an appropriate song, even if she did think it a bit soppy.

'Oh, let me call you sweetheart, I'm in love with you . . .'

They all sang with her except Davy, whose serious approach to life was against this kind of thing. His mind was on a fair maiden and a sunlit pool.

The singsong became prolonged, Danny quite a performer on the mouth morgan, and Annabelle letting herself go in company with her Walworth friends, whom she found infectiously extrovert. Dumpling got herself into such a celebratory state that after half an hour she said they all ought to do a knees-up. Danny obliged with 'Mother Brown' on his mouth organ, and away everyone went, again except for Davy, who couldn't think why Ethel liked making an exhibition of herself.

Up came Mrs Shaw from downstairs, a landlady kind and tolerant, but not too tolerant of rowdyism on a Sunday evening.

'Excuse me, Mr Thompson,' she said, 'but what's goin' on, might I hask?'

'We're celebratin' an engagement with a bit of a knees-up,' said Danny.

'Well, I don't know what it's doin' to your floor, but me hubby says it's bendin' our ceiling something chronic, and rattling our china cupboard as well. And it's makin' our wireless set sound funny. There's all sorts of noises comin' out of it. Could yer give us the pleasure of not jumpin' up and down?'

'Oh, ever so sorry about the noise, Mrs Shaw,' said Dumpling. 'I don't know what come over us, except our friends Cassie and Freddy 'ave just got engaged in Oxford Street. That's them, over there.'

'Pleased to meet you, Hi'm sure,' said the landlady, 'but it's our ceiling, yer see. Me and me hubby don't want it fallin' on us.'

'We'll give it a rest,' said Danny.

'I'd be that obliged if yer would, Mr Thompson,' said Mrs Shaw.

'Never mind,' said Dumpling, when Mrs Shaw had departed, 'we can 'ave some nice talk instead.'

'If you'll excuse us, I think it's time I took Ethel home,' said Davy.

'And I think I'll see Freddy to my door,' said Cassie. 'He needs someone with him when he's out. He's been like it ever since we got engaged.'

'Must be love,' said Horace, 'it's hard on a bloke.' Cassie smiled. Freddy had told her earlier that Horace was gone on Sally.

'What about what us girls 'ave to put up with?' asked Dumpling.

'Oh, I suppose we all suffer, Dumpling,' said Nick.

'Oh, dear, what a shame,' said Annabelle. 'Never mind, you can take me home now, Nick.'

The party broke up. Horace and Ethel left in company with Davy, and as soon as the serious-minded young gentleman was alone in Rebecca's

parlour with Ethel he expressed himself reproach-
fully.

'Ethel, that's the second time you've giggled at
my poetry,' he said.

'Oh, is it, Davy? I don't know why I should, your
poetry's ever so good.'

'I'm disappointed in you, all the same,' said
Davy.

'Oh, I'll make us some nice hot cocoa, shall I?'
said Ethel. 'And it was a nice tea party, wasn't
it?'

'Yes, quite nice, but a bit childish,' said Davy.

'Oh, but we 'ave to let our hair down sometimes,
Davy.'

Davy's spectacles frowned a bit.

'Nick?' said Annabelle on the home-going bus.
They were on the top deck, with only two other
passengers, and she had her arm through his. She
liked contact with him, she liked to feel they
belonged to each other. 'Nick?'

'I am awake,' said Nick.

'Oh, good, I'm flattered. Tell me what you
thought of "beauteous form divine".'

'I thought whatsisname – Davy – was taking the
mickey out of poets, but he wasn't. He was serious.
Did you see Cassie's face and Freddy's grin?'

'I don't think Davy liked hearing the giggles,'
said Annabelle. 'He's very serious, but shy. I don't
know much about him, or Ethel, I've never met
them before, but isn't she a dainty girl? And quite

206

sweet. And I liked her brother Horace. He looked as if he couldn't make out why his sister was going steady with Davy. But there's nothing wrong with a young man being serious. You could do with a bit of seriousness sometimes.'

'How much, half a pound or so?'

'What did you really think of "beauteous form divine"?' asked Annabelle.

'Not as much as "The Boy Stood On The Burning Deck",' said Nick.

Annabelle smiled and cuddled his arm.

'Listen,' said Freddy to Cassie on their way to her home, 'has that bloke Davy seen you in your liberty bodice on some occasion I don't know about?'

'Here, d'you mind?' said Cassie. 'I'm out of liberty bodices, I'll 'ave you know.'

Freddy said he'd not had the pleasure himself of seeing her out of them. If Davy Williams had, he said, he supposed that was why he was able to talk about her form divine. He also supposed Davy would want to paint it next. Cassie said help, if she let him she might get hung in a picture gallery. So might Davy, from the ceiling, said Freddy.

'Freddy love, are you jealous?' asked Cassie.

'Well, Cassie, I can't tell a porkie, you've grown up sort of special to me, and I ain't keen on anyone paintin' you except me.'

Cassie said if anyone tried to paint her without any clothes on, her dad would have him executed at the Tower of London. Freddy said he thought he'd buy a box of paints, anyway, for when he was married. Cassie laughed. But what a crackpot Davy Williams was, said Freddy, imagine poor old Effel landing herself with a bloke as barmy as that.

'Well, like Annabelle's Uncle Boots told me once, we're all a bit barmy,' said Cassie, as they walked up King and Queen Street. 'Still, you ought to be grateful, Freddy.'

'What for, all of us bein' a bit barmy?' asked Freddy.

'No, for my form divine,' said Cassie. 'Freddy, is it really true that Orrice is a bit gone on Sally?'

Freddy said yes, but that it had turned Sally ratty. Cassie said she couldn't think why, because Orrice was a nice bloke.

'Much to me sorrow, seeing I like Orrice meself,' said Freddy, 'Sally reckons she could do better with a muffin man, so she's givin' Orrice a hard time. By the way, I've just thought of something.'

'What something?' asked Cassie.

'I think I might get to like bein' married to you,' said Freddy.

'Honest, Freddy?'

'Well, just lately,' said Freddy, 'well, for the last ten minutes or so, I keep thinkin' about your form divine.'

Davy might have been pleased that his poetic phrase had left its mark on Cassie and Freddy, and Annabelle and Nick. He might, as long as he didn't know it had been a giggle to them.

Chapter Thirteen

Horace popped into the ladies' dress shop at ten-past-five on Monday. Sally was attending to a customer, but the entry of Horace made her grind her teeth. Miss Lomax came forward.

'Good afternoon, sir, may I help you?' she smiled.

'Hello,' said Horace, 'I think you're the manageress.'

'Yes, I'm Miss Lomax. Can I help?'

'If you're busy, I'll wait till Miss Brown's free,' said Horace.

'I'm not at all busy,' smiled Miss Lomax, 'and the shop will be closing in twenty minutes.'

'Ah,' said Horace.

'I'm not sure what that means, sir.'

'I'm thinking you run a very nice dress shop,' said Horace.

'What's that young man doin' in here?' whispered the customer to Sally.

'I really don't know, madam,' said Sally.

'Suspicious, I call it. You'd best keep your eye on your till.'

'Yes, you just can't tell what some people will get

up to,' said Sally, loudly enough for Horace to hear.

Miss Lomax requested Horace to make known his want.

'D'you sell stockings?' asked Horace, giving up his delaying tactics.

'Stockings?' Miss Lomax smiled again. There was no stopping this young man. Noting the departure of Sally's customer she said, 'Yes, we have an excellent selection, and as Miss Brown is free now, she'll serve you while I check the till for the day. Miss Brown?'

'Yes, Miss Lomax?' said Sally.

'Would you serve this gentleman, please?'

'Very well, Miss Lomax,' said Sally, and ground her teeth again. Horace advanced and they eyed each other over the counter. Sally was in a fighting mood, Horace in a persevering one. Stump me for a duck, he thought, I can't help it, I like her when her blood's up.

'Hello, Miss Brown,' he said, and Sally regarded his smile darkly.

'Yes?' she said.

'Did you get my letter and poem?' asked Horace, and Sally drew a hissing breath.

Miss Lomax being out of earshot, she breathed, 'I never read such drivel. I suppose you thought it was funny? Well, it wasn't, and if you don't tell me what you want, I'll order you out of the shop, d'you 'ear?'

'I'm after a pair of stockings,' said Horace.

Finding that unbelievable, Sally breathed,

'Stockings? Stockings? Oh, you ha'porth of suet puddin', I hate you more each time I see you, d'you know that? You ought to be chucked off the top of Nelson's Column. You've come in here just to mess me about again.'

'I take the opportunity of refutin' that remark,' said Horace.

'You what?'

'I'm a customer,' said Horace, 'and I'm askin' after stockings.'

'Oh, and garters as well, I suppose,' said Sally with pointed sarcasm.

'Why, d'you sell garters?' asked Horace.

'Go away, d'you 'ear, go away,' said Sally.

'Listen,' said Horace, 'it's Ethel's birthday next month. I usually buy her hankies. This time I thought I'd treat her to a pair of come-on stockings.'

Sally, breathing hard, said, 'What d'you mean, "come-on stockings"?'

'Yes, you know, the kind that make a feller's eyes blink twice,' said Horace. 'And she's got the kind of feller who needs something to take his mind off poetry now and again. By the way, Ethel's what my mother calls petite, which is about five feet nothing, so you probably know what size stockings would fit her. What about silk? I won't mind if they're expensive. It's her twenty-first, and I'll be buying her something else as well. The stockings would be an extra touch, but I wouldn't want anything like cheap lisle.'

'Now look, are you serious?' asked Sally.

'On me honour,' said Horace.

Miss Lomax was looking, so Sally said, 'Well, sir, if it's her twenty-first, it should be silk. What colour do you have in mind, might I enquire?'

'You've got me there,' said Horace. 'Tell you what, as it's near your closin' time, you sort out a few pairs of different colours for me, and I'll come back tomorrow and inspect them.'

'Oh, no you don't,' whispered Sally, 'that's just an excuse to come and lark about with me again.'

'Have a heart,' said Horace, 'have I larked about ever? Have I stood on me head or performed a clog dance on your counter? I've only ever been in here as a customer.'

'Well, you're the first customer that's ever tried to drag me off on a Sunday morning to a smelly old rubbish dump,' said Sally.

'Wait a minute,' said Horace, 'how about you bein' the first shop assistant to throw a customer's Sunday boater into a dustbin?'

'Oh, you – you rotten piece of haddock,' fumed Sally, 'that was your own fault, not mine. Stop tryin' to make me feel ten years old.'

'Me?' said Horace. 'Would I be havin' sleepless nights if you were only ten years old?'

'Miss Brown, I think the gentleman was after stockings,' called Miss Lomax, hiding a smile. Not even a single pair had been produced.

'Yes, Miss Lomax, I've been tryin' to find out what colour he wants,' said Sally.

'She's a great help,' said Horace, 'but I've been

mumbling a bit. It's new to me, buying ladies' stockings, and I'm probably blushin' about it as well as mumbling. D'you get many blushin' customers, Miss Lomax?'

Miss Lomax, in difficulty, retreated hastily into the back room, where she strangled hysterical laughter.

Sally, eyeing Horace pityingly, said, 'If you end up with your big head in a loony-bin, serve you right.'

'Could I call you Sally?' asked Horace.

'No,' said Sally.

'I'm Horace.'

'That's not my fault. Now, if you really want a pair of silk stockings—'

'Yes, I really do,' said Horace, 'and I'll be grateful if you could sort out some suitable colours. Holy Moses, look at the time, you'll be closin' in a tick, and I've got to scarper. I'll be back tomorrow to look at the selection. So long for now, Miss Brown.' Horace made for the door.

'Come back, d'you 'ear?' Sally almost yelled at him. 'Come back, I'm not havin' you – oh, the rotten faceache, look at 'im.'

Horace had the door open and was sidling out into the street, having given himself an excuse to call back tomorrow. Miss Lomax reappeared.

'He bought the stockings, Sally?' she asked.

'Oh, I'll kick his legs off,' said Sally, 'he's comin' back tomorrow for them, just like 'e did for that blessed rotten boater.'

'My word, Sally, what a campaign he's running,' said Miss Lomax. 'I can't help wishing him luck.'

'Luck? Luck?' said Sally. 'D'you mean me suffering the agony of letting him take me out?'

'There are some very good films showing at the moment,' said Miss Lomax, going to the door and fixing the catch.

'Oh, don't mind about me dyin' a death,' said Sally bitterly.

But a funny thing happened to her on the way home. She stopped suddenly.

Joseph Burns, living in his tormented world, stiffened in his chair beside the window. He drew a breath and his hands clenched. There she was, at a halt only a few yards away and looking, he was sure, straight at his window. A bleedin' Jerry fräulein, getting herself ready to strike. So he got himself ready to spring. But then she was moving again. Up she came and passed his window and his straining eyes. He exhaled breath.

Sally, walking towards Manor Place, had stopped when she was hit by a sudden feeling of exhilaration. Now she was talking to herself. I won't let him win tomorrow, I just won't. He did it on me again today, he had it all worked out. He knew just what he was going to do, he knew if he came in late and spent enough time gassing to me, he could give himself an excuse to come back tomorrow. I know why he's persecuting me, it's because I didn't fall for his fatal charm when he first tried it on with me. Some fatal charm. Blokes who think they're God's

214

gift don't have any charm at all. Well, wait till you come in tomorrow, Horace Cooper, I'm going to look down my nose at you and not say a single word except professional ones like good afternoon, sir, and the door's over there, sir. He likes getting me going, it's his way of having his own back. I'm not falling for that any more. I'll just ignore all his remarks.

It really was exhilarating, thinking of one more confrontation with the bigheaded gasbag. It perked her up no end.

She was in a much better mood that evening, and Mrs Brown said to her husband how nice it was that Sally was herself again. Something's cooking, said Mr Brown. Mrs Brown asked what he meant, and her resilient better half said he didn't exactly know, except he'd been long enough around females to have suspicions when one of them went about with a secret smile on her face. What, said Mrs Brown, your own daughter? I know, Bessie, said Mr Brown, but she's also a female. I hope you're not suggesting Sally's going to rob her own shop, said Mrs Brown. No, more like some bloke's going to cop a fourpenny one, said Mr Brown. In a manner of speaking, he said. Oh, you silly old sausage, said Mrs Brown.

*　　*　　*

Tuesday, and George Carter was sweating. The cheques had bounced and all three upset creditors

215

had issued summonses against him. As soon as the other creditors got wind of this, that would be it. He'd be in the bankruptcy court and ruined. Nor would he be able to start up in business again until he'd cleared his debts. He could put something into the firm's bank account if he sold out to Sammy Adams, if he parted with his business lock, stock and barrel to that clever cocky sharp-nosed sod. But that wouldn't wipe out all his debts and he'd sooner eat his own grandmother than hand over his factory and everything else to Sammy, who'd been lifting customers off him regularly by undercutting him year in, year out. If there was one bloke who wasn't going to profit from all this, it was Mister Bleedin' Sammy Adams.

He'd got to find a buyer and he'd got to find a mint of money, and quick.

★   ★   ★

Sally checked her wristwatch. Nearly five o'clock, and that drivelling beast hadn't shown up. He was going to do it on her again, he was going to make her feel all frustrated by not arriving. What a specimen.

Miss Lomax was dealing with a young housewife, and Sally was attending to a fussy customer, a woman who had been in and out of the fitting room six times, trying on a different dress on each occasion. Out she came for the seventh time, wearing her latest choice, a ruby red creation. It suited her, but Sally was betting she'd found something wrong with it.

'I'll have this one, yes,' said the customer, doing a walk up and down the shop in fancy fashion. 'It looks just right, don't you think? Mind, I'm not sure the bodice isn't a bit tight.'

'No, it's fine, madam, really,' said Sally, professional training and patience going hand in glove with sincerity.

'Well, I like it myself,' said Horace, and Sally swung round. There he was, he'd just come in, looking as cheerful and cocky as ever.

'Oh, it suits me and fits all right, d'you think?' said the woman, who was in her early thirties and obviously not averse to being admired. 'I'd be glad of a man's opinion.'

Some man, thought Sally. Windbag, more like.

'Suits you all the way,' said Horace, 'and it's a lovely colour, like port wine.'

'Well, fancy you saying that, I like a drop of port,' said the woman.

'If I'd known, I've have brought a bottle with me,' said Horace, and Sally wanted to scream. Well, it wasn't unreasonable, a fuming desire to yell at him when he looked and sounded as if he'd taken the shop over and one of its customers as well. And trust him to make up to the woman, to let her know he was God's gift.

'Well, I must say you're a nice feller,' said the woman.

'I could do with that kind of reference,' said Horace.

Miss Lomax, hiding a smile, saw her own customer out of the shop, then addressed Sally.

'I'll see to Mrs Turner now, Miss Brown,' she said, 'and perhaps you'll attend to the young man.'

The switch was made with smooth professional dexterity by the manageress, who dealt with Mrs Turner at the far end of the shop, leaving Sally to cope with one more attempt by the persistent Horace to win her over. Normally, Miss Lomax would have firmly discouraged that kind of carry-on taking place in the shop, but she quite liked Horace, and if only Sally would stop playing hard to get, the two of them could meet in a normal way instead of having these absurd arguments in the shop. Still, the confrontations had their funny side.

Horace advanced on Sally, and Sally drew herself up, remembering she meant to resolutely defend her status as an experienced and respected assistant and not to let him get her goat.

'Good afternoon, sir, may I help you?' she said, and the plum in her mouth was smooth, firm and polished.

'Hope so,' said Horace cheerfully. 'Stockings, wasn't it?'

'Very good, sir,' said Sally, and from a tray under the counter she produced four pairs of silk stockings packaged individually in colourfully printed cellophane. 'Black, grey, white and navy blue, sir, all in a suitable size, and silk.'

'That's done it,' said Horace, 'I'm not goin' to be able to make my mind up, not all at once.'

'I'm sorry,' said Sally, and placed the stockings back in the tray under the counter.

'What's that vanishing trick for?' asked Horace.

'Good afternoon, sir, the door's over there,' said Sally, nose in the air.

'Hold on,' said Horace, 'I haven't—'

'Good afternoon, sir.'

'Wait a minute—'

'We're very busy,' said Sally, polished plum in a settled position, 'but thank you for calling. Good-bye.'

'What a demon,' said Horace. Mrs Turner departed with her ruby red dress, and that left Miss Lomax free to covertly observe how Sally was coping with her resilient admirer. 'Let's see those stockings again,' he said.

'If you insist, sir,' said Sally, and placed them back on the counter. Horace viewed them with an inexperienced eye.

'I'm just not sure,' he said, 'I think I'd better—'

'Go elsewhere?' said Sally. 'Very good, sir.' And away went the stockings once more. 'Thank you for calling.'

'Don't keep saying things like that,' said Horace, 'and stop muckin' me about.'

'The door's over there, sir,' said Sally, sticking to her predetermined approach.

Miss Lomax, her back to them, was killing herself.

'Now look here,' said Horace, 'I'm only askin' to take my time about which colour Ethel might like best, and I'd appreciate—'

'Good afternoon, sir.'

'Give over,' said Horace, 'what about my valuable rating as a regular customer?'

'We're very busy, sir, and I can't stand about talking,' said Sally.

'I'm not having this,' said Horace, 'I'm coming back tomorrow to have another go.'

'Very good, sir,' said Sally.

'What d'you mean, very good?' said Horace. 'There's been nothing very good about what you've been doin' with those stockings, playing Jack-in-the-Box with 'em. That's a fine way of treatin' a regular customer, I don't think.'

'We can only hope, sir,' said Sally, nose as high in the air as she could get it, 'that if you come back tomorrow you'll know what you want. Good afternoon, sir.'

'Well, I give up,' said Horace, and out he went.

'Sally, you minx,' said Miss Lomax the moment he'd gone.

'Me, Miss Lomax?'

'That was disgraceful. While I can't approve of him taking up your time unnecessarily, he did want to buy something, and that makes him a customer. You forgot one of our important rules. A customer's wishes are our wishes.'

'But, Miss Lomax, we don't want him comin' and goin' all the time, do we?' said Sally, keeping to herself the fact that the comings and goings were now enlivening her.

'If he has a purchase in mind, we can't discourage him,' said Miss Lomax. 'You should have helped him to make his choice of the stockings.'

'But he was goin' to take ages over it, just to get my goat,' said Sally. 'I never knew anyone more aggravatin'. Anyway, he's comin' back tomorrow.'

'In that case, Sally, make sure you give him the service any customer is entitled to. And let's close up now.'

'Yes, Miss Lomax,' said Sally, feeling she'd triumphed, even if she had disgraced her professional standing.

She was delighted with herself all the way home. She'd found out how to take the smile off Horace Cooper's face. And she'd forced him to come back tomorrow. She'd give him more of the same. Except she'd better make the sale or Miss Lomax might lay the shop assistants' law down.

She had no idea Horace had gone home laughing to himself. Sally Brown, what a character, what a performance. Well, he knew one important thing about her. She didn't have any serious attachment. Somehow, he'd got to bowl the maiden over. If he couldn't, his cricket might go to pieces. Then what? He'd have to join the ruddy Foreign Legion and march about in all that hot sand.

Rebecca could hardly believe the latest goings-on between Horace and Sally. It seemed utterly absurd to her. Yet Horace appeared to be enjoying it, even though he wasn't getting anywhere.

'Horace, are you sure this isn't becoming too ridiculous?' she said over supper. 'You'll end up being evicted from the shop.'

'Not while I go in as a customer,' said Horace.

'What did you ask for when you went in today,' enquired Ethel.

'Oh, something or other,' said Horace.

'Sounds all right,' said Jim. He knew, and so did Rebecca. Only Ethel was ignorant.

'I don't know how something or other can sound all right,' said Ethel. 'Fancy anyone askin' a shop assistant for something or other. No wonder Sally wouldn't serve him. Orrice, she'll hit you one day. Crikey, a promisin' cricketer sportin' a black eye in public. You won't like that, Orrice. Can't you find someone else?'

'I'm beginning to feel you should, Horace,' said Rebecca.

'He probably will,' said Jim, 'he's at the age when a young man's fancies are pointing him at the fair sex alone. Stamp collecting won't do, nor even a good book.'

'Here, Orrice,' said Ethel, 'did you know that Daisy Peters down the street writes poetry?'

'No, I didn't, Ethel, but nice of you to inform me,' said Horace.

'Well, then?' said Ethel.

'I appreciate the information,' said Horace.

'We all do, Ethel,' said Jim.

'Poetry's nice,' said Ethel with the fixed emphasis of a girl who was trying to convince herself she'd fallen in love with it.

'Unfortunately,' said Jim, 'Daisy Peters doesn't happen to be Sally Brown.'

'There's only one Sally Brown,' said Horace.

'Sally's ever so cheerful again, love,' said Mrs Brown to Mr Brown later that evening.

'Yes, singing, I noticed, when she went out,' said Mr Brown.

'She 'asn't met somebody new, I suppose,' said Mrs Brown.

'She'd tell us if she 'ad,' said Mr Brown, 'and bring him 'ome.'

'It's nice Freddy's got himself engaged to Cassie at last,' said Mrs Brown.

'Laugh a minute, that girl is,' said Mr Brown.

'And ever so sweet, really,' said Mrs Brown.

'Reg'lar caution, more like,' said Mr Brown, 'but a real pet, and I reckon the good Lord made 'er for Freddy. They fit like hand and glove, those two, always 'ave.'

'Her dad's goin' to miss her,' said Mrs Brown. 'Cassie's the last of his girls.'

'Freddy?' said Cassie. She was in her parlour with Freddy, and Freddy was trying to come to terms with something that would be in keeping with his future status as a married man. To wit, a briar pipe, a tin of tobacco and a box of matches. Cassie was watching him fondly, in the way of a future wife. 'Freddy?'

'I'm here, Cassie.'

'Freddy, our Charlie's movin' to Northampton next month. He's been offered a skilled job at a boot and shoe fact'ry at a very good wage.'

'Well, good old Charlie,' said Freddy, pushing in tobacco. 'Mind, it'll be a bit quiet without 'im. Every time he turns round, a cup and saucer fall over, or even the teapot.'

'He can't help havin' large hips,' said Cassie. 'Anyway, when he goes and when you and me get married, there won't be anyone here except me dad.'

'No, I suppose there won't, Cassie,' said Freddy, his pipe full. Cassie's sisters, Nellie and Annie, were both married.

'Freddy?' Cassie was hesitant for about the first time in her life.

'I think you want to tell me something,' said Freddy.

'D'you think – I mean, would you mind if me dad lived with us when we move into our married home? He works ever so 'ard on the railways and gets home late sometimes, and I don't like to think of him comin' into an empty house and no meal ready for him.'

'Well, Cassie—'

'I've been to see the landlord that owns lots of the houses in Wansey Street, and there's one goin' to be vacant in March, just a week or so before our weddin'. He said if we put our names down, he'd give us first refusal. Freddy, would you mind if we had my dad?'

'Well, Cassie—'

'He won't be any trouble, he's not an interferin' or grumpy man, and as Nellie and her 'usband have only got a flat, and Annie and Will have got two children, we'd be the only ones that could easily find room for him.'

'Well, Cassie, it's like this.' Freddy had a go at lighting his pipe. Flame jerked and smoke rose. Freddy sucked, took the pipe out of his mouth and gave it an approving look. Cassie watched in admiration of his manliness and hopefully in respect of her dad. 'I happen to 'ave lived with me own dad all me life, and me mum too, and me dad only ever walloped me once, and me mum only ever sent me early to bed twice.' The pipe went out and Freddy put another match to the charred tobacco. He puffed smoke, then took the pipe out of his mouth again. 'So I can't say livin' with me own dad, and me mum, gave me a lot of trouble. What I can say is we owe a bit to our parents, so I reckon you and me could 'ave your dad, Cassie, and give him his own room, but you'll 'ave to make sure he'll want to come. I like yer dad, you know that, but he might prefer to be independent.' Back into Freddy's mouth went the pipe. He drew and sucked, and the tobacco glowed. He coughed, and out came the pipe again. 'Anyway, it's all right with me, Cassie, if he'd like to be with us.' Back went the pipe, Freddy determined to be its boss.

'Oh, ain't you a love, Freddy?' said Cassie, and flung her arms around him. His pipe dropped, and she kissed him. Freddy came out of the kiss looking a bit alarmed.

'Cassie, could yer run for a bowl of cold water? I think me trousers are on fire.'

'Dad,' said Cassie, after Freddy had gone home in his scorched trousers, 'when Charlie's left and me and Freddy are married, will you be able to manage livin' in this house by yourself?'

'Oh, I'll rent a couple of rooms somewhere,' said the Gaffer, a rough and ready man with a heart of marshmallow. 'Don't you worry about me, Cassie, I'll be all right.'

'But who's goin' to do your cookin' and your Monday washin'?' asked Cassie.

'I'll keep me eye open for an obligin' widder woman,' said the Gaffer.

'Dad, me and Annie and Nellie don't want you gettin' up to any larks with a widow,' said Cassie.

The Gaffer, still a ruggedly sturdy man at fifty, grinned.

'Not me, Cassie,' he said. 'Mind, I ain't over the hill yet, me pet.'

'Well, I'm against leavin' you alone so's some flighty and graspin' widow can take advantage of you,' said Cassie.

'Some what?' said the Gaffer, looking comfortably at home in his braces and shirt sleeves.

'You heard, Dad,' said Cassie. 'You'd best come and live with me and Freddy. We'll be rentin' a nice house in Wansey Street, and you can 'ave your own room with a cosy fire and an armchair.'

'Beg yer pardon, Cassie?' said the Gaffer.

'Yes, Freddy says so as well,' said Cassie. 'Before he set his trousers on fire, he—'

'Nearly sent 'is best prospects up in smoke, that did,' said the Gaffer, and laughed.

'I'm talkin' to you, Dad,' said Cassie.

'Course you are, me pet,' said the Gaffer, 'and I'm listening, ain't I? I just wasn't sure I 'eard right.'

'I was tryin' to say that Freddy said he'd never minded his own dad livin' with him, and that he'd like you livin' with us. It's best,' said Cassie.

The Gaffer looked at his youngest daughter, all grown up and pretty in her nineteenth year. And a real pet. He had a very tender spot for Cassie. There she was, offering to look after him now that his old age was just around the corner. Blowed if it didn't give him a bit of a lump in his throat.

'Cassie, that's reg'lar kind of you and Freddy,' he said, 'but you've got yer own lives to live, and married lives at that, which ain't a bed of roses all the time, yer know. There'll be ups and downs, and infants, and I don't reckon a third party in the 'ouse would be a great 'elp, Cassie.'

'I'm not havin' my own dad call 'imself a third party,' said Cassie. 'Crikey, it wasn't a third party that brought us all up after Mum died, and you even made sure Charlie stopped running wild and behaved 'imself. Me and Freddy don't want you livin' alone. I've spoken to Annie and Nellie, and they both said they'd feel better if you weren't by yourself.'

'Well, I tell you what, Cassie love,' said the Gaffer, 'you let me get a couple of rooms and time to see if I can settle down comf'table in them. If I can't, I'll be honest and tell yer so, and then we can 'ave another talk about me comin' to live with you and Freddy, eh? 'Ow about that, 'ow about it bein' the fairest proposition for ev'ryone, eh?'

'But, Dad, in rooms it'll still be who's goin' to do the cookin' and Monday washin' for you,' protested Cassie.

'A gas ring'll see to me cookin', Cassie.'

'A gas ring?' Cassie looked appalled. 'I don't want my dad livin' with a gas ring. It's crummy, it'll make your lodgings smell of food and fryin' fat. Dad—'

'Still, we'll give it a go, me pet,' said the Gaffer. 'Only fair. You ask Freddy. And I can take me washin' to a laundry.'

Cassie felt dismay. She simply couldn't stand the thought of her hard-working old dad living in a couple of rooms all by himself. He'd been such a good old dad, one of the kind who didn't think it was soft to show affection, and who always worked hard to bring home enough wages to see that his kids had the best he could provide. He'd had to belt Charlie a few times, and Cassie on those occasions had felt it really did hurt him more than rowdy Charlie.

'Dad, you'll honestly be truthful if you find lodgings don't suit you?' she said.

'Cassie, I ain't ever set much store by tellin' any of you something that don't 'appen to be true,' said the Gaffer. He got up from the kitchen table, and put his arm around her shoulders. 'You and Nellie and Annie, yes, and Charlie too, what man could 'ave been blessed with better kids, save for a few aggravations from Charlie? I 'ad me years with yer mum, rest 'er soul, and I've 'ad me years with me son and daughters, and they've all been good years. But there comes a time, Cassie, when all the young cocksparrers do what's natural, leave the nest to live their own lives.'

'Well, I just don't think it's natural lettin' you live with a gas ring and a laundry,' said Cassie. 'What's all our friends and neighbours goin' to say if your daughters let you do that? Even Charlie said to me the other day that he wasn't too happy you livin' alone.'

'Charlie's all right,' said the Gaffer, 'turned out to be a bit more civilized than I reckoned 'e would. No, don't you worry about me, Cassie. Just think about me proposition, and ask Freddy if 'e don't think it makes sense.'

'Well, all right, Dad,' said Cassie reluctantly, 'but I'm goin' to come after you and see for myself how you're livin'.'

'I'll be livin' like a lord on Sundays, 'aving a roast

229

beef dinner with you or Nellie or Annie,' said the Gaffer cheerfully.

'Yes, we'll all take turns,' said Cassie, 'you can spend all day Sunday every Sunday with one or the other of us.'

'Well, bless yer, Cassie,' said the Gaffer, and had trouble with another little lump in his throat.

George Carter, heading for bankruptcy, confided his gloom and his resentment to his wife that evening. Mrs Mildred Carter, thirty-two and well-endowed, had helped him spend the money he took out of the business, and all her sympathies lay with him. She agreed that Sammy Adams shouldn't profit by reason of her husband's bad luck. She'd met Sammy several times at rag trade functions, and liked him, but he was sharp all right. George said something ought to be done to make the geezer squirm, and Mildred said yes. And something else ought to be done to him to make him dip a hand into his well-lined pocket as well. She didn't want to lose her home in addition to the Rolls Royce and the business. Think of something, she said.

Ethel was about to read Davy's completed sonnet to Cassie and Freddy.

'It's ever so nice of you to have done it, Davy,' she said.

'I promised I'd try to,' said Davy, 'I only hope it's appreciated. Begin, Ethel.'

Ethel began.

'With apple blossom awaiting
Her beauteous form divine,
Cassie's eyes doth sparkle
Like pools of sunlit wine.
Seated in the garden
'Twixt bubbling water wells,
Her bosom fair sighs gently
At dreams of wedding bells.'

Ethel spluttered and coughed, but to no avail. A giggle sprang forth. Davy's spectacles grew dark and brooding.

'I think that's enough, Ethel,' he said.

'But, Davy—'

'Your levity is too upsetting.'

'Me what?' said Ethel.

'You're lacking serious appreciation of my work,' said Davy, and took the sheet of paper from her.

'But I mean, her fair bosom sighing gently, it's – oh, 'elp,' said Ethel, 'you're not really cross, are you?'

'I'll take the sonnet back to my lodgings and try to make it commonplace instead of Byronic,' said Davy.

'Oh, 'elp,' said Ethel again. 'What's Byronic, Davy?'

'Never mind,' said Davy, 'I'm leaving now.'

'I'll walk with you, shall I?' said Ethel.

'If you want to,' said Davy, so she began to walk with him to his lodgings, doing her best to soothe his ruffled feathers. Davy was very much on his dignity, refusing to be soothed. He walked quickly, Ethel stretching her legs to keep up with him. Stepping up a kerb she tripped and fell. Davy walked on. A young man pulled him up.

'Hold on, feller, your lady friend's taken a fall,' he said, then went and helped Ethel to her feet. 'You all right? Oh, it's you, Effel.'

Ethel, brushing herself down, looked up. The young man, Vic Rogers, was the son of a neighbour, attending evening classes to better himself. He was a bit lean and lanky, but had quite a nice face, sort of pleasant and kind.

'Oh, thanks,' said Ethel, 'I'm all right, I didn't see where I was lookin'. Where's me young man, Davy?'

'Funny bloke to 'ave left you on the pavement,' said Vic, who knew Ethel as a neighbour's daughter and enough to say hello to in the street. She was a slip of a thing at about five feet one, but everybody said what a dainty girl she was.

'Where is he?' Ethel looked. But Davy had gone on. He had turned a corner and was out of sight. Oh, blow, thought Ethel, he's really cross with me. I'd best leave him to his mood, I've hurt his feelings something chronic. But Cassie's fair bosom softly sighing, oh, crikey.

'You're giggling,' said Vic, his peaked cap at a dashing angle.

'Oh, I 'ope not,' said Ethel, 'I've already upset – still, never mind, I'll see him tomorrow.'

'Walk you home?' offered Vic, taken with her at close quarters.

'Yes, all right, I like walkin',' said Ethel, and she began her return home in company with Vic. 'You go to evening classes, don't you?'

'Yes, to the big school on the other side of Kennington Park Road,' said Vic. 'There's all kinds of subjects you can take there. Girls can take shorthand-typin'. I'm doin' automobile engineerin'. I've just left this evening's class.'

'You'll be able to drive a bus when you're older,' said Ethel.

'I'm old enough now,' said Vic, twenty-three, and chatted away with Ethel. He discovered from her ingenuous tongue that her young man, Davy Williams, was a poet and wrote very romantic poems, and was a bit sensitive about anyone laughing at them. But he was a gent, really, and spoke very nice. 'Don't know much about poetry meself,' said Vic, 'but can't say I liked him leavin' you on the pavement.'

'Oh, he was a bit cross with me for giggling,' said Ethel, and said goodbye to Vic as they reached her house.

'Well, look after yourself, Effel,' said Vic and went on his way.

Ethel decided to say nothing to her family about Davy being cross with her.

Davy, on reaching his lodgings, received a question from his landlady, Mrs Albright.

233

'Been out with yer nice young lady again, Mr Williams?'

'Yes, out to her home,' said Davy, spectacles still showing a bit of a brooding look.

'That's good. I've just made me pot of late evening tea, would yer like a cup?'

'No, thanks – well, yes, all right, thanks.'

Over the tea Mrs Albright asked him to do her a favour, to keep an eye on the house this coming weekend on account of her going to her sister's place in Lewisham from Saturday morning till Sunday evening. And could he look after her cat as well, and feed it for her? Davy said he'd be only too pleased, and light arrived in his spectacles that were always the first thing people noticed about him. They were horn-rimmed with round lenses close to his eyes.

'You'll be away all day Saturday and Sunday?' he asked.

'That's it, out after me breakfast on Saturday and back after tea Sunday evening,' said Mrs Albright.

'I'll look after everything, Mrs Albright,' said Davy. 'Oh, I've just remembered something, I'll have to pop back and see Ethel again.'

Back he went to see Ethel, which pleased her, because he took her into the parlour and apologized ever so nicely for his behaviour. He gave her a kiss, and that pleased her more. They parted the very best of friends.

Chapter Fourteen

Mr Gregson, one of the directors of the imports and exports company employing Nick at their offices in St Mary Axe, looked in on him just before three the following afternoon.

'There you are, Nick,' he said. The firm practised a friendly approach to employees. 'Pop along to your old insurance company in Holborn. The head man, your erstwhile chief, wants to see you.'

'Mr Douglas?' said Nick, startled.

'J M himself,' said Mr Gregson.

'Is it a request or a command?' asked Nick, getting up from his desk.

'Well, you know J M. And he's chief shareholder in this company. Preferable not to keep him waiting. Put a suit of armour on.' Mr Gregson chuckled and disappeared.

Nick, donning his hat, made his way to Holborn via Cheapside and Newgate Street. He'd always thought of the awesome insurance company chairman as God. And God was Annabelle's great-uncle. And Annabelle was his favourite relative.

Arriving at the insurance company building, he went up to the fourth floor, the exclusive domain of the chairman. The carpet muffled his footsteps as he entered the ante-room and knocked on God's office door.

'Enter.' The deep voice arrived at the door as a growl, and the door seemed to vibrate slightly. Nick went in. Mr J M Douglas was seated at his massive oak desk. He looked up from his inspection of an insurance valuation. His mane of iron-grey hair and his square features reminded most observers of Lloyd George, although he had a craggier appearance. Seeing Nick, his dark eyes glinted.

'Good afternoon, sir,' said Nick, hat in his hand.

The glinting eyes performed a slow survey.

'So it's you, Harrison.'

'I was told you wanted to see me, sir.'

'So I do, you young scoundrel.' The growl rolled up from the broad chest. 'I've just had lunch with my great-niece, Miss Annabelle Somers. What the devil do you mean by it, eh? Eh?'

'Mean by what, sir?' asked Nick.

'I understand you've had the audacity to inform my niece you mean to officially propose to her on her birthday. You damned scoundrel, you upstart, do you have the unmitigated gall to consider yourself good enough for my niece?'

'Well, sir—'

'Don't mumble, get on with it.'

'I'll have to say, sir, that modesty prevents me from answering your question,' said Nick.

The broad chest rumbled.

'Damned if you're not more of an impudence

than you were before. Let me tell you, Harrison, that genuine modesty would induce you to withdraw your suit. My niece, a young lady of virtue and light, was never born to marry a pipsqueak.'

'I couldn't agree more, sir.'

'Oh, you couldn't, could you?' God was rumbling awesomely. 'What d'you mean by that? Be careful how you answer.'

'I'll only say, sir,' said Nick, 'that I don't see myself as a pipsqueak.'

The glinting eyes surveyed him menacingly.

'Damn my boots, Harrison, it's as I feared, you've got above your puny self. You've got some idea that you're Napoleon, I suppose?'

'Beg to differ, sir. I don't fancy Waterloo being just round the corner. I've already settled for just being me.'

'And you think that's enough, do you?' growled God.

'Well, I've improved my prospects, with your help, Mr Douglas.' Nick knew now that God had invested in the imports and exports company, and must have been the man behind his advantageous move to the firm. 'Many thanks, sir.'

'What? What?'

'For getting me a position with my present firm—'

'Rubbish. Nonsense. Poppycock. By God, Harrison, your belief that you can support my niece in a reasonable fashion is a confounded impertinence. How do you propose to live?'

'I thought in a house with a garden and an apple tree, and a climbing rose outside the front door,' said Nick. 'I'll just about be able to manage a deposit and a mortgage on my present salary.'

'I'm speechless,' said God. He wasn't, of course, and he proved he wasn't by going on without so much as a second's pause. 'You have in mind some semi-detached hovel in the bowels of Peckham, do you?'

'No, not much, sir, I don't know the bowels of Peckham. I know Peckham Rye, it's not bad there, but I thought of somewhere leafy.'

'Leafy?' The growling chairman looked as if a village idiot had wandered into his sanctum and was dribbling all over his carpet. 'Leafy?'

'Yes, a few trees up and down the road, sir. Annabelle and I are—'

'Miss Somers?'

'Yes, we're both quite fond of trees, Mr Douglas. There's some in Sunrise Avenue, where she lives. As a matter of fact, I wouldn't mind settling on a house there, and her parents wouldn't mind, either. They're fond of Annabelle. Well, so am I, of course.'

'God help the blind,' said the chairman. 'And my niece,' he added. 'May I be allowed to ask how you intend to keep her?'

'As best as I can, sir. We might have to make do with rissoles and baked beans some evenings, but—'

'Say that again,' breathed God heavily.

238

'Well, mortgage repayments will have to come first, Mr Douglas, and that might mean we shan't be able to eat like lords of a manor, but Annabelle says she quite likes homemade rissoles and baked beans. Meat rissoles, not fish. She'll make them from cold meat.'

'Are you serious, Harrison?'

'Yes, sir. We both are. Annabelle says she'll seriously interfere with my well-being if we're not married by this time next year. I think she means she'll put me in hospital. I think you know she's not a weak-minded young lady, sir.'

God made the kind of sound that came from grinding his strong teeth.

'You scoundrel,' he said, 'I believe you're trying to get an insane laugh out of all this. As to what I think, between the two of you I'm not sure if I can think at all. You stand there talking about keeping my niece on a starvation level, and tell me you're serious? Have you discussed with her the cost of furnishing your proposed residence? Do you realize that one piece of furniture she has in mind is a piano?'

'I believe she plays a little, Mr Douglas, and—'

'Can you afford anything but a broken-down relic?'

'Not at the moment, sir.'

'So you can't support my niece even to the extent of properly feeding her or supplying her with a piano?'

'I think I could afford a flute,' said Nick.

'A what?'

'It's just a thought, Mr Douglas.'

'The thought of an idiot, Harrison. I despair for my niece. Will nothing induce you to give up your impertinent idea of marrying her?'

'No, nothing,' said Nick.

'Say a cheque for a hundred guineas, then?'

'I didn't hear that, Mr Douglas.'

'Standing on your integrity, are you?' he rumbled. 'Very well, Harrison, off you go. I've nothing further to say to you.'

'Mr Douglas, will you be at the wedding?'

God growled something gravelly, and Nick left. Coming out of the anteroom he ran into Annabelle, a picture, of course, in a light autumn coat and hat, and a smile of sweet innocence on her face.

'Oh, hello, darling, what are you doing here?' she asked.

'As if you didn't know, you saucy angel. I've just been trodden into the Almighty's carpet for having the gall to consider marrying you.'

'Oh, I like the sound of that, marrying me,' said Annabelle. 'Let's go to that teashop and have tea and toasted crumpets, like we did when you first dragged me there.'

'I've got a job to get back to – listen, wait a minute, I didn't drag you to any teashop.'

'Oh, I didn't mind at the time, I thought oh, thrilly, what a tall strong silent bloke, he doesn't care what he does as long as he gets me there.' Annabelle's smile knocked Nick sideways. 'And never mind about getting back to your job, Uncle John is seeing to that. Come on.'

Down the stairs they went and out into busy Holborn, the air breezy with advancing September, Annabelle's arm linked with Nick's. They made for the Exchange Teashop in Fetter Lane, where Annabelle had first used her brown eyes and playful lashes to captivate him.

Over tea and aromatic toasted crumpets, Nick recounted his interview with her great-uncle. Oh, don't, begged Annabelle, I'll have hysterics. Nick said he didn't feel like having any himself, he felt more like he'd been run over by a bus. God was dead against the marriage.

'Of course he isn't, you silly,' said Annabelle.

'He offered me a hundred guineas to duck out of it.'

'Crikey, as much as that?' said Annabelle. 'Did it tempt you?'

'Leave off,' said Nick, and a hand squeezed his knee.

'Nick, you must be really gone on me to turn a hundred guineas down,' said Annabelle.

'It wouldn't have made any difference if he'd offered five hundred,' said Nick.

'Oh, what devotion,' said Annabelle.

'On the other hand, if he'd offered a thousand—'

'Don't spoil it or I'll pour tea all over your suit,' said Annabelle. 'But about Great-Uncle John, he simply wanted to see if you'd stand up to him. He said if that pipsqueak didn't stick his chest out like a man, he'd move heaven and earth to get you transported. Did he growl and roar at you?'

'Several times,' said Nick, eating buttered crumpet slowly, as if he wasn't sure what it was or where he was.

'Good. You stood up to him, then. He always growls and roars at me when I do the same. Did he ask you if you could keep me in the manner to which I want to become accustomed?'

'Not half,' said Nick, and recounted the relevant exchanges. Annabelle choked on a bite of her second crumpet.

'Oh, no, I don't believe it,' she gasped. 'You told him we'd eat rissoles and baked beans most evenings, and that if you couldn't afford a piano you'd buy me a flute?'

'He didn't think much of any of that, especially the rissoles. He said the flute was the suggestion of an idiot, and that he despaired for you. I flopped then.'

'I bet you didn't,' said Annabelle, 'I know you. Nick, I do like you, you'll never be as silly as your dad. Doesn't fate do wonderful things? I mean, if it hadn't got me stuck in the lift that time, we might never have met. And Mum said once that if my Uncle Boots hadn't had his tonsils out when he was fifteen, she might never have met Dad. Well, she met him when she was visiting Uncle Boots in the hospital. Bless me, if she hadn't, I might never have been born. Wouldn't that have been a terrible blow to you?'

242

'I'd be thinking of doing away with myself,' said Nick.

'Well, yes, your life wouldn't be worth living without me, would it?' said Annabelle. 'But imagine you telling Uncle John you'd buy me a flute if not a piano. Well, you needn't worry. That's going to be his wedding present to us.'

'A flute?' said Nick.

'No, you daft thing, a piano.'

'Pardon?' said Nick.

'Oh, you blessed ha'porth,' said Annabelle, 'can't you get it into your lumpy loaf of bread that Uncle John likes you?'

'He's going to give you a piano?'

'Not me. Us.'

'Well, I – here, who's pinched half of my second crumpet?'

'Me,' said Annabelle. 'You've been thinking and mumbling too much.'

'You've done it on me again,' said Nick.

'Well, I'm sort of fond of you,' said Annabelle. Sitting side by side with him, she murmured, 'Give us a kiss.'

'Annabelle, did you have a tipsy lunch with him?'

'No, of course not. I just like being here with you. Oh, come on, no-one's looking at us in this corner.'

'Well, you're the sugar in my tea, I suppose,' said Nick, and gave her a quick one on her lips. She tasted of buttered crumpets.

'Lovely,' she said, and squeezed his thigh.

'Crikey, lovely muscles as well. I'll let Chrissie Dumpling know.'

Waitresses looked and patrons looked. The two young people at a corner table were laughing out loud.

'There's a Mrs Carter on the line for you, Mister Sammy,' said Nancy Griggs from the general office switchboard.

'Carter?' said Sammy. 'Oh, right, put her through.'

Mrs Carter came through.

'Sammy Adams, is that you?' she asked.

'It's me, Mildred,' said Sammy. He knew the lady. She had a fine figure and expensive tastes.

'You've got George with his back against the wall,' said Mrs Carter.

'Now, now, Mildred, not yours truly,' said Sammy.

'Well, he thinks it's you,' said Mrs Carter, and went on to say that if Sammy was willing to listen, she could put him in the way of getting her husband's business and his factory without any more palaver. Sammy said he'd made George a decent offer, and that George had turned it down. He wasn't going to up the offer, he said, it was hurting him and the shareholders enough as it was. Mrs Carter said she knew all that, and she could stop it hurting if he'd care to come and see her. Say tomorrow.

'Kind of you, Mildred,' said Sammy, 'but what can you put on the table that George can't?'

'Well, Sammy, fifty-one per cent of the shares are mine, and the company owns the freehold of the factory. I've a way to settle this that won't upset George too much when he gets to know. So can we talk? Say tomorrow afternoon here at the house?'

'All right, Mildred, if there's a chance it can be settled without George gettin' heartburn, I'll take meself to your doorstep,' said Sammy, willing to lend a friendly ear without letting himself be overcome by her eau de Cologne. 'I think you're in Highgate. Am I right?'

'You're right, Sammy,' said Mrs Carter, and gave him the address. 'Say about three?'

'Put the kettle on at five-to,' said Sammy, and Mrs Carter laughed and hung up.

Sammy informed Boots of the arrangement.

'I see,' said Boots, 'she's found a way, has she, of selling out to you without upsetting her old man?'

'I don't know if you've noticed,' said Sammy, 'but female persons happen to be different from us, and can find ways we never know about.'

'I think I've noticed,' said Boots, 'and I think it accounts for some of the fireworks that go off from time to time.'

'Indubiously,' said Sammy.

'I think you mean indubitably,' said Boots.

'Same thing,' said Sammy.

'Regarding fireworks, the ones to look out for in business, Sammy, are the ones that go off behind our backs.'

'Don't I know it,' said Sammy. 'Well, I'll have a

friendly chat and a cup of tea with Mildred. She likes a friendly chat more than fireworks.'

Sally had gone home when the shop shut at one o'clock, early closing time as it was Wednesday. That blessed bloke Horace Cooper hadn't shown up. He was playing the same kind of game with her. He'd made her all frustrated again.

The eyes of the watching man with the dark and disordered mind flickered as she went past his window. She didn't look, but he was sure she always knew he was there, so he kept his head down. You had to when you were in a trench and a Jerry sniper was waiting for your head to show. He didn't know why this female Jerry stalked him at this time of the day, like she did occasionally, seeing she was nearly always on the prowl early in the evening. Trying to catch him out, trying to make him careless enough to show himself, that was her game, he'd lay a whole packet of fags on it.

His wife called.

'Come and 'ave yer bite to eat, Joe.'

He waited half a minute, then made his way to the kitchen, brooding a bit.

Ethel had a better time with Davy that evening. He came early to the house and took her to the pictures. He said he knew she liked the pictures, and that they could give poetry a bit of a rest. Ethel said yes, she really did like going to the cinema, but that didn't mean she didn't like his poems. Davy said they'd get back to poetry in a day or so. Ethel said that would be nice.

Rebecca and Jim were in favour of Ethel enjoying herself. It was a fact that although their daughter and Davy were a quaint pair, Ethel obviously found his company to her liking. He's quite a young gentleman, said Rebecca. His manners are a credit, said Jim. It's his poetry that makes my hair curl, said Horace.

After the football committee meeting that same evening, Freddy wrote a letter in his parlour, Cassie sitting beside him. She had spoken to him about her dad, and Freddy said her dad had made sense, and that they should leave it to him to decide where he wanted to live. Cassie said well, all right, but she wasn't very happy about it. So Freddy gave her a little pat and said not to worry, her dad wouldn't fall in love with any lodgings.

Now he wrote to the relevant landlord of certain Wansey Street properties, asking for first refusal on renting the house that was being vacated in March according to information supplied to his fiancée, Miss Cassie Ford.

'That'll do, I think, Cassie,' he said.

'Oh, put "who I'm going to be united with in holy wedlock at Easter,"' said Cassie.

'What for?' asked Freddy.

'To show you're goin' to be a respectable married man that won't fall behind with the rent,' said Cassie. 'Landlords don't like takin' on tenants that might dodge payin' the rent and then do a bunk. They like respectable married tenants best.'

'Well, I've got to say you're not just a funny face,' said Freddy, 'you can think as well, Cassie, which is a nice surprise to me.'

'Stop soundin' like Sammy Adams, or I'll bite your ears off,' said Cassie. 'D'you want that to happen?'

'Well, no, I don't actu'lly, Cassie, me ears are important to me,' said Freddy.

'Then don't sauce me,' said Cassie, 'just put in what I said.'

Freddy added the suggested words, then signed the letter. Cassie said she'd best sign as well.

'What for?' asked Freddy.

'The landlord knows me, he met me when I called on 'im,' said Cassie, 'and he quite liked me. Besides, we both ought to sign to show we're makin' an application as a future holy wedlock couple.'

'All right,' said Freddy, so Cassie appended her signature, adding 'fiancée' to it. Freddy inspected it. She'd signed above his own name. 'Why'd you do that?' he asked.

'Well, I'm more important,' said Cassie.

'Come again?' said Freddy.

'Yes, wives are always more important than 'usbands, didn't you know that, Freddy?'

'No, I didn't actu'lly, I—'

'Never mind, Freddy love, you know now. I mean, your mum runs things, and so does Nick's mum, and they're both wives. Then there's Queen Mary, she runs Buckingham Palace, being the King's wife.'

'Do I take it, Cassie Ford, that you're goin' to run me?' asked Freddy.

'It's just called lookin' after, Freddy, and makin' sure you go off to work with a good breakfast and clean socks.'

'I bet it's goin' to be more than that,' said Freddy, 'and I've got to tell you, Cassie, I'm puttin' my foot down 'ere and now. In short, Cassie, it's me that's goin' to wear the trousers.'

'Yes, of course, Freddy.'

'I ain't just sayin' that, Cassie.'

'No, of course not, Freddy.'

'All right, then, now who's goin' to be the important one when we're married?'

'Me,' said Cassie.

'I'll never learn,' said Freddy, 'I ought to 'ave known I should've saved me breath.'

'Never mind, Freddy,' said Cassie, 'you'll always have something to treasure.'

'What something?' asked Freddy.

'Me,' said Cassie.

Horace arrived in the shop just after twelve the following day. He had to wait. There were customers. It was pinching minutes off his lunch hour, but that didn't worry him. He was smitten. All else was insignificant, especially now the cricket season was well and truly over. That Sally Brown, there she was, smiling at her customer and looking so tasty he could have eaten her. Ruddy Adam and Eve, he thought, she could even make a Walworth backyard turn into a Garden of Eden if they shared it with each other. Funny thing about girls, you saw them everywhere all your life, down the street, up the street, in the market, in the parks, on a tram or riding a bike, and you thought well, they're sort of nice to have around, but there's other things. Then suddenly, wallop, you come face to face with a particular one, and your life's ruined from then on unless she's felt the same wallop.

Horace idled about, hoping Sally would be free before Miss Lomax was.

'Good morning, sir, can I help you?'

He turned. Sally's customer was leaving, and Sally was looking at him, but from behind her glass-topped counter. She felt safer with that between them. Horace came across and tried a smile.

'Hello, Miss Brown, I'm back. Couldn't get here until the afternoon, and then, of course, you were closed.'

'Wednesdays are always early closing, sir,' said Sally, professional plum firmly lodged. 'Let me see, was there something, sir?'

'I'm watchin' you and your tricks,' said Horace.

Sally, still determined not to be drawn into his kind of cross-talk, and aware that Miss Lomax had an ear turned her way, said, 'Oh, yes, I believe you had a purchase of silk stockings in mind, sir.'

'Well, that's very kind of you, Miss Brown,' said

Horace, determined to woo and win, even if it took him until next cricket season. 'Might I see the selection?'

'Very good, sir,' said Sally, and produced them, black, grey, white and dark blue. She spread them for his inspection, and Horace regarded them like a wise old owl regarding its chicks, his head bent. He wore no hat and Sally noted the crisp look of his dark hair. And he had a sort of fresh open-air smell. A little of that exhilaration touched her, this time simply because she knew he must be potty about her, or he wouldn't be constantly popping in and out of the shop, using his sister's name as an excuse.

'What d'you think, what colour would you choose?' asked Horace, looking up.

'All of them,' said Sally.

'Do what?' said Horace.

'Well, sir, for different occasions,' said Sally.

'Could I have a look at what you're wearin' yourself for your work?' asked Horace.

Sally's plum moved up a degree to touch the roof of her mouth.

'Hi must hask you, sir, not to make such requests,' she said, adding a couple of aspirates to emphasize her proud defence of her dignity.

'Understood,' said Horace, 'I just thought it might be a help. You look nice in your workin' outfit, did you know that?'

'Do you wish to make a purchase, sir?'

'Well, yes, I do,' said Horace. 'How much are the stockings?'

'One-and-fourpence-three-farthings a pair, sir,' said Sally.

'How much?'

'I must remind sir they're silk.'

'I could buy a weekend's supply of cockles and mussels for one-and-fourpence-three-farthings, and for four people,' said Horace.

'Please do, sir, if that's your wish,' said Sally, and Horace gave her a look. Eyes met eyes. One pair were enquiring, the other pair haughty. 'Shall I put the stockings away?'

'Did you say you'd choose all four pairs?' asked Horace, lingering, as usual, over the confrontation.

'All four colours, sir, for different occasions.'

'That 'ud cost me nearly six bob,' said Horace.

Miss Lomax, helping her customer to make up her mind about a Sunday dress, cast a glance at Sally. Sally, still holding her own, said, 'I'm sorry, sir, if the price is too much for you.'

'I'm savin' up to get married, y'know,' said Horace.

'Pardon?' said Sally, startled, and her plum wandered about.

'That's if I can make a go of it with the right girl, if I could meet the right girl,' said Horace. 'You're not married, are you? I'm askin' that privately, of course.'

Sally swallowed her plum and her head fell off. Well, in a way it did.

'Oh, you rotten funny-cuts,' she breathed, 'you know I'm not married, and you're comin' it again.

D'you want me to push these stockings into your big mouth?'

'No, I want to buy them,' said Horace. 'But listen, if you ever do want to get married, could you come round and see me and talk to me about it?'

Sally wanted to kick him then, except the counter was in the way, and all kinds of funny things were happening to her. A strange sound escaped her lips. Horrors, she was giggling, and at her age.

Miss Lomax cast her another glance, and found her with her hand over her mouth. A new customer came in, saw that Sally was engaged with a male person, and went to the end of the shop to await Miss Lomax's attention.

Sally struggled with herself and won.

'Now look here,' she said to Horace. 'I ought to have served you by now, and you'll really get me into trouble if you don't make up your mind about these stockings. I don't want to listen to any more comical stuff, d'you 'ear?'

'Nothing comical about gettin' married,' said Horace.

'You'll be lucky if anyone marries a bloke as daft as you,' said Sally. 'Now what about these stockings?'

'I did say I wanted to buy them,' said Horace.

'What, all four pairs?' said Sally.

'Well, you did say—'

'Oh, two pairs would be more than enough for any girl, you silly man,' said Sally, then frowned at herself.

'Yes, but which two pairs?' asked Horace.

Sally played him at his own game then.

'Look,' she said, 'you can take all four pairs and show them to your mum. She'll know which two colours Ethel would like best. Then you can bring the others back tomorrow.'

'Well, good on yer, Miss Brown,' said Horace.

'But don't mess me about, d'you 'ear?' whispered Sally.

Horace said he'd pay for two pairs now, that was only fair. Sally said she'd be appreciative of that, she said she couldn't complain about him not ever paying up, it was just his Clever Dick stuff that got her goat. But she'd trust him to come in tomorrow, she said. Horace said what a nice kind girl she was, and that he'd recommend her shop to the whole Surrey cricket team. Sally said she could hardly wait for them to come in looking for cricket flannels and cricket boots. Putting the stockings into a bag, and receiving three shillings, she gave him his change of tuppence-ha'-penny.

'Good afternoon, sir, thank you for your custom,' she said.

'I suppose—'

'The door's over there, sir.' Her plum was back in position. It didn't depress Horace. He had a little grin on his face as he left. He felt he was winning. He'd actually made her giggle. There were a lot of giggles about lately.

254

Chapter Fifteen

The house was in a select part of Highgate and not far from Hampstead Heath. The Heath was an old stamping ground of the Adams family in respect of Bank Holidays. Mostly, such days had been spent on Peckham Rye, for it had cost Chinese Lady less to take them there. But there had been times at Hampstead, where the Bank Holiday funfair had always been larger and more varied than at Peckham Rye.

Sammy rang the doorbell of the imposing house. The afternoon was fine, and approaching autumn hadn't yet introduced any premature chills.

The door opened and revealed the attractive wife of the beleaguered George Carter. Sammy blinked.

'Is that you, Mildred?'

'Hello, Sammy.' Mildred Carter smiled. She was wearing an ankle-length robe of soft white fluffy towelling, complete with a belt. Her face was delicately made-up, her auburn hair piled high, a gold bracelet around her left wrist, her fingernails a light shade of pink.

'Are you havin' a bath?' asked Sammy.

'Not now, I'm out of it,' said Mildred. 'Come in,

Sammy. We don't see each other very often, but when we do it's a pleasure, I hope.'

'Pardon me for askin',' said Sammy, stepping into an oak-panelled hall, 'but d'you always bath at this time of the day?'

'No, not always, just sometimes, depending on how I feel,' said Mildred. 'Oh, I'm dressed up to a point under this robe, by the way, or I wouldn't be receiving you, would I?'

'Me foot wouldn't have put itself over your doorstep if you weren't decent,' said Sammy.

'Sammy, I'm a married woman,' said Mildred. 'Come through to the garden, it's quite warm, and there's a drink waiting for you.'

'Tea?' said Sammy, aware of a scent that was either from bath soap or a bottle of French stuff. Very nice to the nose.

'Tea?' Mildred laughed as they emerged from open French doors on to a terrace that provided a wonderful view of Hampstead and its greenery. On a garden table were a bottle and two glasses. On one side of the terrace was a little summerhouse. Good investment, a house and a garden like this, thought Sammy, but who owned it, George or Mildred? Mildred certainly had something in mind regarding how to part George from his business and his factory to the advantage of the enemy. Which is me myself, plus the shareholders, thought Sammy. And she was going to place the proposition before him in a setting that was all of peaceful and relaxing. What with the seclusion of the well-kept garden and the view, a sort of cultural balminess hung about and offered to take him to its bosom. Watch the lady, Sammy. 'You don't really want tea, do you, Sammy?' she said.

'It's the wrong time of the day for a bottle with a label on it,' said Sammy, observing the view again, which was a lot more relaxing than Mildred. Mildred was scented, fresh from a bath, and glowing with friendship. That sounded all right, but it wasn't relaxing. Dangerous, more like, to a reputable businessman whose prime reasons for living were his wife, his children and his turnover. 'You've got a picture of a place here, Mildred,' he said, turning to her. She smiled, came close, something white travelled downwards with a soft but alarming rush, and the lady, naked, wound her arms around him and kissed him ardently on his mouth. Sammy nearly did himself an injury. He nearly took off for the sky over Hampstead and for a fall from there to the gasworks. Ruddy Mother Hubbard, her assets were all bare, and it felt as if a well-arranged set of velvet cushions were making themselves at home against his suit. Not only that, she was eating him into the bargain.

However, not being in need of this kind of relationship outside of marriage, and not being in favour of it, either, Sammy emerged from temporary paralysis after a few moments, got rid of the ringing in his ears, and put his hands on the naughty lady's ribs. She pressed closer. Sammy stiffened his sinews, the right ones, and pushed her off. The push was strong enough to make her let go.

'Sammy—'

'You've been at the port,' said Sammy, and picked up her robe. He shook it out and held it in front of her to keep his eyes from hurting. 'Put it on,' he said.

'Don't be feeble, let's get together,' said Lady Godiva. 'You'll like me, and I know I'll like you. Pleasure before business, Sammy.'

'I'm disinclined,' said Sammy, 'it'll muck the business up. Put this on.'

Mildred, starkers, ducked under the robe and reappeared in front of him, and a hell of a lot too close again. Bloody hell, what a shocker of a female woman, thought Sammy.

'Hello, lovey, how's your corpuscles?' she said.

Sammy dropped the robe and executed a wise bunk. He disappeared through the open French windows into the house. Mildred went after him. In the hall, Sammy retrieved his hat, opened the front door and shot out.

'Just remembered another appointment,' he said.

'Well, sod you,' called Mildred and slammed the door shut.

I think I've just escaped a fate worse than death, thought Sammy, and just in the nick of time. So that was her proposition. I get her and she gets me to double my offer so that she and George can live happy ever after. On the other hand, George said I wouldn't get the business at any price. Fishy, Sammy old lad, fishy.

He drove back to Camberwell, where he acquainted Boots with Mildred's Lady Godiva performance.

'Let's see,' said Boots, 'I think I mentioned fireworks.'

'So you did, old-timer,' said Sammy, 'but you didn't mention rockets. I nearly took off on the tail of one.'

'I suppose the idea was to roll you over, Sammy, give you a lively afternoon, then threaten to tell George you'd sown the wild oats of a married man suffering a seven-year itch unless you made the kind of offer acceptable to him.'

'I have it on prime authority from Bert at the fact'ry that George Carter wouldn't consider any offer acceptable from me,' said Sammy.

'He might if it was an offer to pay his debts full stop,' said Boots.

'Leave off,' said Sammy. 'Pay his debts on top of paying for his business just for letting Mildred roll me over? Which I wouldn't have allowed, anyway, on account of me honour as Susie's lawful wedded husband and the respected father of her children. Susie would leave home and take the kids with her, but not before she'd hit me with the chopper.'

'Good point, Sammy,' said Boots.

'What's good about the point of a chopper,' asked Sammy.

'No, I'm thinking of your mention of Susie,' said Boots.

'You're not the only one with Susie on your

mind,' said Sammy. 'If she'd seen what went on in only the space of a minute, she'd never let me into me own castle again, never mind me innocence and me hot flushes.'

'Yes, you've got it, Sammy,' said Boots.

'Got what?'

'Mildred, perhaps, would have threatened to tell Susie.'

'Strike a light,' said Sammy, 'I'm acquainted with one married female woman that puts green into Susie's eyes. My old friend Rachel Goodman. I don't want to be considered familiarly acquainted with another. If I 'ad mixed business with pleasure this afternoon, and Mildred let Susie know, I'd be a drownin' man. I mean, you ever tried puttin' a porkie over on Susie? Can't be done.'

'Well, you played the wise virgin, Sammy, you ran,' said Boots.

'Like a ruddy greyhound, believe me,' said Sammy. 'But kindly refrain from mixin' me up with virgins, I've got enough on my mind as it is. Well, I'll say what I said before, Boots, female women are different from us, and some can be fatal to a bloke.'

'Count your blessings, Sammy.'

'I'm still busy at the moment countin' me hot flushes,' said Sammy. 'Mother O'Reilly, what an escape.'

'I'm doing some appropriate amendments to the sonnet,' said Davy that evening to Ethel. They were taking a walk, which Ethel always enjoyed. She was physically frisky and liked exercise.

'What sonnet, Davy? Oh, the one to Cassie and Freddy?'

'I felt perhaps it was too ambiguous,' said Davy.

'Crikey, what's ambiguous?' asked Ethel, new boater on her head.

'A bit too meaningful for some people to understand.'

'Davy, you're ever so educated,' said Ethel.

'Is that amusing?' asked Davy.

'Oh, no, I'm very admiring,' said Ethel.

'Well, thank you, Ethel. I've got the sonnet at home. If you like, you can come to my lodgings on Saturday afternoon and help me with my amendments. You know Cassie and Freddy better than I do, so you'll be a great help, I'm sure.'

'Davy, that's really nice of you,' said Ethel, and Davy looked at her and his spectacles smiled at her. A young man approached as they strolled along the Walworth Road. He smiled.

'Evening, Effel,' he said.

'Oh, 'ello, Vic,' said Ethel, 'it's a nice evening, isn't it?'

'Nice for a walk,' said Vic, glancing at Davy as he went by. Davy smiled at him, then asked Ethel who he was.

'Oh, he's Vic Rogers,' said Ethel, 'he lives down our street, he's doin' evening classes.'

'Good for him,' said Davy, 'it's a way of bettering himself.'

'Yes, he's quite nice too,' said Ethel, 'not loud or anything.'

'Now you're making me jealous,' said Davy.

'Oh, you don't 'ave to be jealous,' said Ethel.

'That's good,' said Davy, and they strolled on.

Meanwhile, Horace was taking advantage of Ethel's absence to get Rebecca's opinion on the selection of stockings. Rebecca, utterly intrigued by this latest development, which seemed to indicate Horace had actually begun to make progress, didn't take long to suggest he should buy the black pair and the dark blue pair. Horace asked why. Rebecca said those colours were smarter, that Ethel was very neat and particular, and when there were occasions that deserved the wearing of silk stockings, they'd be the kind of occasions when smartness counted. Jim said every colour looked all right to him. Well, yes, all silk stockings could be worn with confidence as long as the particular colour didn't clash with one's dress or skirt, said Rebecca.

'Well, OK,' said Horace, 'I'll—'

'I really don't like OK, Horace,' said Rebecca.

'Understood, Mum,' said Horace, 'will "very well" do?'

'Very well will do very well,' said Rebecca.

'Pass very well,' said Jim.

'Very well,' said Horace, 'I'll treat Ethel to all four pairs, seeing she's turned out quite a decent sister.'

'Horace, that's really very nice of you,' said Rebecca.

'Handsome, I'd call it,' said Jim.

'I'm fond of our Ethel,' said Horace, and Rebecca gave him an affectionate look. Horace winked. 'I'm going through fire and water for her,' he said.

'But you're still alive,' said Jim.

'Only just,' said Horace.

If Sammy had escaped a singular worse than death fate, he didn't escape trouble. A City messenger boy arrived at the offices the following day with an envelope addressed to Mr S Adams and marked PRIVATE.

Opening it at his desk, Sammy drew out three postcard-sized photographs. They immediately brought back paralysis. Two showed him locked in the arms of a naked woman, her mouth glued to his. The third showed her close to him and inside the bath robe that he was holding up behind her. Jesus give me strength, thought Sammy, I'm going to faint for the first time in my innocent life. I'm innocent all right, but Susie might not think so. She'll kill me.

There was no letter, no note, just the photographs.

His phone rang. He picked it up, reversing the prints as he did so.

'Yes?' he croaked.

'It's Mrs Carter,' said Nancy Griggs, the switchboard girl.

Delilah herself, thought Sammy, and asked Nancy to put her through.

'Sammy?'

'You forgot to enclose a letter, you female spider,' said Sammy.

'Oh, they've arrived, have they, lovey?' cooed Mildred. 'But I didn't send them. A well-wisher did. D'you like them?'

'I'm thinkin' of framin' them and puttin' them on me mantelpiece,' said Sammy.

'You mean you like them enough to settle George's debts for him?'

'So that's the game, is it?' said Sammy. 'Well, I'm not in the mood. In fact, I'm grievously disapppointed in you, Mildred, grievously. Who took them?'

'The well-wisher,' said Mildred. 'You'll have to settle, Sammy. You wouldn't want large prints sent to Susie, to your competitors, to your local newspaper and even your dear old mother, would you?'

Ruddy earthquakes, thought Sammy. Susie? Chinese Lady?

'I hope you're jokin', Mildred.'

'Send the cheque to me, Sammy. The amount you offered, plus another thousand. Leave the payee blank. I'll fill it in.'

'And what do I get for that?'

'Why, the negatives and the other prints that were done. Can't say fairer, can I, Sammy?'

'And George still keeps his business?'

'Yes, and his factory, Sammy.'

'He's got a hope, and so have you,' said Sammy.

'Oh, I think you'll be reasonable,' said Mildred.

264

'You can have until Monday to make up your mind. Only Monday. I need the cheque before George has to appear to answer a summons or two, and I don't want it to bounce, lovey. Phone me Monday. Oh, by the way, if the photographs have to be sent to your near and dear ones, they'll be delivered by hand, not through the post. Have we got a deal, Sammy?'

'You've got a mucked-up mind, Mildred, I'll say that. Ain't you ashamed of yourself?'

'Not while George is fighting for his life, Sammy. Ring me Monday. I'll be in all day. Have a nice weekend.' Mildred hung up. Sammy replaced his phone and took another look at the photographs. Crucifying, all three of them. He gathered them up, slipped them into the inside pocket of his jacket and went to consult Boots, whose brainbox was what it should have been as head of the family, always allowing for Chinese Lady's place on the family pedestal.

Boots was on the phone, talking to Harriet de Vere, chief buyer for Coates, affluent and profitable customers of Adams Fashions. Harriet was coming across with sweet nothings in between strict business stuff, and Sammy had to wait before Boots was able to end the conversation.

'You're in trouble, Sammy,' said Boots as soon as he'd replaced the receiver.

'It shows?' said Sammy.

'Looks like toothache from here,' said Boots.

'It happens,' said Sammy, 'to be a bit more than

that.' Making sure the door was shut, he produced the photographs and placed them on Boots's desk.

'Well, well,' said Boots, 'what have we here, Sammy, the latest naughty picture postcards from Paris?'

'Would you mind keepin' it serious?' said Sammy, and recounted his phone conversation with Mildred. He followed that up with a more detailed account of what had taken place on Lady Godiva's garden terrace. More detailed than yesterday's. It explained the photographs.

'A well-programmed piece of chicanery, Sammy, which set up a nice line in blackmail,' said Boots, and emulated Sammy by reversing the photographs.

'Here, give over,' said Sammy, 'your Lord Muck education is interferin' with me comprehension, and I ain't in the mood for anything except plain English.'

'Well, in plain English, Sammy, are you paying up or not?'

Sammy said that his prime consideration was to make sure none of the photographs ever got within a mile of Susie and Chinese Lady, and that his secondary consideration was to save his personal bank account from diabolical ruination. Thirdly, he said, he was dead against helping Mildred and George to live happy ever after. Boots said he was in favour of that himself. Accordingly, there was only one thing to do, and that was to lay hands on the negatives and any other prints that had been made.

Sammy said he liked the sound of that, but would Boots kindly explain how to do that without getting this ruddy well-wisher up against an alley wall and knocking Charley-Harry out of him? Boots said well, you know who the well-wisher is, don't you, Junior? You know who took the photographs, don't you?

'Frankly, Boots, me thinkin' apparatus is in a state of collapse at the moment.'

'Since I doubt if he'd let a third party lay eyes on his wife in the altogether, George was bound to have taken the photographs himself, and from some close point or other,' said Boots. 'After all, they don't show you and Lady Godiva too far away from the lens.'

'The ruddy summerhouse,' said Sammy, and smacked his forehead.

'So where's he keeping the negatives and other prints?' asked Boots.

'Under his bed bolster?'

'Sammy, you said a City messenger boy delivered the photographs by hand. They came direct from George, of course, and I think that puts him in the City, in his factory. He'll expect you to make a beeline for his house, perhaps in company with Tommy and me, with the idea of making Mildred disgorge the negatives. Where's Mitch?' Mitch, an old West Kents comrade of Boots, was the firm's van driver.

'Out delivering orders from our fact'ry to our shops,' said Sammy.

Boots suggested Mitch was to get back to Camberwell as soon as he'd finished his deliveries. In the meantime, Sammy was to phone Bert at the factory and ask him if he knew whether or not George had a safe in his factory office. If he didn't know, Sammy was to ask him to find out. Sammy said his comprehension was improving, and he was beginning to follow Boots. Boots said he was glad to know it. Sammy suggested Boots had burglary on his mind. Boots suggested Saturday night. Sammy suggested it might need a team. Boots suggested Bert could rustle up the right kind of team, plus Mitch and his van.

'What's the van for?' asked Sammy.

'If Bert's team can't crack the safe, it'll have to be carted away in the van,' said Boots. 'But listen, neither Mitch nor Bert are to enter the factory, but to lie low, just in case the police cop the team. Ask Bert to hire a couple of East End professionals who'll be willing to risk it, and shut your eyes to the expense. I'll look after some pocket money for Mitch. Don't go near the place yourself, just put Bert in charge. He and Mitch will know how to keep out of the hands of the police if they do turn up.'

'Hold on,' said Sammy, 'I'm not sure I want a couple of professional cracksmen gettin' a butcher's at the saucy French postcards.'

'They won't be lying loosely about in the safe,' said Boots, 'they'll be packeted and probably sealed. Bert's to tell the team simply to take

268

everything that's in the safe. There'll be no money. George hasn't got any.'

'I'm now concernin' myself with the suspicion the goods won't be in the safe, if there is one,' said Sammy.

'Well, we'll have to bet there is,' said Boots. 'But if it can't be cracked and has to be carted away, Mitch will be under instructions to bring it to these offices on Sunday morning, and we'll meet him here. We'll use an acetylene torch on it. If it can be opened, however, Mitch will bring the contents straight to me.'

'Now listen, Sir Jasper,' said Sammy, 'if the contents do include the photographs, and they end up in your mitts, I'm against Em'ly gettin' a look at Lady Godiva climbin' all over me purity and innocence.'

'She won't get any kind of a look,' said Boots, 'and I'm against them ending up anywhere near Susie.'

'So am I, twice over,' said Sammy.

The phone rang. Boots answered it.

'It's Mrs Susie Adams,' said Nancy. 'She wants to talk to Mister Sammy. Is he there?'

'He's here,' said Boots, and handed the phone to Sammy. 'It's Susie,' he said, and Sammy had a sudden horrendous feeling that calamity had already struck.

'Er – Susie?' he said, dredging his voice up from his hurting chest.

'Sammy? Are you all right?' asked Susie.

'I think I've got a touch of tonsillitis,' said Sammy, slightly hoarse.

'Don't be daft,' said Susie, 'you don't have any tonsils. You had them out ages ago.'

'So I did,' said Sammy. 'Some of me breakfast cornflakes must've stuck.'

'Oh, dear, what a shame,' said Susie. 'Never mind, I'll sandpaper them for you tomorrow. Listen, I forgot to get my copy of *Woman's Weekly* when I was shoppin'. Could you be a love and buy a copy for me on your way home? Only there's some special recipes in it this week.'

'I'll do that, Susie.'

'There's a good boy,' said Susie. 'Some mothers do have them, don't they? 'Bye, lovey.'

'See you, Susie,' said Sammy, and replaced the phone.

'Still hurting you, is it, Sammy?' smiled Boots.

'It's all me hot flushes again. Ruddy ailments, I feel like a woman comin' out of perberty.'

'Puberty, Sammy.'

'You and your educated dictionary,' said Sammy. 'Still, I'm appreciative of you being the original cool cucumber, old lad.'

'Well, I'm not robbing the safe myself,' said Boots, 'I'm delegating.'

'And you ain't turnin' a single ruddy hair,' said Sammy.

'Lap of the gods, Sammy. Go and ring Bert. I'll speak to Mitch when he gets back.'

'Well, as I don't fancy any lunch,' said Sammy,

'I'll talk to Bert.' He phoned his factory maintenance man, and Bert caught on after being given no more than the essentials.

'Got yer, guv. No worries. And you don't 'ave to say more'n you need to. You want a job done. Good enough for me. And I can tell yer now, George Carter's got an office safe. A Henry Lockwood.'

'What's a Henry Lockwood?' asked Sammy.

'A safe that can't be cracked, guv.'

'That's not good news,' said Sammy.

'It's what the makers say,' said Bert.

'And what do you say, Bert?'

'Not the same as the makers, guv. Leave it to me. I know the blokes you need. Still, let Mitch come with 'is four-wheeler, just in case. Tell 'im midnight tomorrer. The sailors'll be back in port by then, not round the back of the fact'ry with their fancies. What about yer brother Tommy?'

'Keep it all quiet on the Western Front as far as he's concerned, Bert. I'll leave everything to you, then?'

'Pleasure to do yer a favour,' said Bert, who had done Sammy several over the years. What Bert didn't know about the East End's prolific amount of talent could be written on a postage stamp.

Boots spoke to Mitch later, and Mitch, an obliging old soldier, who knew Bert well and Boots even better, decided that what was afoot was a job to be done. If Bert was in favour and Boots wanted it, Mitch would lend a hand.

'Fiver all right?' said Boots.

'Well, you still owe me for bein' me sergeant,' said Mitch, 'but the price of a drink for me and a double Guinness for me missus'll do. You look after me in me job, I look after you in any extra carry-ons, and we both look after me missus in 'er partiality for Guinness.'

Boots gave him a couple of quid, which Mitch thought fair and square, and proved you could rely on some old sergeants to honour one's missus. Especially a Walworth-born sergeant. Good old Boots, not a bad bloke at all. Good at getting things done, even a safe-cracking job. Well, it was a cut-throat business, the rag trade.

Chapter Sixteen

Horace, free of his labours at the time, appeared in the shop at ten minutes past one. Miss Lomax was snatching a quick lunchtime sandwich in the back room. Sally had two customers, two young working women looking for dresses during their lunch hour. One had settled on her choice, the other was in the fitting room, trying on a very economically priced dress for everyday use.

Sally quickened at the entry of Horace. Her settled customer, waiting for her friend, eyed him with interest. Noting her friendly optics, and that Sally was engaged, he spoke.

'Afternoon, how's yourself?' he said. He had an agreeable approach to all and sundry.

'Oh, pleased to meet yer,' said the young woman.

'Same here,' said Horace.

'I don't see many like you in a dress shop, except someone's 'usband now and again,' said the young working woman. 'You someone's 'usband?'

'Well, no, not yet,' said Horace.

Sally, waiting near the fitting-room, felt her temper rise, and it sort of fumed about. That was him all right, he was trying to pick someone else up now.

'Bet you got a girl, though,' said the young working woman.

'I'm trying,' said Horace, 'but not much luck so far.'

'You mean there's a girl but she don't fancy yer?'

'No, not much,' said Horace.

'Wants 'er brains testin',' said the young working woman. 'I mean, you talk friendly, and you don't 'alf look brown and 'ealthy. You spent the summer down in Margate or Southend?'

'No, I've spent it workin',' said Horace, 'I have to take my summer holiday in October. You been to Margate?'

Sally had a job not to throw something heavy at him. Oh, the rotten Romeo, he didn't have any principles at all, he was making up to that flirty thing as if she was Clara Bow from Hollywood.

Out came the other young woman then, and Sally had to give her all her attention. But she couldn't help hearing continuing chat. Next, out came Miss Lomax from the back room. She summed up the situation at a glance, gave Sally a nod and advanced on Horace, divorcing him from his conversational companion.

'Good afternoon,' she said, 'can I help you, Mr Cooper?' Sally, having discovered who he was, had mentioned his name.

'Hello, Miss Lomax, how d'you do, nice to see

you,' said Horace. 'Did you know about the stockings?'

Miss Lomax said she did, that she knew he'd taken four pairs away, had paid for two and was to bring the others back. Horace said he hadn't brought any back, he was keeping all four pairs and had come to pay what was due.

'My, you're becoming quite a prized customer,' said Miss Lomax.

In came another customer, and then one more, and Miss Lomax had no option but to let Horace settle his account, which he did. Sally was still engaged with her original customer. Miss Lomax, handing Horace some change, said she hoped the shop could be of service to him again sometime.

'I'll think of something my mother might like,' said Horace. 'Of course, it would help if you sold gents' natty suitings. Well, you're busy, so I'll buzz off. Could you give Miss Brown my personal regards?'

'Certainly,' said Miss Lomax. 'Goodbye, Mr Cooper.'

Later, when they had a moment to themselves, Miss Lomax gave Sally the personal regards of her young man.

'My young man?' said Sally. 'He's not my young man, and I don't want his personal regards. Did you see how he was tryin' to get off with one of those two women?'

'No. I saw he was talking to a young woman when I came out, I didn't see him trying to get

275

off with her. You sure he wasn't just passing the time with her?'

'I'm sure I don't care if he was or wasn't,' said Sally, 'but I suppose he found an excuse to come in again tomorrow, did he?'

'No, not a word about coming in again, unless he thought of something his mother might like.'

'He's barmy,' said Sally. 'Anyway, I know about 'is mother, she adopted him, and 'is sister. She's superior and I don't think she'd let anyone buy anything for her in the way of clothes. Anything she wanted she'd buy herself. My mum knows her and says she's very tasteful in what she wears.'

'Then we might not see the young gentleman again,' said Miss Lomax.

'Well, hooray,' said Sally, and then got cross with herself because the thought of no more up-and-downers with him over the counter took away the little exhilarating tingles she'd experienced lately.

When the shop closed for the day, she made her way home. She felt a bit fed up. She wasn't short of friends, young men as well as young women, but she was short of the kind of excitements that made life that much more enjoyable. She was short, in fact, of a feller she could really take to. At twenty-two, that just wasn't fair on a girl.

A little light rain began to fall.

Horace, on his way home himself saw her ahead of him as he turned into Braganza Street.

Joseph Burns saw her from behind his curtains as

276

she stopped to open her umbrella. Jesus Christ, there she was, right outside his window and reaching for something. He'd been twitching all day, and Mrs Burns had been watching him. He sprang now, out of his chair, out of the room and out through the front door after yanking it open. He'd got to get her, he'd got to get her before she got him. The guns were going off, and their roar was in his ears and pounding at his head.

Horace could hardly believe his eyes as he saw a large man in shirt, braces and trousers rush from a house and bear down on Sally, who was opening up her brolly. He made violent contact with her. She staggered. Horace began to run. The man took hold of Sally. She screamed. He wound his arms around her, lifted her up and threw her like a sack over his left shoulder. He turned and rushed with her back into the house. Horace, athletic, piled on the pace. He shot like an arrow into the house through the unclosed door. He heard Sally, and she sounded as if that madman was choking her. The noises were coming from the front room, the parlour. Horace burst in. There she was, on the floor, on her back, the man kneeling astride her, his breathing heavy and hoarse, a cushion in his hands, a cushion that was over her own hands. And her own hands were pushing at it to prevent it smothering her.

No weapon leapt to Horace's eyes except an umbrella that lay on the floor. In a flash he slipped off his right shoe, took hold of it by the toe, and dealt the man a solid blow on the back of his head with the heel.

Joseph Burns sagged and fell sideways off Sally. The cushion tumbled away, and Sally, eyes huge and dilated, looked up into the face of Horace.

'Did you see, did you see?' she gasped. 'He's mad.'

'I know, I know, I couldn't believe my eyes,' said Horace, 'he was right off his head. Are you badly hurt?' He went down on one knee beside her and Sally, shocked and shaken though she was, at least managed to give an embarrassed little yell and to push at her disordered raincoat and skirt.

Mrs Burns hastened in then.

'Oh, Lord above, what's 'appened?' she gasped as she saw the dramatic tableau of her unconscious husband, a grounded young lady and a kneeling young man. 'Oh, what've you done to me 'usband?' she gasped to Horace. 'Who's that girl, and who are you? Oh, poor Joe, look at 'im. He's a shellshock case.' Down she went on her knees beside him and cradled his head. He was still out cold.

'Help me up, would you?' asked Sally of Horace, and only too willingly he brought her to her feet. She was very shaken but unhurt. 'Oh, me gawd, I thought I was done for, but I'm all right, and I was never more glad to see anyone.'

'Sit down for a minute and take it easy,' said Horace.

'What 'appened, what 'appened?' begged Mrs Burns, and Horace told her while Sally sat down and let herself recover. Mrs Burns sighed. 'Oh, you shouldn't 'ave hit Joe's head,' she said. 'That's where all 'is troubles are, in 'is head. He can't ever get rid of the noises of the Great War, he nearly got buried alive when 'is trench was blown up. Oh, I'm that sorry for what 'e did to the young lady, but he 'as times when he thinks the Germans are creepin' up on him or there's one of them snipers about. I'd be downright thankful if you wouldn't go to the police about 'im, only he'll get took away and won't get looked after like he is here at 'ome. I'm Mrs Burns, and I can tell yer Joe's a good man.'

'But he might murder someone,' said Sally, 'I was sure he was goin' to murder me.'

'He's never gone right off 'is head before,' said Mrs Burns.

'He's a danger, though, isn't he?' said Horace.

Joseph Burns uttered a little sigh and his eyes opened. He blinked.

'I've got an 'eadache,' he said.

'There, it's all right, Joe love,' murmured Mrs Burns.

'Is that you, old lady?' he asked.

'Yes, course it is,' said Mrs Burns, his head in her lap, his eyes blinking away.

'Where am I?' he asked.

'At home,' said Mrs Burns.

'It's bleedin' quiet,' said Joseph Burns.

'Well, course it is, Joe, the war's over.'

'Is it? Well, not before time, I tell yer. Blimey, am I still alive?'

It was his wife's turn to blink.

'Joe, you're talkin' quite a bit,' she said.

'I've got an 'eadache,' he said again.

Mrs Burns looked up at Horace.

'It's because you hit 'im,' she said. 'You shouldn't 'ave, not on 'is head.'

'Sorry, missus, but it was the only thing that occurred to me at the time,' said Horace. 'I think you ought to get a doctor to look at him.'

'Oh, yes, I will,' said Mrs Burns, 'me lodger'll go round to the surgery as soon as 'e comes in, which'll be any minute now. I'm honestly sorry Joe acted like he did, but—'

'We'll leave it to you, Mrs Burns,' said Horace. 'Well, shall we do that, Sally, leave it to Mrs Burns? It's your say more than mine.'

'Yes, you see to things, Mrs Burns,' said Sally. 'I'm sure you'll do what you think's best. Yes, and see what the doctor says.'

'Oh, Dr Parsons knows Joe all right,' said Mrs Burns, 'he knows Joe's only a danger to me ornaments mostly. Joe, what come over you, doin' what you did to this young lady?'

Joseph Burns stood up, put a hand to the back of his head, winced and looked at Sally.

'Well, I'm that sorry, miss, if I upset yer in some way, but I can't remember a thing,' he said, 'everything's gone all quiet. I just dunno what's been 'appening.'

'Come on, Sally, I'll see you home,' said Horace,

picking up her umbrella. 'You take care of things, Mrs Burns.'

'I'm ever so sorry,' said Mrs Burns, and Horace and Sally left her to look after her unhappy problems.

Sally, her umbrella up to shield her from the drizzle, was quiet and a little pale, and Horace let several minutes go by before he spoke. They were in Manor Place by then.

'Bit of a nightmare,' he said soberly. 'You sure you're all right?'

'Just shaken,' said Sally. 'That poor man. I mean, I've 'eard of shellshock.'

'Yes, some old soldiers never get over it,' said Horace, 'and you're a forgivin' girl to look at it like that.'

'Still, I don't think I'll walk home this way again,' said Sally, 'I'll go round by Penton Place in future.'

'Will you tell your parents?' asked Horace.

Sally thought before saying, 'No, I don't think I will. Dad might want to do something about it, even though he's an old soldier 'imself. It'll upset him that another old soldier went off his head, and he'll want to go and talk to him, and that poor woman's got enough troubles.'

'I feel sorry for them both,' said Horace.

A little more brightly, Sally said, 'Here, I wonder if it did her 'usband a bit of good, you bashin' his head with your shoe?'

'I shouldn't think so,' said Horace, 'that sort of cure only happens in films.'

'Yes, and it happened in a book I read once, called *Random Harvest*,' said Sally.

They crossed from Manor Place into Browning Street, and from there Horace saw her to her front door in Caulfield Place. The row of old but solid terraced houses showed roofs glistening in the rain.

'Well, you're home safe and sound,' said Horace.

'Yes, thanks ever so much,' said Sally, the incident still chasing around in her shaken mind.

'Only too pleased I was behind you at the time,' said Horace.

'Yes, thanks.'

'So long, then,' said Horace. He wasn't going to worry her by talking out of turn. This wasn't the time to engage in his usual kind of persuasive chat. He'd find some excuse to visit the shop again.

'Goodbye,' said Sally, not very with it at the moment. Horace left and she entered the house. She called to her mum that she was home, and her mum called back from the kitchen that she was a bit late, wasn't she? 'Oh, I got held up a bit,' said Sally, and went up to her room, where she sat down on the bed and drew several long breaths.

She felt better then, just from drawing air into her lungs in the familiar haven of her bedroom, and her pity for that caring woman and her shell-shocked husband took over. She wished Mrs Burns all the best in coping with him. Oh, and next time Horace Cooper popped into the shop, she'd have to let him know she really was grateful for him arriving in the nick of time. That sort of thing was in films and books too, the nick of time. Say just in time to save a heroine from something or other.

Crikey, she thought, does that make that Cheerful Charlie a hero?

Saturday saw Dumpling in high spirits. The Rovers were playing a ding-dong local derby match in the afternoon. One of her wedding presents had been a rattle, and she was going to make full use of it when cheering the blokes on.

Ethel was looking forward to visiting Davy in his lodgings after she'd come home from work and had had her meal. She was going to help him make suitable amendments to his sonnet to Cassie and Freddy.

Sally, having slept like a top after feeling she wouldn't sleep at all, woke up with recharged spirits, especially as a bright Saturday had followed a drizzly Friday. Walworth didn't really take too kindly to rain, drizzle or fog. Well, it was old and aged, and probably thought it was now entitled to bask in the sun, just as its old codgers reckoned they were entitled to a comfy chair by the fireside through the days of winter. There were a lot of old codgers in Walworth who'd lived there all their lives, in bad times and not so bad times, and didn't want to live anywhere else. Her mum was like that. She'd lived in Walworth all her life, and whenever Dad suggested she might like to move to Peckham, say, she always said she didn't mind going to Peckham Rye on Bank Holidays, but she didn't want to live there as she'd miss the East Street market and all her friends and neighbours. Mum was what people called a contented woman, and sort of proud that Susie and Will, her elder son, had both made good marriages.

I wouldn't mind having a nice loving husband, thought Sally. Susie's mother-in-law had told her once it was what God ordered for every woman, but that some husbands forgot about God and went drinking with the Devil. The Devil's got a lot to answer for, Sally, she'd said, and I always made it my duty to bring my sons up not to have anything to do with him. Mind, I still have to watch that Sammy, he can still disrespect what's right and proper, but never mind, Susie keeps him in fair order mostly.

Sally smiled and slipped from her bed.

When Horace managed to get to the shop at twelve-thirty, it was crowded. That is, there were four customers present, and four represented a crowd to any bloke who wanted to make a name for himself with the fair-haired assistant.

Sally, seeing him, felt a perky feeling arrive. Her recharged spirits put her into just the right frame to give as good as she expected she'd get from that tongue of his. For the moment, however, she and Miss Lomax had to attend to customers.

Horace sort of idled about. Miss Lomax caught

his eye and smiled at him. He smiled back, then watched a girl inspecting dresses depending from their hangers on a rail. Sally's fund of goodwill took a bit of a beating at that point because he began to exchange some cheerful words with the girl. Sally, trying to get on the right side of a fussy customer, actually heard him tell the girl that blue would suit her best.

'Oh, d'you think so?' said the girl.

'I like blue myself,' said Horace.

'But you're wearin' brown,' said the girl.

'Forgot myself,' said Horace.

Oh, the rotten faceache, he was the worst bloke she'd ever met, he just couldn't stop trying to get off with every girl within reach, even ones as plain as that girl was.

Horace, actually, was only trying to pass the time. In doing so, he was giving the girl quite a lift, so much so that she took his advice and chose a light blue dress for trying on. Sally ground her teeth when the girl came out of the fitting-room and actually asked Horace if he thought it suited her. Her fussy customer departing satisfied, Sally took the girl out of the wicked clutches of the devious Romeo and began to attend to her. Horace put himself out of the way.

It was another fifteen minutes before he was able to make his mark. Sally, the moment she knew she was next in line for his fancy talk, took shelter, as usual, behind her counter.

'Hello,' said Horace, 'are you—'

'I don't want to keep you if you want to follow that girl 'ome,' whispered Sally fiercely.

'Pardon?' said Horace.

'Oh, I never knew any bloke who tries to pick up more girls than you.'

'Pardon?' said Horace.

'Don't keep sayin' pardon, d'you 'ear?' said Sally, voice low enough not to reach the ears of Miss Lomax, busy with a mother and daughter. 'You – you didn't ought to be allowed in a ladies' shop.'

'Have a heart,' said Horace, 'I only ever come in here in the hope I can take you to the pictures. Anyway, are you still feelin' all right? I worried about you all through yesterday evening.'

Sally's sense of umbrage fell to pieces. He was asking kindly, she could tell.

'Oh, yes, I see,' she said a little weakly. 'Yes, I'm all right, thanks, I'm fine.'

'Well, you look it, which is a relief to me,' said Horace. 'Lots of young women would've fainted and taken days to get over it, and who'd have blamed them? No wonder I like you.'

'Well, you like all the girls.'

'They're nice to have around,' said Horace, 'but I'm not savin' up to get married to all of them.'

'Now you're being daft again,' said Sally. Two women came in. Saturdays were always busy.

Horace, noting them, said, 'Well, I'd better get out of your way. Glad you've perked up. I'll be watchin' your brother Freddy's football team this afternoon, as I've finished for the day, just by way of a change. Hope to see you around, Sally. So long.' He left, and Sally felt she'd let herself down, that she really ought to have been nicer to him, especially after what he had done to rescue her from that poor mad bloke in Braganza Street.

Oh, blow it.

Chapter Seventeen

'Well, I'm off to see Davy now, Mum,' said Ethel at fifteen minutes past two.

'Yes, all right, Ethel dear,' said Rebecca.

'You're lending him some of your poetic talent, Ethel?' smiled Jim.

'Me?' said Ethel. 'Some hopes, Dad, I can't write poetry. Still, I can sort of tell Davy what I think might not sound right. Like – like, well, beauteous. I just know that'll make Freddy laugh, and as for Cassie, she giggles at everything. Well, nearly everything. I'll see you both later, and fancy Horace goin' off to watch that Browning Street football team when he likes cricket best.' She was on her way out of the kitchen at this stage, and her voice went with her to dance about in the little hall.

'She's sweet,' smiled Rebecca.

'Davy's sober,' said Jim.

'Serious young men have their own virtues,' said Rebecca.

'Sammy Adams, what's up with you?' asked Susie of the reputable businessman who was always trying to convince himself he was the better half of their marital relationship.

'Me, Susie?'

'Yes, you keep standin' about lookin' like you've lost a pound and found a penny,' said Susie. 'You're supposed to be playin' games with the children.'

'So I am,' said Sammy.

'Listen, my lad,' said Susie, 'what's on your mind?'

'Oh, just the kind of games that won't make me finish up with all our kids on top of me,' said Sammy, and made himself disappear before it became necessary to try to put a vital porkie over on Susie, which wasn't possible. The point was, he couldn't help thinking about those photographs and the negatives, and if Boots was right in guessing they were somewhere in George Carter's factory. Well, with the help of Mitch and Bert, they'd find out. Bert had called at the Camberwell offices this morning to collect the dibs required to remunerate two professional gentlemen engaged to perform the break-in, and to put Sammy up to date with arrangements. Bert had asked no questions. What Sammy wanted him to do, Bert would do.

Boots had decided everything was now in the lap of the gods, and that if the gods failed them Sammy would have to go to the police as a put upon Mr X. Accordingly, he took himself off with Ned and Annabelle to watch Nick's team play their local derby match in Brockwell Park. Annabelle had the glow of a young lady in love with life. Boots thought

Annabelle showed her feelings as much as Lizzy, her mother, always did.

Dumpling was a prominent figure among other girl supporters on the touchline. That is, there was more of her, and she bounced with energy and enthusiasm, her rattle making itself heard. Horace was there, much to Dumpling's delight, for she still saw him as a potential member of the team. Cassie introduced him to Boots and Ned, and within a minute or so Horace discovered Boots was the man who had driven his mother home when she took a tumble in the Walworth Road. That led Boots to tell Horace he'd met his sister Ethel when she stopped to watch the tennis in Ruskin Park. She'd had a young man with her. Horace said that would have been her steady.

'Name of David Williams?' said Boots, eyes on the game, a vigorous one.

'Davy Williams,' said Horace. 'He's a bit of a poet, and Ethel's struggling to find out how long she can live with it. I think she sees the stuff he writes as a bit of a giggle, but doesn't want to upset him by sayin' so. I can't make him out myself.'

'H'm,' said Boots, and thought about a certain incident at the firm's offices back in April. A young man had entered his own office without being announced or invited. Boots looked up from his desk and asked to what he owed the pleasure of being interrupted. The young man gave his name and said he'd come about a job. Boots said if there was a job going, he didn't know about it himself.

The young man said he'd called on the off-chance, as someone had told him Adams Enterprises was a very thriving firm always in the market for keen job applicants. He could keep books, he said, and prided himself on being conscientious and efficient. Boots acknowledged he looked intelligent, and that he might well be all he said he was.

However, he perforce had to tell him that the firm at present had no vacancy for a bookkeeper, and he advised him as pleasantly as he could to try elsewhere. The young man, polite up to that point, began to look offended. He suggested that if he was being turned down, it wasn't something to be amused about. Boots assured him he wasn't amused. The young man asked what he was smiling for, then, and went on about life being serious, and that it was even more so if one was out of work. Boots said he quite agreed, but still couldn't offer him a job.

There were a few more words followed by the young man suddenly shouting he didn't like being treated as a joke. He stormed out and crashed the door to behind him. In the corridor he then managed to walk straight into Gwen Fuller, one of the general office girls. Gwen, carrying a tray on which stood cups of tea she was taking to the bookkeepers, was knocked down, tray and china flying. The young man, neither stopping nor offering any apology, stormed on, went down the stairs to the street and pulled the door shut so violently after him that a panel split. He left in his wake a scene of minor chaos. Boots, out of his office, helped Gwen to her feet and apologized profusely for the young man's manners and bad temper. Although he'd taught himself to be tolerant of people's imperfections on the grounds that he was far from perfect himself, he nevertheless promised himself to kick that young man's backside if he ever saw him again.

Well, he had seen him again, with Horace's sister Ethel, during that tennis game in Ruskin Park.

'You're doing some thinking, Mr Adams,' said Horace, struck by the fact that this likeable man had suddenly stopped being conversational.

Boots, giving more thought to what was on his mind, said, 'Well, you mentioned your sister doesn't like upsetting her young man, this Davy Williams. I wonder if that's an instinctive feeling?'

'Pardon?' said Horace.

'It may be none of my business, Horace, but if I were your sister, I'd be very careful about upsetting that young man.'

'What makes you say that?' asked Horace.

'I upset him myself once,' said Boots.

'Tell me more,' said Horace.

'I think I should,' said Boots, and told Horace exactly what had happened when Davy Williams applied for a job, was turned down, demonstrated a violent objection to not being taken seriously, and created havoc during his exit. He seemed to imagine he was being laughed at. 'He even objected to the smile I gave him,' said Boots.

'He did all that?' said Horace, astonished. 'He crashed doors shut, knocked one of your office girls over and left her there, on the floor?'

''Fraid so,' said Boots.

'Just because he thought he was being laughed at?'

'It's as well to know he's sensitive,' said Boots.

'That's puttin' it mildly,' said Horace. 'You mean he's got an ugly temper. Would you have given him a job if there'd been one goin'?'

'No,' said Boots.

'Why?'

'I didn't take to him,' said Boots.

'Well, I suppose he's not everyone's cup of tea,' said Horace, 'and he's not mine now. I think I'd better warn Ethel, but I'm not sure she'll believe me.'

'I've a feeling I should have minded my own business,' said Boots.

'No, I'm glad you told me,' said Horace.

The football match went on in the afternoon sunshine.

It was nearly half-past-three when Davy knocked on the door of the house in Wansey Street. Jim was at the Servicemen's club, keeping a managerial eye on things until six, when he'd hand over to the night manager.

Rebecca answered the door to Davy. The young man's spectacles had a worried glint.

'Where's Ethel, Mrs Cooper?' he asked. 'Hasn't she left yet?'

'What do you mean?' asked Rebecca.

'She was supposed to come to my lodgings, to be there at half-past two,' said Davy, 'but she hasn't turned up.'

'There's some mistake,' said Rebecca, 'she left here at two-fifteen.'

'That's over an hour ago,' said Davy.

'It's absurd,' said Rebecca, 'she must be there. Is she with your landlady, perhaps.'

'My landlady's out,' said Davy, 'she's gone to her sister's for the weekend. I wonder if Ethel thought I was meeting her somewhere else?'

'I don't think so,' said Rebecca, 'she mentioned she was going to your lodgings just before she left.'

'Oh, that's something to go on,' said Davy. 'She must have got held up somewhere. I'll go back to see if she's arrived, and keep my eyes open for her on the way. Don't worry, Mrs Cooper, I'll find her.'

A little worry showed itself in Rebecca's expression.

'Davy, I think I'll come with you,' she said, and she put on a hat and coat and accompanied Davy back to his lodgings. On the way their eyes searched high and low for Ethel. They saw nothing of her, but when they arrived at Mrs Albright's house, Rebecca noted the front door was ajar. 'Does that mean anything, Davy?' she asked.

'Only that I left the door open in case she arrived while I went round to see you,' said Davy. 'I thought if she did arrive, she could go in. Of course, she could have used the latchcord, but I thought an open door would be more inviting to her. And I left a note for her.'

'Well, do see if she's there now,' said Rebecca, worry increasing.

'Yes, come in, Mrs Cooper,' said Davy, and Rebecca stepped in with him and found herself in his landlady's living-room. Davy called. 'Ethel? Ethel? You here, Ethel?'

There was no answer.

'I don't like this,' said Rebecca. 'I can only think she had some kind of accident.'

'Oh, d'you think she might be in hospital?' asked Davy, spectacles dark with anxiety.

'What other answer is there?' said Rebecca. She lifted her voice. 'Ethel? Ethel?'

Still no answer.

'Let's go up,' said Davy, 'let's see if she's been here and has seen my note and left one herself.'

'Yes, we had better make sure,' said Rebecca, and she followed Davy out of the room and up the stairs. On the table in his room lay his note, telling Ethel he'd gone round to her house and to stay until he came back.

'No, she's not been, the note's still where I left it,' he said. 'Mrs Cooper, she just hasn't turned up.'

'Davy, you stay here,' said Rebecca, 'while I take a tram to King's College Hospital. That's where they'd have taken her if she'd had an accident.'

'But if she'd been taken to hospital, wouldn't someone have called at your house to let you know?' said Davy.

'I shall go, anyway,' said Rebecca, now deeply concerned.

'While you do that, I'll ask the people in this street if any of them have spotted Ethel,' said Davy.

'Yes, do everything you can to find out, Davy,' said Rebecca.

He followed her down the stairs and through to the front door.

'Mrs Cooper, I'm sorry,' he said, 'I know you're really worried.'

'Yes, I am, Davy,' said Rebecca and hurried away, wishing Jim was with her. In the Walworth Road she caught a tram that took her to the hospital, where she made enquiries. No, no-one of the name of Ethel Cooper had been admitted to Casualty this afternoon. Nor any young lady. Try St Thomas's. Rebecca asked if someone could help her by telephoning St Thomas's, and the receptionist, sympathetic, obliged. St Thomas's reported in similar fashion. No young woman had been admitted this afternoon.

Her worry mounting, Rebecca returned to Davy's lodgings in the hope that Ethel had turned up. Davy was at the open front door, looking deeply concerned.

'Did you find her at the hospital, Mrs Cooper?' he asked.

'No, Davy, I didn't,' said Rebecca, 'and she's obviously not arrived here. Did you find out if anyone saw her?'

'Everyone I asked hadn't seen anything of her,'

said Davy, spectacles peering forlornly at Ethel's handsome mother.

'I'm going to phone my husband,' said Rebecca, 'I need his help.'

'I think I'll go round to the police station,' said Davy.

'Yes, please do,' said Rebecca.

'Well, someone ought to,' said Davy, 'it's coming up to five o'clock. I'll go now, Mrs Cooper.'

'And I'm going to find a public telephone,' said Rebecca.

'There's one in the Walworth Road, near—'

'Yes, I know,' said Rebecca and away she went again.

She made contact with Jim from the phone box, and Jim, given the details, said he'd come at once, that he'd meet her at home. There was a faint chance Ethel might be there, he said, that for some reason she had returned home. If not, he and Rebecca would begin a new search for her. Jim spoke in a reassuring way, disguising his own worry.

Rebecca hurried home. It was twenty minutes past five when she arrived, but there was no sign of Ethel. Suddenly struck by the possibility that there was a self-motivated reason for her daughter's disappearance, Rebecca went up to the girl's room and looked for a note, although she knew that Ethel, uncomplicated and in many ways naive, simply wasn't the type to indulge in dramatic impulses, especially not the kind to cause worry to her family.

The room was neat and tidy, like Ethel herself, and there wasn't the slightest sign of a note.

She heard the front door open then, and she ran from the bedroom, heart beating fast. Rebecca's attachment to her adopted son and daughter was that of a natural mother.

'Ethel, is that you?'

'No, it's me, Mum,' called Horace from the little hall. He was back from the football match.

'Horace? Oh, I need you,' said Rebecca and hastened down the stairs. Quickly, and slightly staccato in her worry, Rebecca acquainted Horace of Ethel's alarming disappearance. She inserted a reference to her greatest worry, to the possibility that his sister might have fallen into the hands of a horrible kind of man.

'Kidnapped, you mean?' said Horace, his concern showing. He shook his head. 'In the middle of Walworth on a Saturday afternoon? Only if—' He stopped. He'd been going to say only if she'd gone to Braganza Street, where there lived a shellshock casualty of the Great War. But Ethel would have been nowhere near Braganza Street. She would have been in the heart of Walworth all the time, its busy Saturday afternoon heart. 'Wait a moment,' he said, and thought about what a certain Mr Adams had told him. He thought too of the look on the face of Davy Williams at the tea party given by Dumpling and Danny to celebrate the engagement of Cassie and Freddy. He'd quoted the opening line of his sonnet, a line that had brought giggles and amusement, and he obviously hadn't liked the idea that he was being laughed at. And he certainly didn't like Ethel giggling at any of his poetry.

'Horace, must you stand there?' asked Rebecca.

'No, I mustn't,' said Horace, 'I'm off to Davy's lodgings. When Dad gets here, tell him—'

A key turned in the front door lock then, and in came Jim.

'No luck?' he said, expression grim.

'Let's not waste time,' said Horace, 'we've got to get to Davy's lodgings, and I'll tell you why on the way.'

And on the way he told them of the conversation he'd had with Mr Adams, the man Rebecca had come to know consequent on her tumble.

'You shouldn't feel unhappy, Ethel,' said Davy, 'you should feel happy. You've been my lady of shining waters ever since we met, you know that.'

He was sitting on the bathroom stool, gazing at Ethel through his expressive spectacles. The steam in the bathroom had clouded the lenses at first, but the water was a lot cooler now. Well, it should be, it was two-and-a-half hours old. Ethel, bound and gagged, lay in the bath, which was full to the overflow pipe. Only her head was above the surface. The water itself blurred the shape and colour of her clothes. He had hit her fifteen minutes after she'd arrived, and in a way that knocked her out. When she came to, her ankles and knees were bound, and so were her arms and ribs. Under the thin rope, her hands were lashed at the wrists. In her mouth was a thick linen gag. And she was in the bath, and the bath was filling up with a mixture of hot and cold water. Davy was watching her, and she thought herself the victim of a horrible dream. She struggled and squirmed as the level of water climbed and climbed, drowning her legs, her thighs, her clothes, her body until it reached her neck, when Davy turned the taps off.

Her eyes were huge now, staring at him, listening to his reproachful voice gently scolding her for laughing at him, for giggling at his poetry, and for being a very disappointing lady of the lakes. She could still squirm, she could still struggle, but she was desperately afraid it would cause her to slide and for her head to be covered. She would drown then, for she was even more desperately afraid he would not prevent it. In his offended mood, he kept shaking his head at her, and the gleaming glass of his spectacles seemed to Ethel to flash with evil light.

'I believed in you, Ethel, I believed that your devotion to poetry, to my poetry, was sincere, but you laughed and giggled, not once but two or three times. You let others giggle. My fair lady of limpid waters, you betrayed me.'

Ethel's staring eyes begged and pleaded. The level of the water was horrifyingly threatening, gently heaving around her neck, gently slapping at her chin.

'However, I shall let you remain my lady of the

lakes to the end, Ethel, and then one day I'll go on my way, yes, to Scotland, I think, to the deep lochs. I think your parents will be here in half an hour, and I shall go down and meet them and help them to look for you. They think I'm at the police station. I shall tell them that on my way I met a woman who said she had seen you, and that I went looking for you and came back here again when I couldn't find you. They won't look in here, Ethel, in the bathroom. Why should they? Your mother has been up and has seen my room. When she arrives again, this time with your father, I shall bring them both up to my room and then suggest we go to the police station together. During the night, when no-one's about, I shall carry you to somewhere like the market and leave you there for the police to find you and to puzzle their brains out about how you got there. Your mother will confirm you were never here.'

Ethel's horrified eyes begged anew. Davy began to recite.

'There she stood on shining pool,
The lady of my dreams—'

He broke off to lean forward. His hands slipped under the almost cold water, and he placed them on her submerged shoulders. Her wet gagged mouth issued a gurgle as she tried to scream. She knew what he was going to do then, push her beneath the water to make his poems come true.

Her bound, immersed body struggled.

'And slowly then her fair form sank

To join the water queens.'

His hands began to push slowly but firmly.

He had, however, forgotten one thing, the front door latchcord, and the use Walworth people and their neighbours made of this form of gaining entry. At this point it was pulled hard, and the door crashed open. Jim, with Horace on his heels, rushed through the living-room and up the stairs, their suspicions inflamed by an urgency born of Rebecca reminding them that Davy Williams's landlady was away for the weekend.

Davy hissed an exclamation of sheer fury, and all his psychopathic tendencies surfaced. He pushed violently and Ethel's head sank and was submerged, her helpless body frenziedly writhing. Landing doors were flung open. The bathroom door smashed back, and Jim showed himself. He made an instant leap, took hold of Davy and hurled him away. Davy hit the floor. Horace rushed in as Jim lifted Ethel clear of the bath with his one arm and hugged her to his chest. He seated himself on the stool, sat Ethel on his lap and untied the gag. Ethel coughed wetly. Davy scrambled up, but went down again, Horace felling him with a violent blow.

'Don't try to say anything, Ethel,' said Jim, and as Horace began to untie her bonds, Ethel managed a very weak smile, her sopping clothes transferring cold wetness to her dad's jacket and trousers. Rebecca appeared, stared at the scene, took in the fact that Ethel was preciously alive and that Davy had obviously been knocked out. Her relief was enormous. Rebecca had never wavered in the care and affection she had given to Ethel and Horace.

'Bring her out, Horace,' she said, 'and put her on the bed in the back room. Jim, look after that creature on the floor, and thank your God that Horace arrived home in time from the football match. Be gentle with her, Horace.'

Ethel, body and clothes soaked, but free of her bonds, looked up at her brother as she was transferred to his arms and carried from the bathroom to the rented room.

'Orrice, that's the – that's the last time I want to be anyone's fair lady of any lakes,' she said.

'Bless you, Ethel darling,' said Rebecca.

'Twice over,' said Jim from the open bathroom door.

'You're all right now, Ethel,' said Horace, placing her down on Davy's bed. Rebecca took over from there, shooing him out and closing the door. Then her voice was heard.

'Jim – Horace – find warm clothes, blankets, anything. And towels.'

'I'll do that, Horace,' said Jim, snatching a towel from the bathroom rail, 'you keep your eye on that crazed specimen.' Out he went, leaving Horace standing guard over Davy, now stirring and twitching. Hell and the devil, thought Horace, two ruddy madmen in the same week? The difference was, of course, that one was the unfortunate victim of the war, the other a calculating and dangerous case for an asylum.

The police took charge of Davy Williams, who was to prove to be David Morgan of Monmouth, with a history of very erratic behaviour. He had left home nine months ago, after becoming such a menace to his sisters that his parents made arrangements for men in white coats to interview him. He skipped before the interview took place, experienced the trials and tribulations of homelessness for a while, then found himself a job and lodgings in Walworth. He also found a naive girl.

★   ★   ★

It was ten minutes after midnight in Shoreditch and elsewhere in London when a dark figure edged up on Bert Roper and nudged his elbow.

'That you, Bert?' whispered Mitch.

'It's me,' murmured Bert. 'Where's yer van, old cock?'

'Down the road. Best, I thought, not to park it 'ere. If we need it, I'll go and fetch it. Then it'll only be 'ere a couple of shakes. Where's yer team?'

'Where'd yer think?' said Bert.

'Already in and on the job, are they, Bert?'

'Well, they're pros, Mitch, and Sammy Adams said don't spend time 'anging about.'

'Knows 'is onions, does Sammy,' said Mitch, 'but it's Sergeant Adams who's the Duke of Wellington in the Adams outfit. What's first prize in the safe? Did Sammy say?'

'No, 'e didn't say,' said Bert, 'and I didn't ask.'

'Sergeant Adams didn't come across, either,' said Mitch, 'and sometimes, Bert, I don't ask no more than you do.'

'I'm just waitin' and watchin', Mitch.'

'Seen any rozzers about?'

'Not yet,' said Bert, 'but keep your ears open, mate.'

Inside an office in the darkened factory, the professional gentry were at work. One gent was Flash Ferdy, who always wore very thin and very expensive kid gloves, the other was Mr Buggins, so called on account of looking smart and managerial. Well, he always wore a good suit and a collar and tie whenever he was on a job. He was holding a torch, and Flash Ferdy was at silent war with the combination lock of the safe.

'Ain't beatin' yer, is it, Flash?'

'Mr Buggins, kindly keep your cakehole shut.' Flash Ferdy had his sharp ear trained on the tumblers, his thinly gloved fingers moving slowly. He'd already been at the lock for fifteen minutes, and Mr Buggins was sweating on the possible loss of his sidekick's reputation.

Click.

Another smile.

'Yer done it, Flash?' whispered Mr Buggins. Flash Ferdy continued to gently fiddle. 'You ain't done it?' said Mr Buggins.

'Your cakehole is aggravating me,' said Flash Ferdy. His fingers were still at work, his listening

305

apparatus still highly tuned. He detected the tiny sound of one more click. Then another. 'Well, well,' he murmured, and took hold of the safe's lever-like handle. He pressed. The handle remained rigid.

'You still ain't done it?' whispered the anxious Mr Buggins.

Flash Ferdy blew on the fingertips of his right glove, then murmured, 'Forgetful, forgetful. It's a Henry Lockwood, of course. Double chamber. Let me see now.' He gave the combination lock one slow full turn.

Click.

He pressed the handle again. It moved and he pulled the safe door open. Mr Buggins illuminated the interior with his torch. It was empty save for a cheap tin petty cash box. Flash Ferdy drew it out. He gave it a little shake, and it gave off a tiny rattle. He put a hand around the lid.

''Ere, no opening, nor lookin'. Strict orders,' said Mr Buggins.

'Unfortunately,' said Flash Ferdy, 'it's my belief we might have a pig in the poke here.' He opened the lid and the torch disclosed a solitary penny. 'All right for a distressed lady that's run out of them, but not what the doctor ordered on behalf of our clients, Mr Buggins. Would you pay a hundred quid to earn yourself a penny?'

'It ain't in our contract to ask ourselves questions,' said Mr Buggins, 'only to 'and over the safe's contents. It ain't our fault it's only a cash box and a copper coin.'

'Something was supposed to be in the safe,' said Flash Ferdy. 'I don't consider a penny represents services properly rendered. Hold on.' He lifted out the twin container, one side of which was for coppers, the other for silver. Notes were usually kept beneath the container. There weren't any. But there was a brown envelope, postcard size, which fitted in neatly. 'There we are, Mr Buggins.' He placed the container back in the tin box, closed the lid and shut the safe. 'We can now depart.'

'Yer a bleedin' marvel, Flash,' said Mr Buggins.

'I have that honour,' said Flash Ferdy.

A few minutes later, the professional pair were out of the factory and making contact with Bert in the darkness. Flash Ferdy gave brief details of the operation, then handed over what he'd brought out.

'That's all?' whispered Bert.

'On me oath,' said Mr Buggins.

'What's your oath worth?' asked Mitch.

''Alf the bleedin' fee, fifty smackers,' said Mr Buggins.

'Just for a ruddy cash box that feels empty?' said Bert.

'It ain't much,' said Mitch.

'I grant it's not a grand piano,' said Flash Ferdy, 'but it's promising. It holds one copper coin and a brown envelope.'

'That's it, you reckon?' said Mitch to Bert.

'Could be,' said Bert.

'Might payment be forthcoming?' asked Flash Ferdy, with the population of Shoreditch, tucked up in bed, sleeping off the pub revels of Saturday night.

Bert paid up, having collected the ready from Sammy during the morning. The professional gentry, having made known their services were always available providing they weren't guests of His Majesty, God bless him, melted away into the dark hollows and looming shadows of the East End. Bert handed the box over to Mitch, and they parted company, Bert to go home and Mitch to drive to Boots's house off Denmark Hill.

Boots was up and waiting for him. They exchanged a few words, and Boots took the cash box into his keeping. Mitch said goodnight. Boots said he was obliged.

'Me pleasure, Lord Wellington,' said Mitch, and drove off in the van.

Boots took the box into the kitchen and found what it contained. He pocketed the penny with a smile, and with everyone else in the house fast asleep, he opened the envelope. There were three photographs identical to those delivered to Sammy, and three negatives. He held each negative in turn up to the light. Satisfied, he lifted the hob lid of the kitchen range and slipped the photographs and negatives into the slow-burning fire. He pulled out the damper. The hot dusty coals began to glow. The photographs began to burn, the negatives to melt. He watched their destruction, replaced the hob lid, pushed in the damper, switched off the kitchen light and went up to bed.

Emily woke up when he inserted himself between the sheets.

'What's goin' on?' she murmured.

'Nothing dramatic,' said Boots.

'Have you only just come up?'

'Couldn't put the book down,' said Boots.

'You've been readin' all this time?'

'It's what a good book does to you, Em.'

'That's your story,' murmured Emily. She thought Boots could be very deep sometimes, but she was too comfy and dreamy to start a conversation about it now. She simply snuggled up and went back to sleep.

Boots rang Sammy first thing on Sunday morning, and that enabled Sammy to spend the day happy ever after.

Chapter Eighteen

Rebecca insisted on Ethel spending Sunday in bed. Horace went up, sat on her bedside chair and chatted to her. Ethel said he was being a fusspot. Horace said he, Mum and Dad were all fusspots at the moment, but would get back to being normal tomorrow. Ethel kept thinking about Davy, of course, and she kept saying things like what a sly beast he'd turned out, and what a brute for wanting to drown her.

'It was all about his fair lady of the waters, it all got stuck in his queer mind,' said Horace. 'I don't myself think you ought to talk about it, sis.'

'Of course I ought to,' said Ethel with surprising acumen, 'it's the only way of gettin' it out of me system. Orrice, you don't have to sit up here with me, not on a nice day like this, specially a Sunday. Why don't you go round and see Sally Brown?'

'Oh, I think I'll let her have a restful day,' said Horace.

'What's she want a restful day for?' asked Ethel. 'She's not old.'

Horace thought that Sally, like Ethel, needed a quiet time for a while.

'I'll probably see her in the shop sometime tomorrow,' he said. 'I'll need an excuse, of course.'

Ethel, relaxing on her back beneath the bed-clothes, her hair a dark pattern on the white pillow, said, 'Oh, you daft 'a'porth, Orrice, you don't have to 'ave an excuse every time, do you?'

'I feel safer with an excuse,' said Horace.

'Safer?' Ethel grimaced as she remembered how safe she'd always felt with Davy, because he seemed like a young gent. 'She's not goin' to hit you, is she, if you go into the shop without an excuse?'

'She's threatened to once or twice, even when I've been a customer.'

'Orrice, you're both barmy,' said Ethel. 'Crikey,' she said, 'so must I 'ave been to think what a nice bloke Davy was.'

'Well, how could you have known he wasn't?' said Horace. 'He fooled all of us, even Dad. We just thought he was a serious type, that's all.'

'Yes, but when you think, most of his poems were a bit funny,' said Ethel. 'Funny peculiar, I mean, always about a fair maiden that kept drowning 'erself. Well, he always made her sink under the water to join mermaids or something.' Ethel grimaced. 'And he always said the fair maiden was me. Crikey, I didn't want to join any mermaids. Orrice, he must 'ave bats in his belfry.'

'Yes, they'll put him and his bats somewhere safe,' said Horace. 'Would you like a mug of hot Bovril, sis?'

'Yes, I'd like that,' said Ethel. 'And Orrice, tell

311

Mum I'm not goin' to stay in bed all day, just till dinner-time, that's all. Then I'm goin' to get up.'

'Sure?' said Horace.

'Yes, ever so sure,' said Ethel. 'Weren't the police kind last night?'

'Well, I think they did us all a kind turn by takin' Davy away,' said Horace.

'Yes, I think it's best for him to be locked up,' said Ethel, 'then he can spend all his time writin' more poetry.'

'I hope his keepers don't giggle,' said Horace and went down to the kitchen to see about the hot Bovril.

Ethel thought about Davy and sighed for that poor silly young man.

She was up and standing at the gate in the middle of the afternoon. She was thinking how glad she was to be alive, and how nice the street looked with its air of Sunday quiet. Little white autumn clouds were actually doing a bit of a dance above Walworth. She thought again of Davy and what a shame it was that he wasn't right in his head. As Horace had said, he'd be locked up in one of those places that looked after sad cases like him. Well, at least she wouldn't have to read any more poetry to him, and she found that a bit of a relief. Well, even more than that, she found it made her feel quite light-hearted.

Rebecca appeared at the open door.

'Ethel dear, I'll be making the afternoon pot of

tea in five minutes, and the weather's fine enough to have it in the garden.'

'That'll be nice, Mum,' said Ethel, and Rebecca thought how resilient the girl was under her ingenuous front. But then, that was common to most Walworth people, resilience. Yes, and courage too, and the ability to endure. Ethel and Horace both had those qualities. Ethel might have given way to nightmarish hysterics, but hadn't.

'In five minutes, then, Ethel,' smiled Rebecca, and went back to her kitchen.

A young man came strolling.

'Hello there, Effel,' he said.

'Oh, hello, Vic,' said Ethel.

'Waitin' for someone?' said Vic Rogers, healthy of mind and body.

'No, just enjoyin' the fresh air,' said Ethel.

'I've been havin' some of that,' said Vic, 'choppin' firewood in our backyard.'

Ethel looked at him. He seemed very much like a bloke who could do a good job of chopping firewood.

'D'you like poetry?' she asked.

'It's not me fav'rite pastime,' said Vic.

'Would you like a cup of Sunday afternoon tea?' asked Ethel.

'Beg yer pardon?' said Vic.

'We're havin' one in a minute.'

'You askin' me in, Effel?'

'Well, me mum won't let us have it out here,' said Ethel.

'But what about that bloke of yours?' asked Vic. The news that would break in tomorrow's papers was not common knowledge yet.

'I don't like 'is poetry,' said Ethel, 'I've gone off it, and him as well.'

'Well, I'll come in for a cup of tea with pleasure, Effel.'

'Yes, come on, me fam'ly won't mind,' said Ethel, having decided a young man who chopped wood and didn't call after her in the street would be a nice change from someone who poetized about fair young maidens sinking into limpid pools.

Her resilient spirit pushed the lamentable pictures of Davy out of her mind as she took Vic into the house and asked him if he could tell her how to enrol at his night school for shorthand-typing classes. Vic said he'd take her to the school when he went for his next lesson on Tuesday evening, and Ethel said oh, good, my mum and dad will like it if I take up shorthand-typing. I'll like it as well, said Vic, we can go to the school together when you start next term.

Out into the backyard they went, Vic blinking at the sight of the little garden, the little oasis in the heart of Walworth, where Rebecca, Jim and Horace were seated around the table.

'Hello, Vic, how's yourself?' said Horace.

'Oh, I've asked 'im in for a cup of tea with us,' said Ethel.

'Well, that's nice,' said Rebecca.

'You're welcome, Vic,' said Jim.

'Oh, I hope so,' said Ethel. 'Vic's like me, he doesn't go much on poetry.'

Laughter sprang then from the little oasis, and Horace thought good old Ethel, one more nightmare's bitten the dust.

Cassie and her dad entertained Freddy to Sunday tea. The Gaffer remarked, not for the first time, that he was highly pleased about the engagement.

'Done our Cassie proud, you 'ave, Freddy,' he said. 'Made 'er look blooming.'

'Dad, I already bloomed ages ago,' said Cassie. 'It's Freddy who's bloomed now.'

'You sure?' said the Gaffer. 'I mean, do blokes bloom? I can't recollect I ever did.'

'Freddy's put on a proud and 'appy look since our engagement,' said Cassie. 'That's blooming.'

'What was 'is look like before, then?' asked the Gaffer.

'Oh, it was just any old look mostly,' said Cassie. 'He's a lot better now.'

'Well, I can't say Freddy ever struck me as wearin' any old look,' said the Gaffer.

'Sometimes it was a sort of anxious look,' said Cassie. 'That was when he was worryin' that a rich bloke might enter my life and fancy me.'

'Don't mind me,' said Freddy, 'just talk as if I'm not 'ere.'

The Gaffer smiled. Freddy had always been as comical as Cassie, which had made him Cassie's one and only soulmate. There they were, the two of them, all those years together as inseparable pals, and now together with marriage in front of them. They wouldn't have a lot of money, but they'd have each other, and the Gaffer couldn't see either of them doing without the other.

Freddy was enjoying his tea. He was always very much at home with Cassie and her dad. He liked the Gaffer, and he understood Cassie's concern for him if he went to live in lodgings.

Freddy decided to bring the subject up, simply because he knew that although Cassie had agreed to let her dad give lodgings a try, she still wasn't happy about it. They talked about it over tea, and the Gaffer was still insistent he could manage all right. Cassie, pleased with Freddy for mentioning it, said that wasn't the point.

'It's just not right,' she said.

'It's sensible,' said the Gaffer.

'Well, I agree,' said Freddy, 'but it's not what Cassie wants.'

'I thought I'd give lodgings a go first,' said the Gaffer, 'I thought we'd settled that.'

'Yes, but settling it like that has unsettled me,' said Cassie. 'Oh, come on, Dad, live with Freddy and me.'

The Gaffer looked at Freddy.

'Be pleased to 'ave you,' said Freddy. 'Well, while I agree givin' lodgings a go is sensible, I don't always reckon bein' sensible is the best thing. I know 'ow you feel, Gaffer, but I know 'ow me and Cassie feel too.'

'Well,' said the Gaffer, a little gruff on account of being very touched, 'if you and Cassie can put up with me—'

'Dad, it's not puttin' up with you,' said Cassie, 'it's wantin' to have you. You've always been nice to live with, and you're not goin' to turn awkward or behave different. Besides, me and Freddy are still young, you know, we still need a dad around. Well, Freddy's still a bit simple, poor dear, and I'm not twenty-one yet. You can 'ave your own room and fireside and a flower vase for spring daffodils.'

'Freddy, you sure?' said the Gaffer.

'I'm sure all right, and about the daffodils as well,' said Freddy, 'but you'll 'ave to make allowances for me bein' a bit simple.'

The Gaffer roared with laughter. Cassie smiled. It was properly settled this time, because of Freddy's help. She was going to get married, and she was going to look after the two people she loved best, Freddy and her good old dad. It wouldn't be a problem. One woman could easily manage two men. One woman like herself.

'Mister Sammy,' said the switchboard girl on Monday morning, 'it's Mrs Carter for you again.'

'Again?' said Sammy. 'Who's she, then?'

'I'm sure I don't know, Mister Sammy, except you seem popular with 'er. Shall I put 'er through?'

'Yes, all right,' said Sammy.

Mrs Mildred Carter came through, and Sammy announced himself.

317

'You low-down sod,' she said.

'Is that you speakin', Mildred?'

'You bloody crook,' said Mildred, seething.

'I thought my switchboard girl said there was a lady on the line.'

'Listen, you jumped-up barrow boy from the back streets of flea-ridden Walworth, you wouldn't recognize a lady if you saw fifty of them all in a row.'

'Oh, I don't know, Mildred, I'm in the fortunate position of bein' married to one.'

'Poor cow,' said Mildred. 'You bugger, you did a burglary job over the weekend. George has just phoned me from the factory. Your filthy finger-prints are all over the place.'

'I'm a new-born babe,' said Sammy, 'I ain't out of the cradle yet in respect of being criminally unlawful. Has George had his stock pinched?'

'You know what's been pinched, you second-hand organ-grinder's monkey,' said Mildred. 'You ought to be put under a steamroller and spread all over Camberwell.'

'Sounds nasty,' said Sammy, 'and painful as well.'

'I'm being accused by George of letting you know where that envelope was,' fumed Mildred.

'Envelope?' said Sammy. 'What envelope?'

'Laughing about it, are you, Sammy Adams?'

'Not much,' said Sammy, 'I've got this worry about certain photographs on me mind, but I've decided to be true to me principles and integrity and not give in to your request to settle George's debts. Me pocket would never recover, it's delicate. No hard feelings, Mildred.'

'Do me a favour, drop dead,' said the lady, and slammed her phone down.

Sammy smiled. Good old Boots, he'd guessed right. Boots was a thinker, and downright cagey. He worked things out while looking as if his mind was on something or someone unimportant, like the Prime Minister, who was more unimportant than anybody as far as thinking people were concerned. Boots always worked things out for the good of the family. Chinese Lady always did the same, the good of the family had been her life's work. Boots was her shadow, in a manner of speaking.

At mid-morning, Mr Gregson walked into Nick's office.

'Good weekend, Nick?' he said.

'Well, we won our football match on Saturday,' said Nick.

'Don't tell the other directors,' said Mr Gregson, 'they don't recognize anything but rugger. Let's see, what did I come in here for?'

'For the Newsome Shippers contract?' said Nick. 'I'm still checking it.'

'No, it wasn't that,' said Mr Gregson. 'Yes, I've got it. The directors are giving you a salary rise of fifty pounds a year. Beginning next month. Happy with that?'

'Happy? I don't get it,' said Nick, 'I've already had a summer rise.'

'Well, now you've got an autumn one to keep you warm through the winter,' said Mr Gregson.

'You're my fairy godmothers,' said Nick.

'I think I prefer the sound of godfathers,' said Mr Gregson, who had just taken a phone call from Mr J M Douglas. 'Anyway, you've earned the increment, Nick, and it'll help if you intend to get married sometime in the near future.'

'Which I hope to, next year,' said Nick.

'Well, I'm jiggered, is that a fact?' said Mr Gregson, who knew it was. He had been advised in a deep rumble that the firm of Parker, Rawlings and Gregson Ltd had a civic duty to ensure none of their male employees should be allowed to marry while earning a pittance. I hear, God had rumbled, that your new man Harrison will be married next year. A damned ridiculous idea, Gregson, on his pittance of one hundred and fifty pounds a year. Mr Gregson put forth the notion that many young men got married on less. They're all damned fools, then, said God, and I suggest your board does what is necessary to prevent Harrison falling into the pit of married poverty. Very well, said Mr Gregson. This is confidential, said God, you understand? Mr Gregson did not fully understand, since he had no idea God's great-niece was to be the bride, but he said yes, of course, Mr Douglas. One did not mumble or demur in the face of the chief shareholder, the man who had largely financed the advance of the firm from a private company to a limited one. 'You're really heading towards wedded bliss, Nick?'

'If that's what it is, yes,' said Nick.

'Oh, I've known it myself,' said Mr Gregson, 'and it's recommendable.'

'I'll tell my young lady that,' said Nick, 'just in case she's heard different stories. And thanks very much for the rise.'

'Don't mention it,' said Mr Gregson, and left.

Nick sat thinking. The rise was totally unexpected, especially coming so soon after the previous increase. It put him into a comparatively affluent position. A whole quid extra a week. Had he really earned it at this particular stage? He rang Annabelle at her work. She expressed herself blissful at hearing him. Nick expressed himself staggered at getting another rise, which meant that from next month he'd be earning four pounds a week.

'Rapture,' said Annabelle, 'we can have wisteria round the door as well as roses.'

'Listen,' said Nick, 'have you been speaking to your great-uncle?'

'What about?' said Annabelle.

'About us living on a starvation level?'

'D'you mean have I asked him to use his influence to get you this rise?'

'Yes, have you?'

'Oh, you beast, how dare you,' said Annabelle, and hung up. Then she went straight into Boots's office to let him know how bitter she was that Nick actually thought she'd do the kind of thing he'd accused her of, persuading her great-uncle to see he was given a rise.

'You're flushed,' said Boots.

'I'm upset,' she said.

'Exactly what did Nick say?' asked Boots, and Annabelle repeated the brief conversation. 'That wasn't an accusation,' said Boots, 'that was a reaction. Are you sure you haven't said something to the Growler?'

'Oh, not you as well,' said Annabelle in dismay.

'Out with it,' said Boots.

'Oh, look, when I last had lunch with Uncle John, he asked if I was really serious about marrying a penniless pipsqueak, and I said yes, I was, even if we had to live on bread and cheese. He said just a month on bread and cheese would make me regret I ever met Nick Harrison. So I said never, that it was the best day of my life when I did meet Nick. So he said no niece of his was going to spend her life on bread and cheese. And that's all. I didn't ask him to use his influence with Nick's firm. I wouldn't.'

'That's it, then,' said Boots.

'Uncle Boots, what d'you mean, that's it?'

'Bread and cheese,' said Boots. 'The Growler didn't like the sound of that, not for his favourite young relative.'

'You mean he got Nick this rise because I said I'd marry him even if we had to live on bread and cheese?'

'I'd say so,' said Boots. 'But I'd also say the Growler would have found out if Nick was worth it, if he was promising enough. I don't think he'd go in for charity, not even for you. Tell Nick not to make a fuss, but to count his blessings – your phone's ringing.'

'Love you, Uncle Boots,' said Annabelle and ran to answer the phone in her little office. 'Yes?'

'It's Mr Harrison again,' said the switchboard girl.

'Put him through,' said Annabelle. 'Hello?'

'Annabelle?' Nick sounded penitent.

'Oh, you silly,' said Annabelle, 'of course I didn't talk to Uncle John about any rise for you, and if you've got one, well, just count your blessings, because I'm sure you wouldn't have got it if the firm didn't think you were an asset. I'm counting mine. Well, it means we'll be able to eat pork chops instead of rissoles and baked beans, or bread and cheese. Nick, four pounds a week – let's go looking for the right kind of house on Sunday, shall we?'

'You're on,' said Nick. 'Sorry I jumped in where angels fear to tread. Count my blessings, right, I'll do that.'

'Say something really nice.'

'Glad I met you,' said Nick, 'and by the way, my boss, Mr Gregson, says wedded bliss is highly recommendable. He's had some.'

'Nick, we can't talk about wedded bliss over the phone,' said Annabelle, 'it's private.'

'Saturday evening, then?' suggested Nick.

'Love to,' said Annabelle. 'Will it make me blush?'

'Only in private,' said Nick.

'Oh, well, roses round the door,' said Annabelle.

Horace entered the shop just after one. The more rigorous demands on his time at the Oval had eased a little.

Miss Lomax had a customer. Sally didn't. And Sally for once didn't put herself behind her counter. But she did draw herself up slightly, as befitted her station, which made Horace think not for the first time what a very nice figure she had, which mental note was not out of order in the book of life. It came under the heading of 'Appreciative Moments' in a bloke's existence. A bloke did appreciate certain assets in a young lady, such as a 'pair of sparkling eyes', as per the song, an ability to converse agreeably, and a nicely noticeable figure. Some young ladies, even if they had nicely noticeable figures, didn't get much farther verbally than, 'Oh, you are a one,' or, 'Oh, go on with you.' Horace always found that a bit limiting socially. One thing about Sally Brown, she could converse very verbally, not half.

'Good afternoon, sir, can I help you?' she said.

She's off, thought Horace, and wondered if she'd seen any of the morning papers. The report of the arrest of a young man on a charge of attempted murder had been featured, although no names had been given. But even if she had seen the report, she wouldn't have connected it with Ethel. On the other hand, she might have thought of the shellshocked case in Braganza Street.

'Let me see,' he said, and took up a thoughtful stance.

'Yes, sir?' said Sally, plum in her mouth.

'Well, the fact is, I can't think of anything my mother wants in the way of clothes that she'd let me buy,' he said, trying to look serious.

'Oh, I'm sorry about that, sir,' said Sally, enthralled at the prospect of a real ding-dong. 'Unfortunately, we're very busy, as you can see, and if there's nothing you can think of buying, I simply don't know how I can help you.'

'That's a pity,' said Horace, 'I suppose the next thing will be to tell me where the door is?'

'It's behind you, sir,' said Sally. 'Good afternoon.'

'On the other hand,' said Horace, 'could you think of anything I could buy my mother that she wouldn't bring back on the grounds that it didn't suit her?'

'Pardon?' said Sally.

'Bearing in mind it shouldn't be too expensive,' said Horace. 'I've been lashin' out a bit lately, and as I'm savin' up to get married, I don't want to part with more than a few bob.'

'Well, I do feel terribly sorry for your savings, sir, but I don't think your mother would like anything cheap.'

'That's it, then, I suppose,' said Horace, 'I'm no longer a customer.'

'And I must point out, sir, that this shop is exclusively for people wishin' to buy,' said Sally, with Miss Lomax's customer in the fitting-room, and Miss Lomax herself having silent fits.

'You don't sell anything that would suit me, I suppose?' said Horace.

'I don't think so, sir,' said Sally, 'but I can recommend the gentlemen's outfitters that's just round the corner.'

'Blow that,' said Horace.

'Yes, what a shame, sir,' said Sally, 'it's a pity you're not a lady yourself, then you could try on some nice blouses.'

'Yes, nothing for it, I suppose, but for me to push off,' said Horace. 'Good afternoon, Miss Brown.'

'Good afternoon, Mr Cooper,' said Sally. 'Oh, there's just one thing.'

'A straw hat for a couple of bob, say?' ventured Horace.

'Not for your mother, sir,' said Sally. She rolled her plum about and sort of ate it. 'But if you'd like to come round this evening and ask for my brother Freddy, he'll give you a proper and respectable introduction to his younger sister.'

'Younger sister?' said Horace.

'Yes, Freddy's younger sister would like to go to the pictures next Saturday,' said Sally. 'Good afternoon, sir.'

'Half a mo',' said Horace, 'what younger sister?'

'Me,' said Sally. 'And the door's over there, sir.'

Horace looked at her.

Sally smiled.

Thank goodness, thought Miss Lomax, it's mutual at last.

A week or so later, after Adams Fashions had made mincemeat of the liquidating company owned by George Carter, an open Riley car pulled up outside Somerville College, exclusive to women undergraduates. Rosie, in the passenger seat, looked at Boots. He was looking at groups of young women who had already arrived for the start of the new term. There was a little smile on his face.

'Don't say it,' she said.

'Say what, poppet?'

'That they're a funny-looking lot.'

'Nothing of the kind,' said Boots.

'It's fashionable at Somerville and Girton,' said Rosie.

'What is?'

'To dress seriously,' said Rosie, in a very fetching dark blue costume herself.

'Yes, I see,' said Boots. Seriously seemed to mean an addiction to long ankle-length garments over which thigh-length jackets were worn, everything in dark hues.

'We feel it's one way of letting men know we're serious people,' said Rosie. 'Flighty or fancy rigouts project the wrong message.'

'Can't have that,' said Boots.

'Well, we'll never get anywhere, will we, if we're not taken seriously,' said Rosie. 'I mean, what's the point of obtaining a degree if all it earns us from men is a pat on the head?'

'Not much satisfaction in that,' said Boots.

'You're laughing,' said Rosie.

'Can I beg to differ?' asked Boots.

'No, you can't,' said Rosie, 'because you are laughing, and don't think I don't know it. Never mind, I don't want to change you, and thanks for driving me up. You're a good old sport, and I've had a gorgeous vacation, Salcombe and France, and home and family. Oh, and meeting your lovely surprise, my sister Eloise.'

Boots took his eyes off the groups of chattering young women and looked at his adopted daughter, nineteen and a young woman of extraordinary appeal. A little twinge of regret touched him, for he felt their best years together, their closest years, had gone now. She had shared with him every aspect of her life, and made known her every little wish without ever being demanding. She'd given him a great deal of love, and had always been there at a turn of his head, more or less. University and her aptitude for learning would broaden her outlook and her horizons, and perhaps make a different person of her. But he would stand on a conviction that he and Emily and Tim would never lose her. The ties might loosen a little and stretch a little, perhaps, but never break.

'It's been a delight, Rosie, having you home,' he said.

Rosie, making no move to get out of the car, said,

'I'm a big girl now, and don't say the things I used to say, but I want you to know I love you very much. Oh, I love all the family, of course, but you're the one who's really given me all I've needed or wanted.'

'Well, I love you too, poppet, and always will,' said Boots, 'and whatever you've had from the family, you've given as much and more in return. It's never been one-sided, Rosie. I'd say, in fact, that we owe you more than you owe us.'

'Yes, you would say that, wouldn't you?' smiled Rosie, with Oxford and its colleges awakening beneath a sky full of running white clouds. 'Do you sometimes think university will make me grow away from you and the family? No, never. Never.'

'Rosie, eureka, here you are, bless you.' A young woman whose baggy garments made her look as if she had close connections with jumble sales, swept up to the car. 'My, you've been out in the sun somewhere, you gallivanting creature – oh, I say, who's this you're with?'

'My father,' smiled Rosie.

'Well, don't keep him to yourself. Has he got a secretary?'

'Not one like you, Edith,' said Rosie. 'Daddy, this is a friend of mine, Edith Wells.'

'How d'you do?' said Boots.

'Good grief, I think I'm already running a crush,' said Edith Wells. 'I'll apply in three years time, shall I? You'll like me as a secretary. I'm reading economics.'

'Good luck, then,' smiled Boots, and got out of the car. He lifted Rosie's two suitcases off the back seat. Edith took one from him. Rosie smiled. It was always the same. Women met him, looked at him and tried to get close to him. Even a Somerville undergraduate as ambitious as Edith wasn't immune.

'I'll take the other case, old sport,' Rosie said, and Boots relinquished it. 'There, now I'll let you buzz off. Thanks again for bringing me, you're a love.'

'Pleasure,' said Boots.

'Oh, come up and visit,' said Edith, 'and we'll smuggle you in for tea and biscuits. Well, anything, actually.'

'She's bluffing,' smiled Rosie.

'Good,' said Boots, 'there's something alarming about "anything". So long, Rosie.' He kissed her warmly on her cheek. 'Goodbye, Edith.'

'Yes, perhaps you'd better go, Mr Adams,' said Edith, 'we can't keep meeting like this, not at Somerville. Come on, Rosie, let's make our return noticeable.'

Off they went, each carrying a suitcase, and other undergraduates swallowed them up, although not before Rosie turned and waved. Boots got back into the car, thinking of her and her broader horizons. Then he started the engine, slipped into gear and drove away, heading south for home.

Rosie was not thinking of broader horizons herself. For all the excitements the future might hold, nothing about it would mean as much to her as the years that had gone. Her affection for her family and her love for Boots would never change, and nor would blissful memories ever diminish.

That evening, Mrs Chrissie Thompson, wife of Mr Danny Thompson, set about her husband the moment he arrived home from work.

''Ere, turn it up, Dumpling,' he protested, dodging swipes from her rolling-pin, 'what've I done?'

'What you shouldn't 'ave,' yelled Dumpling, chasing him around the kitchen table.

'But Dumpling me precious—'

'I'll give you precious, you've done it on me, Danny Thompson, the doctor said so this mornin' – oh, stand still, will yer, so's I can make yer life a misery for the next five minutes.'

'What for?' panted Danny, still running.

'I'm goin' to 'ave a baby, that's what!'

Danny stopped and turned. Dumpling, still coming at him, bumped into his chest. Danny just managed to hold his ground and to give her a cuddle.

'Oh, good on yer, Dumpling, I'm proud of yer,' he said.

'Proud?' Dumpling shook the rolling-pin in his face and uncomfortably close to his hooter. 'D'you know what you've been and gone and done? You've ruined me football career and me life as well.'

'Now don't be like that, Dumpling love,' said